MURKY WATERS

Chris Crowther

The Jack Fellows series by the same author
WATERPROOF
STILL WATERS
THE WATER FROLIC
WATER UNDER THE BRIDGE

Published in the U.S.
BLADESTRIKE (thriller)

British Library Cataloguing in Publication Data.
A catalogue record is available from the British Library.

ISBN 978-0-903094-283

First published this edition in 2014
by

Hamilton Publications
Ventulus, Cross Lane, Brancaster
Norfolk PE31 8AE

www.chriscrowther.co.uk

Printed in Great Britain by
Barnwell Print Ltd, Dunkirk, Aylsham, Norfolk. NR11 6SU

Cover photo by Lord Paul Sergent www.photographs-r-us.co.uk
Sketches by Sarah Rogers

PROLOGUE

'Right Jack, this is where it was spotted.'

Navigation Ranger Harry Bentley throttled back the engine and soon the lean bow of his patrol launch was barely stemming the River Waveney's healthy flood tide.

Beside him, fellow ranger Jack Fellows took in the encircling marshes, nearby railway line and slightly rising ground to the east. Ten minutes earlier, they'd passed Oulton Dyke leading enticingly to the broad of the same name. Some distance astern now and beyond one lazy curve of the river, the tower of Burgh St Peter's Church poked its unique three tiers above the treeline, marking the home base of this launch and the continuance of the Waveney towards Beccles. Ahead, a sharp right angle in the river's meander preceded the last straight reach to Somerleyton. On this bright spring day, the fresh southwesterly breeze was a following one, but Jack was still glad to be inside the launch's enclosed wheelhouse.

Or was that slight chill something else, something he'd felt many times in his old police past when first visiting the scene of some mysterious event? It came back to him now, as he looked upriver and down, a mixture of thrill and anticipation as he tried to visualise the strange occurrence here so many years before.

It had happened almost thirty years ago to the day, so, was this whole exercise merely an excuse to flex his old policing skills? Perhaps Audrey had been right in saying he needed another interest. That was why, just a few nights ago, he'd tried his first hand at fishing which had triggered this bizarre investigation in the first place. He thought back to those chilly hours on the Bure, sitting in that small dory, seeing his float move for the first time and hearing Bill Maskell's quiet encouragement.

*　　*　　*

Chapter One

'Looks like you're away, Jack, but give it five seconds before you take in the slack or you might pull the hook out.'

As instructed, Jack paused on the reel and allowed the yellow light of his float to move just a little further downstream. In the normal run of things, he certainly wouldn't have chosen to be out on the river on a cold March night, but his job as a Broads ranger meant he'd constantly encountered the many anglers who fished these waters. They were a friendly, but silent bunch and, for a long time now, he'd been determined to learn more of their seemingly obsessive sport for himself. And so, with Audrey's urgings, he'd signed up for an introductory lesson with local pike-fishing guide, Bill Maskell.

Until then, it had been a fruitless but not unpleasant night, for Maskell had many a fascinating tale to tell of his quest for this big predator. Sitting there in the glow of the small tilly lamp, hands cradling the warmth of a large mug of coffee while their florescent floats lay motionless a dozen feet away, Jack had caught some of the allure in this lonely pursuit. And then, just as the guide was about to fortify their beverage with a tot of rum from his hip flask, Jack's float had moved slightly to the left and the delicate job of playing the fish had begun.

'Okay, start winding down now before it swallows the hook,' whispered Maskell, 'but don't hurry it − gently does it.' Jack felt pressure come on his line. 'Right, now for the strike. Up with your rod and that'll set the hook. Okay, start slowly reeling in.' As he did so, Jack could feel the thrash and pull of some big creature on the other end. And then, suddenly, the reel started paying out, seemingly of its own accord. 'That's the clutch running,' explained the guide. 'It stops her putting enough force on the hook to pull it out.'

'How do you know it's a "she"?'

'Because it takes a fair size to overcome the clutch and ninety-eight per cent of all pike over ten pounds are female.'

'Right.' Jack watched as the line paid out. 'How far shall I let it run?'

'As far as it wants, it'll start slowing soon. There you are, it's stopped. Now start reeling in again.'

The line didn't pay out again and Jack once more played his catch. Soon though, he felt the erratic tugging ease and pressure on the line alter. 'It just feels like a heavy weight on the end now, Bill. Is that all right?'

'Yep, it means she's tiring and on the bottom. Just keep playing her in.'

Jack continued to reel in and minutes later the still waters of the river suddenly erupted into a frenzy of splashing as the fish broke surface just five feet from the boat.

'There she is. As I thought, a good size. That's right, Jack, gently does it. She's slowing now.' As the thrashing ceased, the big fish seemed to lie inert in the water facing her adversary in apparent submission. 'Right, now's the time to bring her alongside. Grab that landing net.'

Still holding the rod with one hand, Jack eased the net under his catch with the other. When the pike was well and truly enmeshed, he put the rod to one side and hauled in with both hands, straining to lift the heavy fish over the gunwale. 'She certainly *feels* a big one, Bill.'

'Yep. Ease her down onto the mat here so I can get the hook out, but watch out she doesn't begin to move about too much. They seem to get second-wind at this point.' Sure enough, the pike had started flapping about in the bottom of the boat. 'That's right, Jack, straddle her with your legs so she doesn't damage herself.' Maskell pulled out a pair of forceps and, while Jack used all his own strength to keep the fish still, reached between the teeth-lined jaws and worked out the substantial hook. 'Good, that's out. Pike might be the number one predator in the river but, strangely enough, they're also the most fragile.' The fish was ceasing to struggle now and the guide took it gently in his hands. 'I reckon about fourteen pounds, but bring those scales over and we'll see for sure.' He laid the pike in the weigh-sling and then hung it from the scales Jack was holding. 'Yep, fourteen pounds, twelve ounces. Not bad, Jack, for a first catch.'

'How does that measure up to other pike caught around here?'

'About average. The biggest caught on the Broads, a year or so back, was forty-five and a half pounds, so you've broken no records.'

'I'm just amazed I hooked one at all. I really didn't expect to catch a thing,' admitted Jack, shaking his head. 'Audrey will never believe this. She'll reckon it's just my first fisherman's tale.'

'Not if we show her the evidence.' Maskell lifted the pike out of the sling and gave it carefully to Jack. 'Here, hold her gently.' There was a flash as the event was recorded on camera, and then the guide was taking the fish back and gently lowering it over the side, where he held it facing into the stream. 'It'll get some water flowing through her gills again,' he explained. 'If we let her go too soon, she might not stay upright and, if she rolls onto her back, she may not have the will to recover. This way...' he paused as the pike once more tensed in his hands, '... we make sure she lives to play again another day. Off you go, my love.' He released his grip and, with a final slap of its tail, the pike was gone.

'Glad to see she's come to no harm,' approved Jack, as calm once more descended onto the black water surrounding them. 'I'd hate the idea of maiming any living creature.' He shook his head. 'Never make a *real* hunter, me.'

Maskell gave him a quizzical look. 'But isn't that just what you used to do, Jack? Hunting?'

'For criminals, you mean?' It was no secret amongst the Broadland community that, prior to becoming a ranger, Jack had been a senior detective at Scotland Yard. 'Not quite the same thing, really, Bill. For a start, it was the villains themselves who instigated the hunt and, unlike the pike, if found guilty, they weren't gently released back into their natural environment.' Jack's thoughts momentarily went back to the harsh world of criminality. 'There's no denying, Bill, this fishing lark is a good escape from the realities of day-to-day life.'

'Making a convert of you are we, Jack?'

'Could be. I'd certainly like to come again, but it won't be for a while now, will it?'

'Not for three months, anyway.' It would soon be midnight on this fourteenth day of March and the start of the closed season when the fish were allowed to spawn. Not until the sixteenth of June would fishing be permitted again. 'So, let's make the most of this last hour,' said Maskell, picking up the oars. 'I reckon we won't get another here now, so we'll move on a little further upriver.'

Slowly edging around the next bend, Jack noticed several other tilly lamps glimmering at intervals along the reach. 'Not the only ones out tonight, Bill.'

'No, it's going to be a long three months for the regulars, so they're all making the most of it by fishing 'til the stroke of twelve,' explained the guide, as he pulled slowly and smoothly at the oars. They were coming abeam one of the other dinghies now, moored close to the north bank. 'Hello, this chap seems to have caught something.' Certainly, one of the boat's two rods was bending as its owner wound in the spool.' Maskell paused on his oars and called across to the other fisherman, 'What do you reckon? A big one?'

'No such luck,' came back the reply. 'More like it's just caught on those tree roots there.' The angler gave a frustrated tug and, suddenly, something gave way, enabling him to reel in. 'There, it's free. Now we'll see what I got hooked on.' Sure enough, seconds later, an object dripping mud broke surface. 'What the hell's this?' groaned the fisherman, as he swung his unwelcome catch to within handling reach to reveal his hook caught on what was obviously a mud-slimed loop of leather. 'Looks like a woman's handbag.'

'Can I see it?' asked Jack, from across the few yards now separating them.

The handbag was dripping mud anyway and all set to make a mess of the fisherman's boat, so he willingly lowered his rod for them to row within reach. 'If it's full of money, I want my cut,' he joked as Jack removed the bag from the hook.

'I shouldn't bank on it.' Jack was making a cursory examination of what was obviously the result of long immersion. 'But, I'll take it back and see if anyone's reported the loss.'

'Well, if you find the owner and she wants to give a nice big reward, Bill knows where to find me,' replied the fisherman, chuckling to himself, as he prepared his line for another cast.

'My only concern is the mess that thing will make of *my* boat,' moaned Maskell, rowing away, but pausing on his oars to pull a used plastic bag from his knapsack. He handed it across. 'Here, stick it in there, Jack. It smells disgusting.'

'You're right, it doesn't half stink.' Jack wrinkled his nose as he shoved the find into the plastic bag and sealed the top with a knot. 'I doubt if anyone would want that back, but we'll see if it's reported lost. A plastic credit card or something might help identify the owner, but I don't think there'll be much else left of its contents, judging by the state of it.' Jack glanced around him. They were a fair distance from the other boat now, but he made a note of its position before again picking up his rod and starting to bait the hook the way Maskell had shown him. He glanced at his watch. 'Still half-an-hour to go, Bill, so let's see if I can catch another pike before midnight.'

*   *   *

'Well, Jack, how did you enjoy your first taste of fishing?'

It was next morning in the Fellows' household and Audrey had already hung out a second load of washing before her husband emerged, having overslept after his late-night angling exploits.

Still in pyjamas and dressing gown and seated at the kitchen table tucking into a fry-up, Jack paused mid-mouthful. 'I did, very much. You'll never believe it, Aud, but I caught a pike this big.' He indicated its size with his hands.

Audrey looked at her husband with an affectionate, but disbelieving, smile. 'You're having me on, Jack. Now, how big was it really?'

'I knew you'd think I was telling a whopper. We weighed it and it was almost fifteen pounds. Bill took a photo to prove it and I reckon when the new season begins, I might take up this fishing lark more seriously.'

'How long will that be?' Audrey poured herself a coffee and joined her husband at the table. There was more than a casual interest in her question. Now that Jack only worked as a seasonal ranger, she was keen for him to find other interests. He was a man who always needed to be kept busy and she hoped fishing might appeal to him, but she'd forgotten that there was a closed season.

'Three months.'

'And when do you take up your ranger duties again?'

'Easter, which is...' Jack glanced at the calendar on the kitchen wall, '... a bit less than two weeks now.'

'So, I've got you under my feet until then,' muttered Audrey with exaggerated frustration.

'Only partly. I'm planning to go out with some of the permanent rangers, just to get back up to speed on what's been happening on the river.' Was it his imagination, or did the faintest flicker of relief cross his wife's features? 'I hope I didn't wake you when I crept into bed in the early hours?'

'No, I was sound asleep.' In fact, the best sleep I've had in a long time without Jack's snoring, Audrey thought, but didn't say. Instead, she asked, 'But what on earth's in that plastic bag you've left by the back doorstep? It looks disgusting.'

'Oh that...' Jack paused to feed their border collie Spike a titbit of his bacon, '... just something one of the fishermen hooked out of the river last night. I think it's a woman's handbag, but I'm going to give it a closer once-over when I'm dressed.'

'Not in here you're not, Jack Fellows. It stinks.' Audrey nodded down the garden. 'Take it to your shed if you must dabble, but I can't see the point.'

'The *point* is that it's lost property, Audrey, and someone might be glad to at least know it's been found.' Jack gave a slight frown. 'Mind you, by the look of it, it's been in the water a long time, so I need to find out just how long before I get checking if it was ever reported lost. And, who knows, there's still a chance I might even find a clue to its previous owner and...'

'... you can indulge in another spot of detective work,' completed Audrey with a sigh. 'I know you too well, so just admit it.'

Jack smiled sheepishly. 'I suppose I do still enjoy a spot of sleuthing.'

'Well, as long as it's in your shed and not here,' she said, wrinkling up her nose. 'And take Spike with you when you go. It'll be better for him than eating all that fatty bacon you keep giving him.' Audrey poured Jack another coffee and adopted a slightly more serious tone. 'But, just make sure this doesn't get out of hand,' she warned. 'I don't mind a bit of lost property but, for goodness' sake, don't go getting involved in another full-blown investigation.'

'As if I would, love. It'll simply be a bag that's fallen overboard, that's all.' Jack took another welcome sip of coffee, hoping it was only Spike who could see the fingers on his other hand, crossed beneath the table.

*   *   *

An hour later, down in his garden shed and wearing a pair of latex surgical gloves, Jack spread a clean piece of polythene on the workbench, and on that, the remains of the handbag.

Just retrieving it from the river bottom the night before had washed off much of the surface mud, but there was still a light coating which Jack wiped away with water and a soft cloth. It revealed surprisingly good quality leather, hand stitched and indented with an intricate design. He opened the flap and reeled slightly as more bottom-mud odour rose from the interior. Gently scooping out the contents, he carefully placed them to one side in an ever-growing pool of liquid ooze. 'What a mess, aye, Spike?' he said to the faithful collie who sat beside the bench pawing his ear. Jack continued to scoop out the inside of the bag and only when he was sure he had removed everything, did he pause to survey the results.

The bag had obviously been in the water for a very long time, but some clues to its contents still remained, such as some wrapping, most probably from a packet of paper tissues, and a clear plastic cover that might have held some sort of card or pass, but now contained only mulch. A small hard-bound notebook held more promise and Jack eased open the covers as though they were made of gossamer thread, but inside was just a litter of dissolved pages.

Some items though had defied the elements, such as the small bunch of keys that Jack now washed in the bucket of soapy water he'd brought into the shed. The steel keys were badly rusted, but the brass Yales, although blackened, were still sound. 'I wonder which locks these used to turn?' he asked Spike, who merely cocked his head on one side. Jack turned his attention to the fob from which the keys hung. It was quite heavy, fashioned from thick metal and with an enamel badge still preserved upon its surface. He took a magnifying glass from the bench drawer and examined the badge more closely. It appeared to be some sort of crest or coat of arms depicting four lions in each corner and with a cross in the centre on which lay some sort of book. Engraved on the other side was just one name: Darwin.

Darwin. Was the previous owner of this bag Australian? Or was it from the settlement of the same name in the Falkland Islands? Perhaps it was just a souvenir of a visit, but that was impossible to surmise with the present data, so Jack put the keys and their ring to one side and turned now to the only other recognisable item amidst the residue on his workbench.

Also of leather, though not of the same quality as the bag itself, it had a solid brass fastening. Jack gingerly eased it apart and opened this mystery woman's purse.

It was, perhaps, too much to hope that her driving licence might still be intact inside, but Jack was hoping there would be at least one plastic credit card bearing her name. In the event, he was disappointed. A close examination of the contents revealed only a few coins and the mushy remains of what had obviously been some banknotes. He removed the coins, washed them in the bucket and placed them side by side on the bench. There were two fifty-pences, three twenties, a five, several one-pence pieces and even two half-pennies. 'Hmm, that's interesting, Spike.' But the collie was more intent on scratching his ear. 'Come on then, old fella,' coaxed Jack, putting the coins and keys in separate food bags before leading his faithful companion back to the house.

*   *   *

As the kitchen door opened, and Jack and his sidekick walked in, Audrey struggled to her feet, wearing yellow rubber gloves and a pained expression. Cleaning the oven was her least favourite task and any diversion was more than welcome. 'Well, what has the great detective managed to deduce?'

'Not a great deal, I'm afraid. A few items are recognisable but, as I expected, most of the contents have perished.' As he spoke, Jack's eyes scanned the worktops for anything to nibble before it dawned on him that the oven had been out of use.

'So, no means of identification then?'

Jack shook his head. 'Unfortunately not, but I do at least know approximately when the bag was lost.'

Audrey wiped back a stray lock of hair, leaving a dirty streak on her forehead. She was the first to discourage Jack from getting involved in any investigation since being retired but, secretly, she loved a bit of intrigue. 'Which was…?'

'… sometime between 1982 and late 1984.'

'Good heavens, how did you work that out, Jack?'

'Because these were still as solid as ever.' Jack jangled the bag of coins and placed them on the worktop. 'Look here, there are three twenty-pence pieces and even a couple of half-pennies which is what got me thinking. You see, twenty-pence coins only came out in 1982, so the bag couldn't have been lost before then, but half-pennies were demonetised in December 1984, which probably makes that the latest it could have been lost.'

'Well done, Jack. You've certainly not lost your investigative touch,' conceded Audrey as she went to wipe any residue from the oven before closing its door. 'Well, after our morning's labours, I think we're both ready for a cup of tea, so be a dear and put the kettle on while I go and clean up.'

By the time Audrey rejoined him, tea was made and Jack was sitting down at the kitchen table, pouring himself a cuppa in his favourite mug. Audrey brought out a packet of chocolate digestives and poured a cup for herself. '1984 is thirty years ago, Jack. Even if this woman reported it lost at the time, I doubt if there's any record of it now.'

'There isn't,' replied her husband, helping himself to a biscuit and then licking some chocolate from his fingers. 'I've already checked with the office, and they have no records left going back that far. I also rang the police, but they almost laughed me off the line and made it pretty clear that the last thing they wanted was a stinking load of sodden leather handed into their lost property department.'

'I don't blame them,' smiled Audrey. 'So, that's that I guess. From what you've said, the bag didn't contain any valuables so, whoever owned it, certainly won't be overly concerned anymore.'

'Perhaps not,' agreed Jack, refilling his mug, 'but I'd still like to find out who she is and let her know her bag has finally been found.'

'Only so you can play detectives again.' Audrey sighed. 'Don't you ever want to give it a rest, Jack? Can't you let go of that old life?'

He looked up and gave an apologetic smile. 'I do try to move on, Aud, and I wouldn't want to be back with the force, but solving mysteries is how I spent my working life. It's just a long-lost bag, love, and I'll probably never find out who it belonged to, but I just hate loose ends and I've still got a couple of weeks to kill before I'm back on patrol.' Ignoring his wife's admonishing look, Jack helped himself to another biscuit. 'And you're the first to admit I need to get out and *do* something, which is why I was trying fishing in the first place.'

Audrey shrugged. 'Fair enough, but how are you going to actually proceed with this? As far as I can see, you've nothing to go on other than a bag of loose change.'

'By following up the only *other* clue I've got, which is a set of keys or, more precisely, the fob they're held on.' Jack produced a second plastic bag containing the crested key fob, and pointed out the name of Darwin inscribed upon it and his theory as to its origin.

'But if this crest is associated with either Australia or the Falklands, surely you're going to have a job nailing it down.'

'Not necessarily. Australia is British Commonwealth and the Falklands, a British overseas territory, so I'm sure the College of Arms in London will know just what it relates to.'

'Intriguing,' admitted Audrey, putting on her glasses to study the crest more carefully. 'Well, good luck, Jack, but, as I said before, don't go and get *too* involved. You know how easily you become obsessed.'

'Of course I won't.' Jack gave a reassuring smile. 'It's just a little exercise in tracing lost property, Aud. How could I get too involved in that?'

*   *   *

It wasn't often that Jack Fellows used his old Scotland Yard rank and position, but calling such an august body as the College of Arms, seemed a time he might have to. But it transpired there was no need, as this ancient order, dating back to the twelfth century, proved to be nothing but helpful. After briefly explaining his enquiry, he was put through to The Herald in Waiting, a gentleman as friendly as he was learned.

'Australia or the Falklands, you say, Mr Fellows,' he responded, after the ranger had explained his quest. 'Well, we still handle heraldic applications from both those lands. The Australians could have had their own heraldic authority like the Canadians and South Africans, but somehow resisted for years. The republican voice of dissent, no doubt.' The herald paused for just a second. 'But, forgetting faraway places, this particular coat of arms you've described is somehow familiar, and I have a hunch I might just be able to help you there. Hang on...' At the other end of the line there was the tapping of computer keys and muttering as the herald read aloud to himself from the screen, '... yes, here we are... "Gules, a cross ermine between four lions passant gardant and, on the cross, a closed book fessways gules clasped and garnished or, the clasps downward." How does that sound?'

'Like a foreign language to me,' confessed Jack.

'Yes, I know.' The herald gave a sympathetic laugh. 'But let me give you the plain English description. "On a red background, a cross of ermine fur between four gold lions walking, but with one fore-leg raised, and facing the observer. On the centre of the cross is a closed book with its spine horizontal and with clasps pointing downward." Does that sound like the crest you have there?'

Jack looked down at the key fob before him. 'That's the exact description,' he marvelled, genuinely impressed. 'How on earth did you manage that so quickly?'

'No great skill, I'm afraid,' admitted the herald. 'I get letters regularly bearing that coat of arms. It belongs to Cambridge University and I often receive correspondence regarding heraldic concerns within their various colleges.'

'Cambridge, good heavens!' Jack exclaimed. He hadn't expected that. 'That's a long way from Darwin, Australia or Darwin, Falkland Islands.'

'Doubtless,' said the Herald, 'but I'd put money on the Darwin you have there as to pertaining to Darwin *College*, Cambridge and not the city or settlement.'

'The college! Of course.' Jack gave himself a mental slap on the forehead. 'Darwin College, named after Charles Darwin.'

'Exactly,' confirmed the herald. 'I hope I've helped.'

'You have indeed,' replied Jack, appreciatively, before putting down the phone. Then he turned to his computer, gleaned some facts from the internet and made a second telephone call, before finding Audrey upstairs changing their bed-linen.

She raised her eyes expectantly. 'Any luck?'

Jack nodded. He took one side of the fitted sheet and stretched it over the mattress. 'Yes indeed, Aud, and you know you've being saying for a long time that you'd like to spend a day in Cambridge?'

'That's right. I've always wanted to walk round The Backs and visit King's College Chapel.' She paused, suddenly realising where this might be leading. 'But I've had the firm impression it wasn't something you were that keen on Jack, so why the sudden interest?'

'Because, dear girl,' said Jack, giving his wife a gentle hug, 'tomorrow we are off to that very city.'

*   *   *

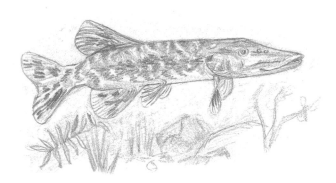

Chapter Two

'Well, here we are after all these years,' sighed Audrey contentedly, as their train pulled into Cambridge Station and she started getting her things together. 'But I should have known it wouldn't happen until it was relevant to some investigation you'd got your teeth into.'

'Hardly an investigation,' protested Jack as the train came to a standstill and he retrieved their coats from the overhead rack before stepping onto the platform. It was a bright spring day and the morning air tasted as crisp as it was invigorating.

'Lovely to be here, whatever the reason,' relented Audrey, before casting her mind back to their departure. 'I just hope dear Spike's okay. He looked particularly down in the dumps when we left him this morning.'

'I know, but he's always like that when we go out,' replied Jack. 'A good run when we get home tonight will soon put the wag back into his tail.'

'It's just that he's been a bit out of sorts lately,' she persisted as they made their way out of the station. 'And he keeps pawing his ear as though it's irritating him.'

'Probably just some foreign body that he's picked up on the river-bank.' Jack gave his wife's shoulders a reassuring squeeze. 'If it gets worse, we'll take him to the vets, but for now, just relax and enjoy your long-awaited day in Cambridge.'

Audrey smiled. 'I certainly intend to.' She looked around her and was immediately struck by an enormous cycle-park crammed with bikes, all looking very similar. Knowing the trouble she sometimes had locating her car outside the supermarket, Audrey wondered how the students were ever able to find which bike was theirs. She turned to share these thoughts with Jack, but he'd moved on and was studying a map of Cambridge.

'Right, love,' he said, pointing straight ahead, 'along that road and then we need to look out for Regent Street.' He took his wife's hand and they set off, both happy to be exploring pastures new.

As they neared a busy crossroads, Audrey pulled on Jack's hand, forcing him to stop so she could look more closely at the notice-board outside an impressive church building on the other side of the road. 'Goodness me!' she exclaimed. 'That's a mouthful - Our Lady and the English Matyrs Church.' Being a regular worshipper herself, she would have loved to look inside, but they needed to press on. 'Isn't this city amazing, Jack? There's just so much to see.'

'Yes, but business first,' said Jack, 'and I'm just grateful the bursar at Darwin is taking the time to see me.' He gave a crafty smile. 'Mind you, I made sure he was a bit intrigued by telling him I was trying to solve a mystery.'

'He probably thinks you're on the trail of Lord Lucan or something,' groaned Audrey, giving him a playful nudge.

'Don't be so disparaging. Just look at it as a day of culture for you and a bit of grey-cell exercise for me.'

By this time they'd turned off the main road and were passing the crested entrances and magnificent historic buildings of colleges they'd heard so much about, but never seen, at the same time having to keep their wits about them as purposeful-looking students hurrying to lectures, filled the paths and bike-lanes on the narrow streets.

'What a privilege for these bright youngsters to study here,' said Audrey, wistfully, 'following in the footsteps of so many academics through the centuries. Doesn't it make you wish…'

'No, Aud,' interrrupted Jack, 'I had no aspirations or the brains for university life. You know I just couldn't wait to get on the beat when I left school.'

They'd turned now into Silver Street and Jack nodded ahead. 'Darwin's just along here.' They walked on together to the centre of Queen's Bridge, which spanned the Cam beneath, and looked down to see a large number of punts for hire. Jack turned to his wife who raised her eyebrows and tilted her head enquiringly. 'No time today, I'm afraid, love. Perhaps we can come back in the summer. Anyway, time we parted company. How about meeting up later at the Anchor pub down there beside the water, and having a bite to eat? The terrace looks nice and sheltered. I'll give you a buzz on your mobile when I'm finished with the bursar.'

'Good idea,' agreed Audrey. 'Don't rush, because I'm off to look around King's College Chapel and then a walk along The Backs. I've heard the spring flowers should look stunning at this time of year.'

'Gosh, my meeting's in ten minutes, so I've got to dash,' prompted Jack, glancing at his watch and giving his wife a quick peck on the cheek. 'Enjoy yourself, love, and see you back here later.'

A short walk the other side of the bridge brought him to the entrance to Darwin College where one of a pair of heavy grey, replica studded outer doors was left open to reveal modern automatic inner ones and a well-lit reception area. Here a porter took Jack's details and called an internal number. Soon a rather stouter, bespectacled man appeared to meet his visitor.

'Mr Fellows? James Watkins, bursar.' He greeted Jack with a firm handshake and friendly manner. 'From your call yesterday, it seems I might be able to help you in some enquiry.'

'I hope so, Mr Watkins. I'm very grateful you could spare the time to see me.'

'Not at all. Let's go to my office.' Jack followed the bursar along corridors, glimpsing the grounds as they passed external windows.

'What a delightful setting,' said Jack, appreciatively. 'Is the college very old?'

'Some of the buildings are, but the college itself was only founded in 1964.' Watkins nodded to a window. 'If you come here and look out, you can see

Newnham Grange and the Old Granary. Those buildings were bought by Charles Darwin's second son, George, in 1885. It was when George's son, Sir Charles Galton Darwin, died in 1962, that the property became available. His widow, Lady Katherine Darwin, and her family, were very happy that their home should become the nucleus of a new graduate college, that it should bear the family's name and be the first to take both men and women.'

'So, all the students here already have degrees from other colleges?'

'Or even some other university,' explained the bursar as they continued along corridors lined with portraits of notable alumini. 'We now have approximately six-hundred students, most reading for either a masters or a doctorate.'

'Obviously smart young people,' remarked Jack as Watkins led him down an off-lying corridor. 'What subjects can they study here?'

'Anything and everything There are no restrictions.' Jack was now being ushered into what was obviously the bursar's domain, where a secretary of mature years sat behind her word-filled computer screen. She nodded a friendly greeting as the two men passed through and into the bursar's own office.

Jack sat in the proffered chair and Watkins behind his own large ornate desk. He put his hands together and leaned forward. 'So, how exactly can I help you, Mr Fellows?'

Jack described the finding of the handbag and handed across the keyring, explaining how its discovery had led him to Darwin College. 'You understand, of course,' he emphasised, 'that this is a purely casual and unofficial enquiry on my own initiative.'

'Hardly casual when you've travelled this far to follow up what is basically a very minor item of lost property.' Watkins looked quizzically over his spectacles. 'Is there some deeper mystery behind all this, Mr Fellows?'

'I hope not,' Jack replied, 'but I was a senior detective at Scotland Yard for years and, even in retirement, I'm always on the lookout for anything, however trivial, that could involve further investigation. I'm hoping you may possibly be able to tell me who the original owner was.'

'Obviously a girl, if these were found in a handbag,' said the bursar, turning the keys and their fob over in his hand.

'Obviously.'

'And you think she was a student here?'

'The keyring suggests she was.'

'What period are we talking about?'

'Probably early eighties which, I realise, was a long time ago.'

'It certainly was,' agreed Watkins, slightly taken aback, 'and well before I came to work here, so I'm afraid I'm not going to be much help.'

'Well, you might just tell me if those keys could possibly be for rooms here,' persisted Jack.

Once again, the bursar turned them over in his hand, while shaking his head. 'Certainly it's the Cambridge University coat of arms, but the keys themselves could be for anywhere.'

'But not with the name of this college engraved on the back.'

'Perhaps an ex-student kept the fob for nostalgic reasons years after she left here,' suggested the bursar with undeniable logic.

Jack nodded. 'I was just hoping that perhaps your old records for those years might show someone reporting the loss of their keys.'

Watkins laughed out loud. 'Every week I have at least one student come in here to report the loss of his or her keys. If we'd recorded every such case we'd need to double our archives.'

Jack smiled. 'Yeah, I can see that.' He paused, reluctant to let go of this one-and-only lead. 'Can you think of any other way you might help me?'

The bursar thought for just a moment. 'Mrs Hendricks, my secretary, started here in the early eighties, so perhaps there's a slim chance she might just remember something.' He picked up his phone and called the outer office. 'Jean, can you join us, please?'

Jean Henricks was a quietly spoken woman who no doubt devoted much of her working life to sorting out student problems. 'I'm sorry, Mr Fellows, but students are always losing their keys so I'm afraid I have no recollections of one missing nearly thirty years ago.'

'Yes, I understand it's a lot to ask.' Jack decided to try a different tack and, after quickly explaining the background to this enquiry, asked, 'How about anything else of significance at that time, Mrs Hendricks? Something that might have stuck in your memory involving a female student.'

'With a Norfolk connection, you mean?' A slight shadow of sadness seemed to pass across the secretary's face. 'There was the rather puzzling business with Samantha.'

'Samantha?'

'Yes, Samantha Waites. I got to know her quite well as she'd had such tragedy in her life and, although I was only a few years older, I rather took her under my wing.'

'Why, what happened?'

'It's a sad story as both her parents were killed in a pile-up on the M6 when she was in her first year at Lancaster University. She was an only child and they were travelling up to see her, which made their loss even harder for her to bear.'

'I can imagine, but she obviously had the strength of character to carry on with her studies.'

'Yes, and in some ways it made her even more determined to excel, and she came out with a first-class science degree before coming here to do a PhD. She was in her final-year at Darwin, which must have been around the early-eighties, when she went to the Broads to carry out some research work and never came back.'

Jack sat up in his chair. 'You mean she disappeared?'

'Not exactly. She just wrote to explain that, for personal reasons, she wouldn't be returning to complete her thesis.'

'Was it common for students to drop out like that in their final year, Mrs Hendricks?'

'Not unknown. Young people quite often decide to opt out or defer their studies as other opportunities present themselves, but I was surprised in Samantha's case, because she'd just secured a large grant to pursue her research project.'

'What research was this?' asked Jack, increasingly interested in Samantha Waites.

'I can't remember for sure,' admitted the secretary, 'but I seem to recall it was something to do with work she'd already done in South America.' She shrugged sadly. 'I'm sorry I can't be more helpful, but at the time I remember feeling a little bit hurt that she didn't get in touch with me and tell me what she was up to.'

'Yes, I can understand that, Mrs Hendricks,' sympathised Jack before nodding in a general direction to the college beyond. 'Would there be anyone else who was here at the time, someone who could perhaps tell me a bit more about this particular student?'

'No, I think I'm probably the only one left here from that era,' explained the secretary. 'The only local person who might just possibly help you would be Doctor Odell.'

'Who's he?'

'A fellow student studying with Samantha at the time and…' Mrs Henricks paused, obviously a little reticent to elaborate.

Jack decided now was not the time to press this slightly nervous lady further. 'Where could I find this doctor, Mrs Hendricks?'

'Not far from here. He runs a second-hand bookshop near the market square called Boffin Books. It specialises in scientific academic works. I could draw you a little map of how to find it if you like.'

'That would be great. Thank you.' Jack turned back to Watkins. 'Not a wasted trip after all, eh?'

'It appears not, and let's hope this Odell chap can help you further,' replied the bursar, standing up and shaking hands. 'It's been nice meeting you, Jack, but work beckons. Good luck with your investigations. I'll leave Jean to see you out once she's helped you all she can.'

Back in her office, Jean Hendricks very quickly sketched Jack a map, slipped on her coat and led him out of the building and into a tranquil garden bordered by a wide brook. It was as they walked down a narrow winding footpath away from the building, that the secretary drew him to one side.

'I hope you don't mind, Mr Fellows, but I wanted to talk to you just a little more before you left, but not in front of James.' A number of students were now

19

moving between the buildings, chattering happily and seemingly oblivious to this senior pair, but Mrs Hendricks indicated a small wooden footbridge leading across the water to a secluded area on the other side. 'Let's go over there where we can talk in private.'

*   *   *

The secretary sat down on one of the wooden bench seats scattered about this island oasis, under a large weeping willow. Although facing the college buildings, they were well out of earshot, the solitude broken only by the chattering of birds in the trees and a pair of mallards dabbling in the brook. Her eyes showed an expression of genuine concern that was mirrored by the catch in her voice. 'The thing is, Mr Fellows, I can see you're a man of profound instinct and I need to know if you think something untoward happened to Samantha?'

'I always avoid jumping to any conclusions,' said Jack, sitting down beside her, 'but yes, Mrs Henricks, I am having some uneasy feelings regarding the loss of this bag.' He fixed the secretary with enquiring eyes. 'And if those instincts you credit me with are correct, you perhaps thought the same thing when Samantha Waites didn't return to Cambridge.'

Mrs Hendricks nodded sadly. 'Only because it was so out of character. Samantha was a brilliant, popular student, all set to get her doctorate within a matter of months and with a bright future ahead of her.' Once more, she glanced about her. 'What I have to say is a little indiscreet. Can I be assured you'll keep it to yourself?'

'Absolutely,' answered Jack, surprised at this last minute intervention. 'Anything you tell me will be treated with the strictest confidence.'

The secretary gave a slight downturn of her mouth. 'Well, as you're about to go and talk to Dr Odell, I want to set the record straight before he twists it because, for all he might imply, Samantha Waites was a decent girl with twice the intellect he ever had.' She shook her head. 'I know he was always making advances toward her, but she just wasn't interested and, to cap it all, she managed to secure funding for her research, whereas he'd managed nothing for his. He found it a bitter pill to swallow and made it clear that he felt very hard done by.'

'I see. So, there was professional jealousy *and* thwarted love. Tell me, Mrs Hendricks…'

'Please call me Jean.'

'Right – Jean – this funding that Samantha had managed to obtain, what happened to it after she withdrew from the college?'

'It was redirected into other areas of research, and you can probably guess who hoped to gain by it.'

'Dr Odell?'

Jean nodded. 'Except he was still just plain Bruce Odell in those days, a final-year student like Samantha.'

'So, it could have been very much to his advantage when she opted out?'

'Yes indeed. He'd made it clear he planned to continue at Darwin once he'd gained a PhD and would need funds to pay for further research.'

'And is this what happened?'

'Partly. He managed to secure his doctorate and, despite his unpopularity, was awarded a grant to carry out a project overseas. On his return, however, the college felt it had been money wasted, so further funding stopped and he was unable to continue.'

'And now, in spite of his academic qualifications, he's running a second-hand bookshop.'

Jean nodded again. 'Yes, I think that says it all, doesn't it?' Suddenly, she seemed to grasp the enormity of what might be construed from what she'd said. 'But, you surely don't think he was in any way connected to Samantha's disappearance?'

'Rejected romantically, academically sidelined and with financial gains to be made,' Jack reiterated, raising sceptical eyebrows. 'People have done bad things for lesser motives, Jean.'

'It's hard to think of anyone harming Samantha,' persisted the secretary. 'She wasn't just a brilliant scholar, but also so well liked by us all.'

'Were you close then?'

'I wouldn't say that but, with no mum to talk to, she did seem to regard me as a good discreet listener when there were things worrying her.'

'What sort of things?'

'Oh, the usual anxieties that concern young women embarking on challenging studies.' The secretary gave a humourless laugh. 'Which usually narrow down to boyfriend problems. Samantha had a quite serious relationship at the start of her studies at Darwin, a modern-languages student at Trinity and in the last year of his naval scholarship. I know they were quite close for a while, even after his graduation, when he went on to begin service in the Royal Marines.'

'A marine, eh? So, what happened after that, Jean?'

'A gradual break-up, from what I could understand. Things seemed to start going wrong once Samantha went off to Peru to study some native specie, and her marine boyfriend was sent down to fight in the Falklands, where he did quite well by all accounts and ended up something of a hero.'

'But not enough of a hero to woo Miss Waites back to his side?'

'No, I'm afraid not. When Samantha returned from Peru, she told me she'd met someone else, a married British financier out there on business and with whom she'd had a relationship.'

'Called?'

'I can't remember, Mr Fellows, but I'm sure Dr Odell will be able to tell you.'

'I hope so.' Jack shrugged his shoulders. 'I suppose these things happen, but it doesn't seem quite in character for the type of girl you've described, to have a fling with a married man while her boyfriend's away fighting for Queen and country.'

'I know. I felt the same way, and I told Samantha so, but she said that it was more than just "a fling" and she gave me the impression that she had some sort of grievance against her old marine boyfriend.'

'What sort of grievance?' asked Jack, somewhat surprised. 'The lad was two thousand miles away fighting, so how could he possibly have offended her?'

'I don't know and she never explained.'

'So, we had *two* very disappointed hopefuls. The rejected marine and the thwarted student. No wonder she had things on her mind.'

'Yes, but it was something far, far worse that was worrying her when her research supposedly took her to her to the Broads.' Jean looked around to check they were well out of earshot of anyone. 'You see, Samantha told me herself that she was actually fearing for her life and didn't know what to do.'

Jack stiffened slightly. 'Her life! Just who was she fearing? One of the rejected suitors or a cheated wife perhaps?'

'I really don't know,' admitted the secretary, shaking her head again. 'I tried to get her to explain more, but she just said it was something she'd have to sort out for herself. In the end, I believe her research project on the Broads was just an excuse to drop out entirely and escape into complete anonymity.'

'How long was there between her returning from Peru and this trip to the Broads?'

'About a year, perhaps two, during which time she was back researching here and continuing the project for which she'd received such generous funding.'

'Did this money come from the college?'

'No, it was far beyond the pockets of our funding. I believe it was given by the financier with whom she'd had the affair. Odell never actually said she prostituted herself for that grant, but he always hinted as much.'

'Strange,' said Jack, almost to himself before giving this informative lady a grateful smile. 'Jean, you've been a mine of information, for which I'm very grateful. But, before I leave, can you try and answer just two more questions?'

'If I can.'

'Do you have any recollection of Samantha having a leather handbag?' Jack gave a brief description of his find and how it must have looked, even though he had little hope of a positive response.

But Jean smiled with satisfaction. 'Yes, surprisingly I can, because she brought me back what sounds like an identical one as a "thank you" for all my support. They'd been handmade for her in Peru with traditional designs worked into lovely thick natural leather.'

'Hmmm,' said Jack, 'not the sort of thing she would part with willingly then?'

'Oh no. She was very proud of that bag, as I was of mine.'

'And this ex-boyfriend of hers, the Royal Marine, do you remember *his* name?'

'Gosh, I've been trying to, but I'm not very good with names, as you can tell, and it *was* a long time ago, but I think it was Greg something or other.'

'Greg what, Jean? Try and remember. This is important,' encouraged Jack calmly, trying hard not to pressurise this most conscientious of women. 'If you can't, then is there any clue you can think of?'

'Oh my goodness. I'm sorry.' Jean rubbed her forehead, as if to stimulate her brain-cells. 'I just seem to think it had some sort of royal connection.'

'Royal!' exclaimed Jack. 'You mean this bloke was connected to the royal family?'

'Oh no,' replied the secretary, quickly and obviously frustrated that she couldn't recall more accurately. 'Just a name that made me *think* of royalty.'

'Okay. Anything else about him that comes to mind?'

'Yes, one thing. I remember that Samantha told me he rowed for Cambridge.'

'What, in the Boat Race?'

'Yes, I think so. I remember her telling me how she often used to go with him to training sessions at the crack of dawn.'

'She *must* have been in love,' commented Jack with a smile, standing up and taking the secretary's hand. 'Jean, you've been more helpful than you can possibly imagine.' He paused to extract a card from his wallet. 'Here's my number. If the actual name does come back to you, give me a ring.'

'I promise I will.'

After a final handshake at the door, Jack set off to map-read his way to Boffin Books, not quite believing his good luck at having gained so much information from his very first contacts.

*   *   *

Jean Hendricks had been correct in saying it was only a short way. Just past King's College, Jack turned off towards the market square and, in a nearby alleyway, found Boffin Books. It turned out to be a somewhat shabby and run-down little establishment. *Specialists in Scientific Works* proclaimed the lettering on the grimy small-paned windows while *Proprietor: Dr Bruce Odell PhD*, above the paint-peeled doorway, hinted that the man himself was still keen to remind of his own academic credentials. Jack entered to the jangling of a tarnished brass bell that would have done credit to a Dickensian play, and an almost-overpowering fustiness.

At first it was difficult to see beyond the rows of bookshelves that heaved under the weight of countless learned tomes, each section alphabetically categorised by a roughly-lettered label pinned to its shelf. Starting with *Anatomy*, they seemed to cover every scientific subject imaginable. Through a gap between *Physics* and *Physiology*, could be seen, seated at a desk, a somewhat round-shouldered and balding figure who now studied Jack with little enthusiasm over half-moon spectacles. 'Can I help you?' he asked in a bored, insincere voice.

'Possibly,' answered Jack with equal antipathy. 'Are *you* Dr Bruce Odell?'

'Yes. And you are…?'

'Jack Fellows.' The ranger showed his ID and detected just a shadow of concern pass across Odell's face when he then added, 'and I'm here to find out about Samantha Waites.'

The bookshop owner shifted a little uncomfortably in his chair. 'How could I possibly help you?'

'Well you knew her at Darwin College, didn't you, and your reaction to her name shows you obviously remember her?'

'Well, p-perhaps I did,' stammered Odell, his blotchy face becoming rather flushed. 'But that must have been well over thirty years ago and I haven't seen her since.'

'Neither has anyone else,' countered Jack, 'which is why I'm here. Perhaps we could start by your shedding a bit more light on her surprise resignation.'

'"Surprise"! It was no surprise to me,' sneered Odell.

'Why was that?'

'Simply because of her complicated private life.' Odell gave a slight shake of the head. 'Do you know, she was carrying on with a married man whom she'd met while researching in Peru?'

'Yes I'm aware of that.' Jack leaned against a bookshelf. 'Just out of interest, what exactly was it she went there to research?'

'The Hydrochoiros.'

Jack frowned. 'I'm sorry. Hydro-what?'

'Cho-ir-us,' repeated Odell, as though he were talking to a five year old. 'Hydro, meaning water and choiros, meaning pig or, to give it its native name, Capybara, the largest rodent in the world.'

'And which, presumably, is indigenous to South America,' concluded Jack, trying to get his head around this previously unheard of creature.

Odell nodded. 'Exactly. Waites was researching the molecular phylogenetics of the specie.' He paused to give a slight shrug of his shoulders. 'A complete waste of resources, of course.'

Jack's eyebrows rose slightly. 'I gather you didn't exactly approve of her choice of research.'

'What people choose to study is up to them. It's the squandering of precious research funds that could be better spent elsewhere, that I can't stomach.'

'But I gather Samantha had found a private sponsor which allowed her to prolong her overseas studies.'

Odell gave an audible scoff. 'By using her undoubted feminine charms to extract money from the wealthy, might be a better description.'

'Which particular "wealthy" person are we talking about here?' asked Jack. 'Not the married man you mentioned earlier, by any chance?'

'Yes, a British international financier by the name of Charles de Courcey, with whom she'd struck up a relationship in Peru.'

'And for whom she'd ditched her previous boyfriend.' Jack fixed Odell with questioning eyes. 'And did *you* have desires in that direction as well, Doctor?'

Odell sat up sharply in his chair. 'I most certainly did not.'

'So, reports that you made several advances towards Samantha Waites, weren't true then?' pressed Jack.

'I liked Samantha, of course, but she – look here, how dare you come in here asking such personal questions?' There appeared to be no heating in his shop and it was quite chilly, but Odell took out a handkerchief and wiped some sweat from his brow. 'Here I am, trying to answer your damned stupid questions, and you dare to start probing into my private life.'

Jack's eyes narrowed. 'All right, all right, calm down. For the time being, let's ignore your own "liking" for Samantha and instead you can tell me why she threw in the towel so unexpectedly.'

'All I know is, she went to the Norfolk Broads to continue her research. I remember her telling me before she left that she was going to stay on a boat.'

'What boat?'

'I don't know, but it was while she was there, she decided to quit.'

'When was this exactly?'

'1984,' replied Odell. 'I remember it was just before I got my doctorate, which would make it June of that year.'

'And can you remember how she let the university know she was giving up her studies?'

'From what I heard, it was by the normal procedure of sending a letter simply saying she'd decided to withdraw from academic life for "personal reasons".'

'Which you assumed…'

'To mean she was going off with de Courcey.'

'Did you see this letter yourself?'

'No, of course not. I was just another student working hard to put the finishing touches to my thesis. Presumably, she sent the letter to her supervisor.'

'I'm assuming this "resignation" was a permanent one,' said Jack, 'but did it have to be? No doubt, there were ways of taking time out if she was having problems?'

'Yes, she could easily have applied for an authorised absence of up to six terms for personal reasons, or asked to extend her time researching in Norfolk.'

'But she chose to do neither?'

'No.'

'Didn't you find that rather strange?'

'Not if her heart was ruling her head,' replied Odell, dismissively.

'And so, after her departure to Norfolk, you didn't hear from Samantha Waites again?'

'No.'

'And never made any attempt to contact her?'

Odell gave a little snort. 'Why should I, when we all assumed she was still having an affair with de Courcey.'

'So, what happened to her sponsorship money when she quit? Was it made available to fund other students? You for example?'

'Er – yes – as it happens.'

'How did you manage that?'

'Simply by writing to de Courcey,' answered Odell, somewhat hesitantly. 'After Samantha had left, I spotted him and his wife in the background of a photo taken at a charity event to raise money for endangered species. It was then I decided he might be just the man to fund my own project, to which he readily agreed.'

'A philanthropist indeed!' observed Jack, smiling, 'but I would have thought that de Courcey would be the last person you'd want money from. What exactly did your own research involve?'

'An examination into whether there was a genomic basis for specification in rhesus macaques.'

'Monkeys?'

'Yes, very important work, on a primate used so much in animal testing.'

'Not something you'd ever find me supporting, Dr Odell,' said Jack distastefully.

Odell gave a little sneer. 'Yes, well you Animal Rights people might think differently if you were a diabetic like me and relied on medical research for your continued well-being.'

'Yes, well there are always two sides to every argument,' conceded Jack. 'But why would this Charles de Courcey so readily agree to redirect funds he'd previously allocated for, shall we say, personal reasons, to your questionable project?'

'Perhaps to outwardly prove to his wife that he had no ulterior motive for sponsoring Samantha and was just as keen to pay out for other students' research projects.'

'Hmmm, you may be right,' acknowledged Jack, stirring himself to leave. 'Seeing how busy you are, Dr Odell, I appreciate you giving me the time you have.'

'Not at all,' replied Odell, completely missing the sarcasm, 'but I know you'd like to compensate me just a little for that time by buying a copy of my book.' He reached behind him to where several piles of paperbacks lay undisturbed under a layer of dust.

'Of course,' said Jack taking out his wallet, 'we all need our share of rhesus genomics, don't we?'

Book in hand, Jack was halfway out when the jangling doorbell served to ring a bell of his own. 'Oh, just one more question, Doctor.' He stepped back into the shop. 'What exactly had Samantha gone to Norfolk to research all those years ago?'

*   *   *

A brisk ten minute walk had Jack back at The Anchor pub where he found Audrey sitting at a table on the outside terrace, patiently sipping a gin and tonic and watching a group of students, venturing out on a self-hire punt, attempting to negotiate the bridge beside her.

'Not another book, Jack!' she exclaimed, noticing the fat volume under her husband's arm. 'What have you bought now?'

'Don't ask,' he said, sticking Odell's work on a spare chair under the table, sinking down gladly on another and taking a long swig of the lager his wife had waiting for him. 'Phew! Thanks, love, I needed that. It's been a hard-working morning.'

'But a worthwhile one, apparently,' observed Audrey.

'Not bad. How about you? Did you get to look around the chapel?'

'Yes, I did and it was more wonderful than I'd even imagined. A beautiful building and, to put the icing on the cake, the choirboys were rehearsing for Easter.' She leaned a little closer. 'But, come on, Jack, you know I'm itching to know. Did you actually find out who owned that bag?'

'Yes, I think I did.' Jack gave a brief summary of the conversations leading to the probability of it belonging to Samantha Waites.

'So, that's an end to it then,' sighed a relieved Audrey. 'Fancy this girl being blessed with personality, brains and opportunity, throwing it all away for someone else's husband.'

'That's how it looks.' Jack paused a few seconds to stare into his glass. 'But there are still parts of this that don't add up. For instance, why would someone, as seemingly grounded as she was and dedicated to fulfilling her late-parents' dreams, suddenly give up the chance of being awarded a doctorate?'

'Because she was in love, Jack, and women do all sorts of strange things when they're besotted. Even marrying a copper.'

But Jack was too engrossed in his findings to even notice his wife's quip. 'Yeah, but to never get in touch with any of your college friends afterwards is a bit strange,' he persisted. 'People don't just disappear completely unless...'

'Jack! Hold it right there!' Audrey leaned across the table. 'I know just where this is going and, for your own good, I'm going to stop it in its tracks.' There was firmness in her words and Jack knew the set of that mouth bode ill for any resistance. 'A rotten old handbag that some girl lost has finally come to the surface. You've found out the likely owner and she probably went abroad over a quarter of a century ago. No-one else is interested and neither should you be and that's an end to it.'

'Okay, love, you're right. I always seem to see the worst in every situation and paint devils on the wall that just aren't there.' He gave his wife a reassuring squeeze of the hand. 'I won't get any more involved except for...'

'Jack, you're not listening to me,' interrupted Audrey. 'There won't be any "except for". Is that clear?'

'Not when you hear what it is I want to find out,' replied Jack. 'Okay, we'll let Samantha Waites ride off into the sunset, but there is something I do mean to investigate further.'

'It must be important, Jack.'

'Not so much important as intriguing. I'm talking about what Samantha Waites had gone to the Broads to research when she disappeared.'

'Which was?'

'You'll never believe this, Aud. I didn't myself when Odell told me.' Jack lowered his voice slightly, 'It was The Waveney River Monster.'

*　　*　　*

Chapter Three

'So, Jack, was there such a thing or is this all just some wild myth from long ago?'

It was the morning after their Cambridge visit and, back in their kitchen, Audrey had just poured two mugs of coffee when her husband emerged from his study.

'Far from it,' said Jack, sitting down at the kitchen table, spooning in some sugar and giving Spike a gentle stroke with his foot. The collie was still pawing his ear and looking a bit sorry for himself. 'I've just been on the phone to Harry Bentley, the ranger on the Waveney, and he remembers it well, being the river inspector there at the time.'

'You mean there really was a monster?' Audrey settled herself opposite, keen to hear the news. 'I like this sort of mystery, so you're on safe ground here, Jack.'

'Good.' Jack took a sip of coffee. 'Well, the basic facts are that in 1984, two Coypu hunters, out in their boat checking traps, spotted something they couldn't explain.'

'Hang on,' she interrupted, leaning slightly closer. 'Coypu hunters?'

'Yep, coypus were semi-aquatic South American rodents introduced into this country in 1929. The idea was to breed them for their fur and several farms were set up, including some in Norfolk. Of course, inevitably, some coypus escaped and re-settled in the wild.'

'If they were water creatures, they must have flourished on the Broads.'

'They did indeed,' agreed Jack. 'So much so that they bred even faster in their new environment and soon became a pest by consuming vast amounts of farmers' crops, particularly sugar beet. In the end, the Ministry of Food decided they had to be eradicated and employed hunters, like our two on the Waveney, to do just that. The scheme was successful and no coypus have been seen in this country since 1989.'

'But are you saying those two hunters saw a *monster* that morning?' asked Audrey, wide eyed. 'What did it look like?'

'I'll find that out tomorrow. I'm going out with Harry on his patrol and he's going to show me where it was seen and what happened.'

'I can't wait to hear all about it.' Audrey paused. 'So, do you think this research was somehow connected to Samantha Waites' disappearance?'

'I'm not sure of that, but it was certainly in line with her speciality, the coypu being from South America, but somehow I feel there was more to it than that. Don't forget that Jean Hendricks reckoned the whole visit was just an excuse to escape whatever threat was causing her so much anxiety.' Jack finished his coffee, but continued to stare into the empty mug. 'I'd dearly like to know what it was that girl was so scared about, Aud. The fact is, I can't help thinking that all her fears were realised.'

Audrey laid a hand on Jack's. 'I know how you feel, but we've talked about this already, love. By all means, find out all you can about this strange monster, but *please* just leave it at that. If you really can't rest until you know what happened to this Waites girl, then why don't you call the police and fill them in with all the info you've collected so far. Your friend Bailey's just been promoted again and posted back to North Walsham, so why not discuss your fears for Samantha's disappearance with him.'

Jack shrugged. 'You're probably right, Aud, but I can see Bailey's face when I dump this on his lap, especially as he's now got the whole CID department to run.'

'Well, you won't know his reaction until you call him.' She leaned closer to give him a peck on the cheek and just as quickly recoiled when hit by a nasty smell. 'Jack, you still stink of that disgusting bag.'

'Of course I don't,' he protested, sniffing his fingers. 'I haven't even touched it today.'

'Well *something* smells. Perhaps it's Spike.'

'I think you're right,' agreed Jack, bending down beside the collie.

'It might be his ear. He seems to have been pawing it even more these last few days?'

'Let's have a look then, old chap.' Jack pulled back and peered into each pointed ear in turn and, on the second, reeled back with a screwed up nose. 'It's this one, Aud. It smells awful.'

Audrey took a small torch from the kitchen drawer and shone it into the offending orifice. 'Yes, and I can see some sort of yellowy puss further down.' She stood up and switched off the torch. 'There's some sort of infection there, Jack, so he needs to see the vet.'

'Right, let's get him booked in then. I'll ring them straight away.'

'No, you go and call Bailey while I talk to the vet on my mobile,' she suggested. 'The sooner you find out what happened to Samantha Waites, the happier you'll be.'

'Okay, love.' Jack rinsed his mug under the tap, went back into his study and rang Bailey's new number.

*   *   *

'Jack, good to hear from you - I think.' Detective Inspector Bailey leaned back in his chair at North Walsham CID headquarters, cradling the phone beneath his chin while he signed some papers just brought in by his female DC. He nodded her into the chair opposite before turning his attention back to his caller. 'So, what can I do for you?'

'Accept my congratulations first,' said Jack, ignoring the slight wariness in the DI's welcome and remembering his own arduous climb up the promotion ladder at Scotland Yard. 'Detective Inspector, eh? You fast-trackers leave us old plodders standing. I guess it won't be too long before you're Chief Constable.'

'Thanks for the confidence,' Bailey laughed, 'but the fact is, Jack, I like what I'm doing and don't want to move for a long time yet.'

'Busy?'

'Always. You know how it is.'

'So you won't exactly relish another enquiry from me?'

'Depends what it is.' Bailey pulled a notepad nearer and clicked his pen. 'Give me the details.'

'A missing person.'

'For how long, Jack? Unless it's a child or there are suspicious circumstances, you know we're not too bothered until they've been gone at least twenty-four hours.'

'How about thirty years?'

'Thirty!' Bailey ran a hand through his hair and gave the patient DC opposite a roll of the eyes. 'Alright, what are the facts?'

Jack left nothing out, including the river monster connection.

'South American research – Falklands hero boyfriend – rich financier – mysterious creatures in our broads – fearing for her life,' groaned Bailey as he finished enumerating the bare data. 'Jack, you sure you haven't been watching too many TV dramas?'

'I wish I had the time. No, Bailey, my gut instinct tells me this girl met with a bad end and I feel we – you – should at least investigate it.'

'Well, you know full well what I'm going to ask next,' said Bailey. 'How come no one has reported her missing before now? Her family, for instance?'

'Because she didn't have any family, Bailey, and contacts of hers in Cambridge were sure she was still secretly carrying on with de Courcey, and assumed she'd opted out for private reasons. She certainly didn't get in touch with any of them again, and there was always the possibility she'd returned to South America to start a new life.'

'Perhaps she had.'

'Yeah. Or perhaps someone ended the one she'd got.'

'Okay, Jack,' sighed Bailey, 'we won't make this official yet but, if you're serious, I'll make some enquiries, starting with checking if anyone *did* report Samantha missing at the time.' He turned around his notes and pushed them in front of the DC. 'But do *me* one favour this time, Jack. Just leave it to us now and concentrate on patrolling those beautiful waterways through the summer months ahead, you lucky blighter!'

'I will,' promised Jack, 'if only to keep Audrey happy. Except, that is, the part of this investigation that definitely does concern me as a Broads ranger.'

'Which is?'

'Investigating the Waveney River Monster, of course,' said Jack, quickly hanging up before Bailey had time to reply.

*   *   *

'Would you believe it, our regular vet's off sick and the rest are so busy that it will be a few days before they can see poor old Spike,' explained Audrey, switching off her mobile, as her husband came back into the kitchen.

'Well, that's not good enough,' complained Jack, bending to give Spike a stroke as the collie once more pawed his ear. 'The poor old chap's obviously in some discomfort.'

'Yes, and they're pretty sure it's canker,' continued Audrey, 'and said he really should be seen to as soon as possible. They've given me the number of a new practice that's opened in the next village, so I've just rung them.'

'And - can they see him?'

'Not immediately, because Mr McQuaid, the new vet, is busy lambing, but Rosemary, the receptionist, has booked Spike in for first thing the day after tomorrow.'

'Good. I'll be glad to see him dealt with. What's the name of this new outfit?'

'VetCare, and very pleasant this Rosemary sounded.'

'Even if receiving her bill might not be,' replied Jack with a grimace. 'Anyway, Spike doesn't seem to be suffering unduly, and he'll enjoy a nice run out tomorrow.'

'You mean we're coming with you to investigate this strange creature?'

'Just taxiing if you don't mind, love. Dropping me off and picking me up further upriver. I'll be on Harry Bentley's launch, but you two can enjoy a nice walk along the riverbank while I'm gone.'

'Well, I'll make sure Spike doesn't dive in to chase any monsters,' said Audrey, smiling.

Beneath the table, the border collie merely buried his head in his paws.

*   *   *

Chapter Four

With the fresh breeze against a fast-flowing tide, the Waveney this morning was producing white-capped wavelets through which Harry Bentley was holding his launch virtually stationary. It was a stretch of river much like the rest but, to Jack, of intriguing significance. 'So, Harry, this is the spot?'

'Yep, about midway between St Peter's and Somerleyton.'

'And you were actually working here in 1984?'

'That's right, as a River Inspector, as they called us in those days, for Great Yarmouth Port and Haven Commissioners, who then had responsibility for the Broads. It was the 19th of March, a bright clear Monday morning and much stiller than today. Two coypu hunters, Colin Denny and Noel Rochford, were out patrolling and checking their traps.'

'So, what exactly did they see?'

'What they first thought was a log in the water, about fifteen yards from their boat. Then they realised it wasn't a log, but a living creature and far bigger than any coypu, estimating its weight at between three and four hundred pounds.'

'Wow! That's certainly big.' Jack turned in his seat and surveyed the choppy waters of the river. 'Just what did this creature look like?'

'That's the weird thing, because Denny hadn't seen anything like it before, having as it did, a head like a moose, with wide nostrils and big eyes. Its back, he reckoned, was about two feet wide and covered in coarse brown fur. They followed it in their boat for about twenty minutes as it swam both on and under the surface, and they had the feeling it was looking at them as much as they were looking at it.'

Jack felt just the slightest prickle down his spine. 'But they didn't feel threatened in any way?'

'Not at all. They were armed with twenty-two calibre pistols and well used to dispatching animals but, strangely, they felt no inclination to harm this fascinating beast, even though they described it as "big, powerful and gruesome".'

'Was this the only sighting?'

Bentley shook his head. 'Not exactly. Rochford reckoned he'd spotted it three or four times before, but after this encounter, it was never seen again.'

Coming around the bend in the river now was a large hire-cruiser. Although early in the season, modern facilities on these big boats made for comfortable and tranquil cruising. As it passed the ranger's launch, the couple on board gave a cheery wave. Jack returned the greeting and nodded after it. 'I can't imagine holidaymakers being too keen on this strange story at the time. Did it have any effect on the boat hire business?'

'Not really, though it did stop people swimming in the river for a bit,' Bentley replied with a chuckle. 'In fact, it actually *added* to the local interest, especially as one of the big hire agencies offered £10,000 reward to anyone producing proof as to its existence, providing...' he paused and smiled, '... they were on one of *their* boats and the creature wasn't harmed. But no-one ever tried to claim the prize.' The ranger glanced at his watch. 'Time to get going Jack or we'll be late at St Olaves.' He slid the engine ahead and the launch once more cleaved down the Waveney. Soon the scene of this very strange happening over a quarter-century earlier was far astern.

Jack took a final backwards glance before turning again to the colleague beside him. 'What did the experts think it was?'

Bentley throttled back very slightly and settled lower in his seat. 'There were several theories. Otters and muntjak deer were two, but the Otter Trust at Earsham said it was very unlikely any of theirs had escaped and there were no *wild* otters or chinese deer at that time. One naturalist suggested it might be a bull Atlantic grey seal that had made its way upriver but, like the deer theory, that was certainly at odds with the description given by the hunters. In the end, it was a local zoologist who came up with the theory that it might have been an escaped capybara.'

'You mean the hydrochoiros?' gasped Jack. 'The largest rodent in the world?'

'If you say so,' acceded Bentley. He gave Jack a quizzical look. 'You seem very well-read on the subject?'

'Oh, just that it relates to the studies of someone I'm trying to locate.' Jack explained the strange disappearance of Samantha Waites and her own capybara research. 'The thing is, Harry, she came to the Broads to follow up this sighting sometime in late June of that year. You didn't, by any chance, meet a young female research student staying on a boat around then?'

Already, they were sliding under Somerleyton Swing Bridge and Bentley waited until they were well clear before answering, 'You know, Jack, I might just well have done.' He frowned in concentration. 'Yes, it's coming back to me now. It was at St Olaves staithe. I think I'd moored up there for lunch, but I definitely remember a young lady coming over to the launch and asking what I knew about the sighting. As you know, we meet thousands of people over the years in this job, but she still sticks in my memory, because she was quite impressionable and seemed incredibly knowledgeable about Capybaras. Nice looking too with deep auburn hair tied back in a pony-tail. I'm sure she introduced herself as Sam something or other.' Bentley smiled at what was obviously a pleasant recollection. 'I couldn't really tell her much more than she could have read in the papers,' he admitted, 'but

34

it was fascinating talking to her just the same, seeing as she'd also studied some such-like creatures in Peru.'

'That's our girl!' exclaimed Jack, hardly able to believe that here was someone putting a face to the name that had been filling his thoughts all this last week. 'Tell me, Harry, was she actually moored up in St. Olaves?'

'Yep, right there at the staithe.'

'In what sort of boat?'

'A big one, if I remember rightly, and smart. Privately owned, not hire. I reckon it was a forty-five-footer, wooden and not painted, but varnished all over.'

'And was Samantha alone on this boat?'

'I think so,' recalled Bentley, pausing to wave to a traditional broads sailing cruiser tacking its way upriver. 'At least, I didn't see anyone else onboard.'

'Sorry, mate, for bombarding you with all these questions,' apologised Jack, aware he was giving his friend and colleague something of the third-degree, 'but they are important. Think back, Harry. Did she seem to be just using the boat for accommodation or was she actually cruising?'

'I really don't know, Jack. She didn't say.' Bentley paused, rubbing his chin with the palm of his hand, eyes partially closed, trying hard to recall events from so long ago. After a brief moment, he said, 'You know, I'm certain she *was* skippering it herself because, now I think about it, I remember we talked about getting through Yarmouth and how to handle the tides. She said she'd had a scary experience there earlier in the week.'

'A heck of a big boat for one person to handle. She must have been very self-assured and confident then.'

Bentley shrugged. 'Yes and no, and that was the strange thing about her. She was extremely capable and full of common sense when it came to handling boats, obviously very knowledgeable about rodents and happy to travel to South America by herself, but she seemed nervous about being on her own *here* in what's a pretty safe environment.'

'Really? What gave you that impression?'

'Just that she seemed eager to be around other people. I remember telling her she could moor quite close to where the creature was seen, but she said she'd rather stay at a public staithe where there were plenty of holidaymakers. Likewise, when I suggested that she'd be better carrying on straight through Yarmouth, she said she'd feel happier staying at the busy yacht station. At first I assumed it was in case she needed help mooring up but, even at the time, I had a niggling feeling it was perhaps because she felt vulnerable being alone.'

'Hmm, interesting,' murmured Jack. 'You don't, by any chance, remember the name of this boat?'

They were coming into the approach to St Olaves itself now and Bentley shook his head. 'Sorry, Jack, not a chance. It *was* thirty years ago you know.'

'Yeah, I understand. I'm thankful for you remembering what you have, but did you get any idea where it was based?'

'Not really.' The moorings and houses of St Olaves were coming abeam now and Bentley throttled back yet more, bringing the speed down to a steady four. 'It certainly wasn't from around here, or else I would have recognised it, and seeing as this Sam girl was planning on heading back through Yarmouth, then it must have been from somewhere on the northern rivers.'

The old cast-iron bowstring girder bridge was drawing closer now. Audrey would be meeting him on the adjacent staithe. There wasn't much time for further questions. 'Harry, are you sure you can't just give me some clue as to the name of the boat?'

With a smart burst of astern power, the launch came gently alongside the staithe and then both men were leaving the wheelhouse for the open working area aft. Bentley grabbed a midships warp and slipped it around the nearest mooring post. It was sufficient to hold them in while he had a final good think. 'Gosh, Jack, I wish I could. I remember it was an unusual name and...'

'... and?'

'It had some sort of decoration painted next to it.'

'What, an emblem or something?' asked Jack, hopefully.

But Bentley shook his head again. 'No, something simpler than that - a flower I think. Yes, that's right, some brightly coloured flower. I remember now how nice it looked painted there on the varnished wooden hull.'

'Well, that's something at least,' replied Jack, before pausing to wave to Audrey who was walking down the grassy bank towards them. He turned back to Bentley. 'Thanks again, Harry. I really enjoyed reacquainting myself with the southern rivers, and the information you've been able to recall about your meeting with Sam all those years ago has been really helpful.'

'You're welcome. Sorry we didn't spot any monsters, but I hope you find your girl.'

'So do I.' Jack hopped ashore, pushed the launch off and watched as it swung back upriver. Running now with the flood tide, it soon disappeared from sight. He turned to meet Audrey but, just as he did so, his mobile rang. By the time he'd answered it and rung off, his wife was by his side.

'Who was that, Jack?'

'DI Bailey, calling to say he needed to talk to me. He's in Norwich tonight, so we arranged to meet up for an evening drink at a pub on the Yare and have a good chat.'

'What about?'

'Hopefully, some inside info on Samantha Waites, but he couldn't discuss it over the phone. Whatever it is, it's urgent and he sounded a bit upset, which isn't like him.'

'Well, you'll find out why, tonight.'

'I will indeed.' Jack glanced towards their car in the pub car park. 'Is Spike okay?'

'Yes, we had time for a lovely walk alongside the river, so he'll be glad to curl up in the car for a while now.'

'Good,' said Jack patting his stomach with one hand and putting the other on his wife's shoulder, 'because I'm famished. Let's go and eat.'

*   *   *

'Well, Samantha Waites seems to have had more reasons than we thought to come to the Broads,' said Audrey, buttering her roll, 'if the naturalist back then reckoned the monster might have been one of those Capi... Capi-whatsits.'

'Capybara, and, yes, what an incredible opportunity for her, as those creatures have never previously been found outside of South America.' He and Audrey were still in St Olaves, enjoying a pub lunch beside the staithe, as Jack related all that Harry Bentley had told him. 'Unfortunately, it could never be proven that it really *was* a capybara,' he stressed. 'I believe those coypu hunters saw *something*, Aud, but just *what*, I guess no-one will ever know for sure.'

'Strange though, that it might have been the very rodent Samantha had been researching in Peru.' Within the *olde-worlde* ambience of the pub, Audrey was finding this whole mystery intriguing to say the least. 'You can well imagine her scuttling here to investigate the possibility of finding one right on her doorstep.'

'Except I'm surer than ever now that she was using that fortuitous sighting as the perfect excuse to hide away from something or someone. Harry reckoned she was keen to have company at all times and he got the impression that she felt vulnerable and insecure, which would certainly tie in with our fears.'

'That she could have been in danger?'

'Exactly.' Jack paused while the waitress delivered their main course. 'I don't think Jean Hendricks was exaggerating when she said Samantha was in fear of her life. I'm sure now she was.'

'But why and from whom?' asked Audrey, taking up her knife and fork. 'Her jilted marine boyfriend, that rebuffed fellow student Odell or the cheated wife of the adulterous rich financier?'

Jack shook his head. 'Odell wasn't my cup of tea, but hardly the type to resort to violence, and I don't think a career officer in the Royal Marines would risk everything to get even. I still haven't nailed who he was, but apparently he'd come out of the Falklands as something of a hero, so I'm sure he wouldn't have been short of female adulation on his return home. No, if it's anyone, the aggrieved wife would be my bet. She'd have the most to lose *and* the money to hire a hit-man.'

'Good gracious, Jack, that would have been a bit drastic, when she could've simply divorced her husband. Surely crimes like that only happen in films. Anyway, I really can't imagine her marriage can have been that strong or she would have gone to Peru with him. No, love, I wouldn't be too quick to dismiss your hero-marine. As a commando, he'd be a trained killer.'

'But also trained to control his aggression,' pointed out Jack. 'Besides, I'm sure active service in the Falklands would quickly have put affairs of the heart on the back-burner. No, Aud, he'd have been too busy fighting Argentineans to have wasted time on bitterness for a lost love.'

'But perhaps, just to spare him while he was away, Samantha didn't tell him until they met again. Who knows what effect those months of combat stress might have had on his state of mind.' Audrey struggled to open her sachet of tartar sauce, in the end using her teeth, before adding further substance to her theory. 'Also, do you remember your Mrs Hendricks said she thought Samantha had some sort of grievance against him. Maybe it was serious and Samantha confronted him with it.'

'Yes, but this was a couple of years *after* the Falklands and, anyway, this is simply conjecture at the moment.'

'Well, what I *do* know, Jack, is that none of this is *your* problem. It's in the hands of the police now,' reminded Audrey, 'and it sounds as though Bailey has found out something already, as he wants to see you tonight.'

'Something's happened, that's for sure.' Jack was still concerned at the downcast tone in the young detective's voice. He glanced at his watch. 'Five hours and I'll find out.'

*   *   *

'Crikey, it's good to be out of the office, and I could do with something stronger than this,' said DI Bailey, sipping his lemonade as he sat down with Jack at a small table in the bar of a riverside watering hole.

Just beyond the window, three hire cruisers lay on evening moorings, their crews at the bar enjoying some jovial refreshment before heading for the dining room. Jack smiled and raised an eyebrow. 'You told me yesterday you loved your work, Bailey.'

'Not today, I didn't.'

'Sorry to hear that.'

'You'll be even sorrier when I tell you why, Jack.' Bailey put down his glass. 'Fact is, I've been ordered to take no further action on your missing girl.'

'You've been what?' Jack's raised voice caused some of the holidaymakers to glance around, and he quickly lowered it and leaned closer. 'Why for goodness' sake, and by whom?'

Bailey shook his head in genuine bewilderment. 'I don't know, Jack. I got my DC to start a computer search of the files as soon as you'd gone yesterday and that must have flagged up something. Anyway, whatever, my Super called me in and told me to forget the whole thing. He didn't say, but hinted strongly enough, that this order had come from the Chief Constable himself.'

'Who must have been leaned on from somewhere even higher up the chain.' Jack sat back. 'And I don't suppose he gave you a clue as to why?'

'I asked, of course,' assured Bailey, 'but the only lame excuse I got was that our budget didn't allow for looking into unreported cases from decades back.'

'That's rubbish and you know it. They're examining cold-cases all the time these days, with the help of DNA.'

'I know, but if I'm to keep my job, I have to obey orders.'

'Of course you do.' Jack glanced about and lowered his voice yet further. 'But that doesn't mean *I* have to. Why don't I take up where you left off.'

Bailey frowned. 'Is that wise? If someone somewhere doesn't want this looked into, then you'll be best forgetting it yourself.'

'That's exactly *why*, I want to. At first, the chances were it could have been a simple case of lost property. But the more I've discovered since, has convinced me there was dirty work afoot back in 1984 and what you've just told me confirms it.' Jack shuffled his chair closer. 'Did you manage to find out anything before the shutters came down?'

The DI shook his head. 'Only that nothing was on file, which means there was no report back then of Samantha Waites as a missing person or of any unexplained deaths.'

It was Jack's turn to shake his head. 'I did a little research myself today on this monster-mystery, and that was genuine enough.'

'You mean there really was a monster!' exclaimed Bailey.

Jack smiled. 'I don't know about that, but the reported sighting happened.' He explained to Bailey all that had transpired during his morning with Harry Bentley.

'So, Samantha Waites really did come to investigate that creature?'

'Yep, and was staying on a boat and scared stiff about something.' Jack sat back in his chair. 'It certainly wasn't the monster, but just what, someone doesn't want us to find out.'

'I'm sure you're right, Jack, and I know you well enough now to realise there's not a snowball-in-hell's chance of you letting this drop. But, on your own and without any resources whatsoever, what hope do you really have of uncovering something that happened over a quarter-century ago?'

'By good old detective work, intuition and, as in most investigations, hopefully a good dose of coincidental luck along the way. And, don't forget, I've got resources of my own that I can use to try and find out what boat Samantha was staying on when she disappeared.'

'Well, I wish you luck, Jack, but be clear on one thing. This time I can't help you in any way.'

'Unless I come up with a way in which you have to.'

'I don't see how.' Bailey's eyes narrowed with suspicion. 'Jack, what devious scheme are you hatching?'

'Never you mind.' Jack tapped the side of his nose and winked before nodding toward the detective's empty glass. 'Time for another?'

Bailey shook his head firmly. 'Thanks, Jack, wish I could, but I've now got to go and make myself unpopular at a local night club.' He stood up, pulled on his jacket and together, the two men went out to the car park. The breeze had died down and, in the stillness of evening, to Jack the river itself seemed to be at rest after its day's toil. Just before climbing into his car, Bailey turned, his expression one of genuine concern. 'Well, just be careful. Someone, somewhere, isn't going to be too happy at you following this one up.'

'And I know who,' answered Jack, putting on a pained expression and pretending to cut his throat. 'Audrey's going to be furious.'

*   *   *

'Jack, you promised!'

'I know, love, but the situation has changed.' Jack settled a little lower into his lounge chair and gave Spike's head a playful scratch. He couldn't help feeling his border collie was the more understanding of his companions right now. On his drive home, he'd tried to rehearse how he was going to break this contentious news to his wife, even considering continuing the investigation surreptitiously. But he'd never knowingly deceived Audrey and he didn't aim to start now. Besides, her own intuition had often served to break through the thorniest of problems and being able to talk them through with her was an asset not to be compromised. And so he'd come straight out with the news and received the expected lecture. Now, with Spike's head on his lap, he played his second card by appealing to his wife's motherly nature. 'Look at it this way, Audrey. The way things are going, no one will ever know what happened to Samantha Waites, which isn't right. Think how you'd feel if this was one of our daughters.'

'But there must be some reason why the police can't investigate, Jack, and you should accept it and not get involved.'

'If anything, it's made me more determined than ever to discover the truth.'

'Oh no, here we go again,' moaned Audrey. 'Knight Errant Jack Fellows to the rescue, except there's no maiden left to help, so what's the point?'

'The point, is the truth, Audrey.' Jack lowered his tone to its most compassionate. 'If I promise not to let it take over my life, what's the harm?'

'The harm is that it always does, Jack.' Audrey threw her knitting to one side. 'Look, love, I know policing's in your blood, but you've just got to let go and move on. I really thought fishing would be a step towards contented retirement, but oh no, you come home with a stinking muddy handbag which stirs up all your old instincts that a crime has been committed.'

'Well, Aud, I know how you feel, but how about letting me take this just a little further and see how it works out. I'm even more intrigued now it sounds as though there was some sort of cover-up by the powers that be. I'd like to challenge that, if nothing else.'

'I must be mad,' conceded Audrey groaning, 'but it's too late to try and change you now, Jack, so if this is what you really want, then go for it.'

'You're an angel.' Jack got up and gave his wife a heartfelt hug.

'Yes, well just make sure *you* don't become one yourself,' she warned. 'So, how are you going to achieve the impossible this time?'

'For a start, I'm going out with the Ludham ranger the day after tomorrow, and his patrol beat takes us close to where the bag was found. I'll get him to stop there so I can have another good look, in daylight this time.'

'Yes, well don't go getting your fellow rangers involved in things they shouldn't,' cautioned Audrey. 'And is that really going to be any help anyway? Surely, even if something bad *had* happened, the handbag might have just drifted to where it was found.'

'Somehow, I don't think it did, otherwise the chances are some boat would have spotted it before it sank. No, love, my thoughts are that the bag was attached to something underwater and only broke free once the angler's hook caught it. I'm going to proceed with the hypothesis that where the bag was found is where an incident took place.' He thought for just a couple of seconds. 'By the way, where's that old watch of mine, the one I dropped on the patio last year?'

'The one that's never worked since? It's in the hall drawer with some of your other junk, but why ever do you want that? You couldn't even get it repaired, so why not just throw it away?'

'Because who knows when it might just come in useful? But first things first. A day off tomorrow, back on the river the next and then, if I get the chance, a bit more investigating.'

'Goodness me,' she sighed, 'can't you just take it easy for once. Come the end of the summer, you're really going to be ready for that holiday.'

'I certainly will,' he agreed absently, before his wife's words actually sank in. 'Hang on, what holiday's that?'

'The wonderful one in the Italian Lakes that you've been promising me for years. I've been checking and there are some great deals going on the internet if we're quick enough.'

'But, Aud – Italy – are you sure we…?' Jack stopped, knowing he'd talked himself into a corner. 'Right, love, I'll have a surf tomorrow and see what's on offer.'

'Good, after we've been to the vets.'

'The vets!' Both Jack and Spike looked up at that news.

'Yes, Spike's got an appointment, remember, to see about his ear.'

'Crikey, I forgot all about that,' admitted Jack. 'But it'll be good to have it looked at. It needs sorting.'

Spike, who like most dogs, was perfectly capable of picking up the sense of a conversation, didn't look so convinced.

*   *   *

Chapter Five

'Right, come on, old boy, this is for your own good,' encouraged Jack, dragging a rather unwilling Spike from the car to the surgery, followed by an almost equally nervous Audrey.

It was next morning and the veterinary practice turned out to be a very modest one, being a fairly small detached house, the ground floor of which had been turned into the surgery and front garden, a small parking area. There was only one other vehicle, a rather battered Land Rover with *VetCare* emblazoned on its side. What this practice lacked in size, however, was more than compensated for by the welcome from the uniformed receptionist behind the counter.

'Ah, you must be Spike,' she said to the trembling border collie whose tail was now firmly tucked between his rear legs. She turned to Jack and Audrey. 'It's all right, they're all the same.' She produced a blank record card. 'Would you mind just filling in the details here please?'

'Are you the young lady I spoke to on the phone?' asked Audrey as she returned the form.

'Yes, that's me,' replied this cheerful young woman with the name *Rosemary* engraved on her identity badge. 'Nurse, receptionist and general administrator rolled into one.'

'Keeps the overheads down while you're building up your patient list,' said Jack, glancing around the still-empty waiting room.

'That's what Gordon says.'

'Gordon?'

'Yes, Gordon McQuaid, the vet. We worked together in Norwich, but Gordon always wanted a practice of his own, and when this property came up so close to where we sail, we took the plunge.'

'You're sailors then?'

'Yes, it's another love we share as well as animals,' explained the nurse. 'A while ago we bought an old wooden sailing cruiser which we're doing up together.'

'That'll keep you busy. What's her name?'

'Jack's a ranger,' broke in Audrey, 'so sorry for the questions, but he prides himself on knowing most boats on his patch.'

'Oh, I don't mind. I'm always ready to talk about boats. Ours is called Foxglove and, yes, you're right about the work. My parents have a modern GRP motor cruiser and Dad thinks we're mad putting all our time and money into a "wooden hulk" as he calls her.' Rosemary smiled enquiringly. 'You'll probably know my parents' boat then, Mr Fellows. She's called Cantuta 3.'

Jack paused, but couldn't recall the name. 'It doesn't ring a bell, but I'll certainly look out for it when I return to work tomorrow. I only patrol part-time during the summer months, as I'm now semi-retired.'

'Well, I'm sure you'll come across her eventually, as Mum and Dad are often out on the river.' Rosemary came around the small counter and ushered them to the door opposite. 'Right, let's get Spike seen to.' She showed them into a spotlessly clean room that must once have been the lounge, but in which the scent of fresh paint already failed to hide the background aroma of disinfectant, sterility and fear. Across a high examination table, a young man in a green surgical top, smiled and held out his hand.

'Hi, I'm Gordon McQuaid.' He nodded down to the subdued Spike. 'How can I help?'

'It's his ears,' explained Audrey. 'He keeps pawing them and there's horrible yellow puss inside that smells really pungent.'

The vet nodded. 'Sounds like a case of canker. Let's get him up here and have a look.'

Jack lifted Spike onto the examination table and soon McQuaid was peering into the collie's ears with his otoscope. 'Yes, as I thought, canker, probably caused by some mites. Nothing that a course of antibiotics won't cure, but first I'll clean out all that gunge before showing you how to apply the ointment.' He called for Rosemary to hold Spike's head still while he probed, but the collie seemed uncharacteristically calm, obviously put at ease by the pair's gentle handling. 'There, that's done,' said McQuaid, tossing the used instruments into a tray and passing it to Rosemary, 'but while he's here and relaxed, I'll just give him a complete once over.'

While the vet deftly felt around Spike's stomach and sounded him out with his stethoscope, Jack glanced around the surgery. There were the usual posters detailing animal ailments plus McQuaid's framed professional certificate. Next to that was a photograph of an old wooden sailing cruiser. As the vet concluded his examination, Jack nodded towards it. 'You're a sailing man, I understand?'

'Yes, that's right.' He put his stethoscope to one side before adding, 'mind you, we've only just got the boat into a condition fit to sail and there's still much to do in the cabin. I'm afraid Foxglove needed a lot of work, because she was in pretty poor shape.' He stroked Spike and gave him a friendly pat. 'Which, I'm glad to say, is certainly not the case with your dog. He's in excellent condition for his age.'

'Oh, that's good,' said a relieved Audrey, who always worried that any medical examination would disclose something serious.

'No, you've got him for a few years yet,' confirmed McQuaid, lifting Spike down and seeing them to the door. 'If the infection doesn't clear up by the time he's finished the course of antibiotics, come and see me again, but I'm sure he'll be fine. Thanks for signing on with us and don't hesitate to ring if you have any worries about Spike in future. Not many vets make house-calls these days, but I'm always happy to come out if you need me. I'll leave Rose to sort out his medication and your bill.'

Ten minutes later and all the Fellows were back in their car and driving home.

Audrey glanced back towards VetCare. 'What a nice friendly practice.'

'Yes, a lovely young couple.' Jack adjusted his driving mirror so he could see Spike, now asleep in the back. 'And very thorough too.' He glanced towards his wife. 'I wonder what their personal relationship is though?'

'Obviously one of mutual love,' answered Audrey.

'You reckon?'

'Yes, of course, it's obvious, as is their love for that boat, Foxglove, which they were keen to tell you about.'

'But, you know, it was Rosemary's parents' boat that I found more interesting.'

'I'm surprised, Jack, I thought you preferred traditional craft?'

'More the name, actually. You know how fascinated I am with the ones people give their boats, and Cantuta 3 is a strange choice. It sounds as though there were two before it, so I wonder what it means?'

'It's a flower.'

'Really?' Jack swung his head round to look at Audrey, surprised that she was able to answer what he thought to be a rhetorical question. 'Are you sure, because I've never heard of it?'

'No, you wouldn't have,' she returned with a hint of smugness. 'Its full name is *Cantuta Buxifolia* and I only know about it myself because, at the Flower Club last month, a botanist gave us a very interesting talk on exotic species. It caught my attention because, apparently, it used to be the sacred flower of the Incas.'

'That's interesting. It's not English then?'

'No, South American. In fact, it's now the national flower of Peru.'

Jack drove on, relieved Spike had been attended to, but also feeling that he'd like to find out a little more about Cantuta 3.

*   *   *

'Stinking day to be back on the river, Jack.' Ranger Arthur Brantley nodded beyond the wheelhouse windows of his launch to where driving rain and low cloud swept across marsh and river alike. 'Not quite your magical waterworld today, is it?'

'Oh, I don't know.' Jack shrugged. It was his first official day back on the river and it would have taken far worse weather than this to lower his spirit. 'One thing I love about Broadland is its constantly changing moods. No day's ever the same and on ones like this, with the marshes deserted and a mist hanging over all, they have an air of indefinable mystery.'

'What, ghosts and ghouls you mean? Well, you're in the right place for those.' Brantley pointed towards the ruins of St Benet's Abbey just appearing on the starboard side. 'Plenty of ghosts there for you.'

Jack knew what he meant. Founded by Suneman in the ninth century, on what had once been known as Cow Holme Island, St Benet's had certainly enjoyed a chequered history. Twice destroyed by the Danes and then captured by the Normans, it had finally met its nemesis in Henry VIII who, though sparing it from Dissolution, had instead taken its funds, forcing it into closure around 1545. Now, only meagre ruins remained of this once great abbey, except for its iconic gateway, obscured this morning in the enveloping greyness and making its stark remains seem even eerier than usual. 'A lonely place, Arthur.'

'Yep, I'll be glad to see some summer visitors milling around again.' Brantley gave an involuntary shudder as they reached the end of the thirty-six acre site. 'I know it's pathetic, but there's an air about this place that fair gives me the creeps.'

'Especially on a day like today.' Jack watched the extensive, but now-empty moorings glide past. Certainly, St Benet's seemed to be somehow brooding with latent foreboding. Or was it the knowledge that they were now getting close to *the* spot, he wondered. For ahead was the mouth of the River Ant and, just a half-mile beyond that, the scene of his first fishing lesson. With all the repercussions that had generated, Jack found it hard to think it was just a week ago. They were at the Ant Mouth now, the limit of the Ludham launch's western patrol, but this was something already discussed. 'You sure you don't mind going that little bit further, Arthur?'

Brantley smiled and shook his head. 'I won't even ask what this is all about, Jack, but if you reckon it's pertinent river work and won't take long, then no problem.'

'Thanks, Arthur. Much appreciated.'

They continued upriver, windscreen wipers slapping to reveal a river whipped into small white caps as the wind gusted through the marshes. Just past Ant Mouth, a community of greylag geese stood on the bank, looking forlorn and desolate as they watched the launch pass slowly by. As it rounded the next bend in the Bure, Jack caught something of their mood.

Perhaps it was the bit of devious practice he had planned, for they were almost there now, the river straightening only briefly before making another almost ninety degree turn northwards. It was in this next short reach that the angler had hooked the handbag. Jack pointed to the stump of the alder. 'Just here please, Arthur.' With the engine brought to STOP, the launch glided towards a location now appearing very different through suspicious eyes.

Bathed in the persistent drizzle, it was hard to imagine this same scene in summer when, Jack recalled, it was a popular place for lone boats to moor. Easy to see why, offering as it did, open country, firm ground to drive your rhond anchors into, and the promise of peace and solitude for a night's stay.

Few trees remained on this northern bank but, right by where they'd hooked the bag, were the exposed roots of a single long-dead alder. Like some mythical creature with its toes in the water, the roots continued below the surface and it was amongst these that the bag must have been ensnared all those years ago. 'Can we go in a bit closer?'

As Brantley worked his launch towards the bank, Jack left the wheelhouse for the open aft cockpit. Soon, he could almost touch the roots. He reached towards them and, as he did so, the old broken watch on his wrist came off and dropped gently into the river. 'Damn!'

'What's up, Jack?'

'Lost my watch,' Jack cursed, hoping his voice hadn't been altered significantly by the tongue in his cheek.

Apparently not, because Brantley joined him in the cockpit. 'We could have a feel with the boathook.'

'Thanks, but not worth it. It was an old one anyway. The damned thing was totally unreliable since I dropped it, so it's time I got a new one. I've seen what I wanted to, so let's get you back on your beat.'

With the launch swung around and heading east, back towards its allotted patrol ground, Jack returned to the wheelhouse, the rain now lashing its aft windows. He took a last look through them at the remote mooring spot diminishing swiftly astern. Turning over in his mind a dozen scenarios of what might have happened there thirty years before, he suddenly remembered something still to be done. He fished out his mobile. 'I need to call Henry Mayhew at registrations and find out who owns a boat called Cantuta 3.'

'Any particular reason?'

Jack wrinkled his nose. 'Just out of personal interest, actually. We took Spike to the vets yesterday and the nurse there said her parents owned a motor cruiser by that name. It meant nothing to me until Audrey told me the name's origin, which stirred my curiosity. Did you know cantuta is the national flower of Peru?'

'No, and I doubt if many people do. A strange name to choose for a Broads boat though.'

'That's exactly why I'm so interested in it.'

'You just can't stop yourself can you, Jack?' chided Brantley before giving a satisfied grin. 'Well, I can save you a call, because I know that boat and just where she's moored.' He paused, enjoying the moment, before adding, 'and, what's more, I can show you on the run home.'

*   *   *

Norwich is one of the few cities in the country to have two cathedrals. From the centre rises the mighty steeple of the Anglican, a symbol in itself, but at the top of Grape's Hill, sitting somewhat incongruously on the site of what was once Norwich's city gaol, is the Roman Catholic Cathedral Church of St John the Baptist. This impressive building was, for three-quarters of a century, the parish church of Norwich's Catholic community. Then, in 1976, it was elevated to the status of mother church of the new Diocese of East Anglia and became the second largest Catholic cathedral in the country.

One of the regular army of volunteers at St John's was Louise Henderson, whose two afternoons a week were mainly spent in the cathedral shop. This was situated in the Narthex, a modern purpose-built centre designed to accommodate the many visitors, some of whom came in organised groups to receive a guided tour. One such group was coming that afternoon, which was good news for Louise, because she was also one of the cathedral guides, a duty she particularly enjoyed. Whenever possible, she researched the background of these groups and, in the hour before they arrived, would walk around the cathedral reminding herself of the many points of interest she thought would be of particular relevance to them. And so, at the same time as the two rangers were turning on the Bure for the second-half of their patrol, Louise was making her way from the Narthex and into the mighty nave.

Now, as always, she paused at its west end and looked along the vast length of the building, between the massive cylindrical columns leading to the triforium and, beyond that, to the great high altar, lit by a pair of beautiful chandeliers. Outside, wind and rain swept across the city, but in here all was calm and still. She continued up the central aisle, made her own devotions at the altar beneath the ascending void of the tower, and then turned left into the north transept. Some short steps here led her into the Lady Chapel, so named in dedication of Our Lady of Walsingham and one of five chapels beyond the transepts. Continuing clockwise into the Unity Chapel and then through the chancel to the Chapel of the Saints of East Anglia with its three modern paintings depicting St. Felix, St. Etheldreda and St. Edmund, she finally stepped into the Chapel of the Blessed Sacrament.

This was the chapel reserved for quiet prayer and reflection, and it was being used as such this afternoon because, as Louise entered, she saw a figure, deep in contemplation, sitting on the front row of chairs. He wore a dark suit and his head of greying hair was bent low and held in his hands. As Louise paused so as not to intrude on his prayers, he slowly stood up and made his way to the hard stone steps before the small altar. Here he knelt once more, completed his devotions, genuflected and then rose, steadying himself as he did so by holding the altar rail. Sensing some infirmity, Louise hastened to his side and offered him a steadying hand.

'Grazie, grazie,' he thanked as he stretched slowly upright, a man in his late sixties with a tanned complexion and whose medium build and broad shoulders seemed to be carrying more than their fair share of woes. 'I am very grateful.'

'It's just that you looked a little shaky. Are you all right – Father?' For, as Louise glanced into this man 's kind but life-worn eyes, she noticed also that he wore the collar of the ordained.

'Si, si.' The priest smiled, obviously keen to reassure her. 'Just a little weary, for I have been travelling from Rome these last three days.' His English, although initially hesitant, was obviously good. He rubbed his legs and forced an even broader smile. 'Too much sitting has made these ageing limbs stiff. My apologies for distracting you...' he glanced at Louise's ring finger, '... signora. And for my manners.' He held out his hand. 'Monsignor, actually, Monsignor Lorenzo Coletti. I am very pleased to meet you.'

'And you also,' responded Louise, introducing herself, but a little unsure how to proceed with this encounter and worried that some protocol had been missed. 'I'm sorry, Monsignor, but does the bishop know of your visit?'

'No, not at all,' said the priest, shaking his head. 'I am here on a fuori programma. How do you say? A casual visit.'

'Well, you are very welcome,' replied Louise warmly. 'And you say you are from Rome?'

The priest nodded. 'Si, signora. I am rector of a seminary there, the Fraternita Sacerdotale dei Missionari di San Carlo Borrameo.' He rolled off the names in lilting Italian, but it was too much for Louise.

'My goodness, I don't think I'll be able to remember all that, Monsignor.' She glanced again at the face of this kindly man of the cloth and saw lines of fatigue running into shadows of worry. And those eyes knew anguish as well as sleeplessness. She nodded back to the Narthex. 'Would you like to come and sit down and have a cup of coffee?'

'You are very kind,' he answered, stooping to kiss the guide's hand. 'That would be good indeed.'

They walked slowly back to the visitor centre and soon Louise had her surprise guest seated at a table in the cafeteria with a large cup of cappuccino in front of him. 'So, did you fly into Norwich Airport this morning?' she asked, once the priest had relaxed and taken some welcome sips of his beverage.

'No, no,' he stressed with an amused frown, 'flying is not for me, and so I came by train, arriving at your Norwich stazione at noon. I took a tassi – a taxi, to this your cathedral to offer my devotions, which have been sadly remiss these last days.'

'Understandable on such a long journey,' said Louise. 'No wonder you look so tired.'

'Not too tired to appreciate the beauty of your lovely cathedral,' replied the Monsignor, graciously. 'It is very old, is it not?'

'Not really,' explained Louise, on firm ground for the first time during this encounter. 'It looks that way because it was designed in the gothic style, but actually it's only just over a hundred years old.' She suddenly brightened at a thought. 'I'm taking a group on a guided tour in about half-an-hour. If you're not too tired, you'd be welcome to join us.'

'Thank you, signora, but no.' The priest gave a kindly smile. 'And, sadly, I will not be able return as my time here is limited.'

'Ah, so you're not here for very long then, Monsignor Coletti?'

'For a week or so.' He took another sip of his cappucino. 'But, initially, only the one day in your Norfolk to stay with an old amico.'

'And does your friend live close to here?' Louise found she was already easily filling in the odd translation.

'Quite close and it will not take long for him to come and collect me once I have called to say I am here.'

'Oh, that's good,' said Louise, glancing at her watch and remembering her guide duties. She was glad to know her visitor would be cared for. 'And after staying with your friend, what then?'

'To your other famous city of Cambridge,' he answered. 'One I have never been to before.'

'Well, there are many wonderful places of interest there for you to enjoy,' enthused Louise, finishing her coffee. 'I hope you'll have the time to explore them.'

'Probably not,' he replied, shaking his head again, 'for I am there on, shall we say, God's work.'

'And my own is calling now,' said Louise, jumping to her feet as she heard her group assembling just outside the cafeteria. 'I'm afraid I must dash, but whatever your plans involve, Monsignor Coletti, I hope you enjoy the rest of your stay. It's been a pleasure meeting you.'

'And you also, signora.' The priest pulled himself to his feet and again kissed the guide's hand. 'And grazie again for all your kindness.' He took a mobile phone from his pocket. 'And now I must call my amico – my friend.'

'I'm sure he'll be delighted to know you're here,' said Louise over her shoulder as she went to join her group. After her introductions and welcome, she led them into the cathedral but, as she did so, she glanced back to see the somewhat sad figure of Monsignor Coletti, talking on his phone. For someone about to reunite with an old friend, he seemed rather melancholy.

*   *   *

'I always come and check down here on the return leg,' explained Brantley, as he turned his launch off the main river and headed down the long waterway known as the Fleet Dyke which led to South Walsham Broad.

To the east now, a huge expanse of grazing marshes stretched away as far as the eye could see. Even from the low profile of the patrol launch, it was easy to see that the water level in the dyke was significantly higher than the

50

surrounding land. Jack stood up and looked about him, marvelling as he always did, at the unique beauty of the Broadland landscape. 'Man's intervention has certainly changed this environment over the centuries, hasn't it, Arthur, what with draining the marshes and digging the peat pits?'

'Thank goodness they used peat for burning all those years ago, or there'd be no broads for us to patrol,' replied Brantley. They were now passing a boomed-off narrow waterway leading to the right. Arthur slowed the launch and nodded towards it. 'Hard to believe now that this was once the original course of the Bure. Back in the days when St Benet's was a working abbey, it did a big horseshoe meander which must've been a real pain for waterborne traffic. So the monks decided to dig out a short cut.'

'Quite a task,' agreed Jack, 'especially as it all must have been done by hand.'

'In some ways, I wish they'd never bothered,' said Brantley, easing the rpm back up to slow cruise. 'That loop would be such a pretty stretch of river, but now it's completely unnavigable.'

Instead, the waterway continued as the Fleet Dyke, a sharp Z-turn bringing them into the final reach, where they passed some public moorings and then a small marina, before entering the ruffled waters of the outer broad itself. Both rangers automatically scanned the scene, checking all was well. At the far end was the narrow entrance to the inner broad, only accessible to the public by boat or via the beautiful Fairhaven Gardens. They made their way towards it by an encircling route that took them past several prestigious waterside homes, but it was towards one of the larger, alongside which a sleek modern motor cruiser lay moored, that Brantley now headed. 'There she is, Jack. Cantuta 3.'

Jack took in the impressive chalet bungalow with its large rambling garden running down to the water's edge and the boat that might just hold the key to his quest. 'Not short of a bob or two are they? What's the owner's name?'

'de Courcey. Sir Charles and Lady Harriet de Courcey.'

Jack stiffened slightly in his seat. 'Do you know them, Arthur?'

'Only to have the odd casual chat when they've been on the boat in the summer. They're obviously pretty top drawer, but friendly just the same.'

I wonder if they'll stay that way when I've made contact, thought Jack. Once again, his instinct had served him well, but it was also the most incredible stroke of luck that, thanks to Spike's canker, he'd managed to locate the very man he was seeking, virtually on his doorstep.

And now it was *Sir* Charles and *Lady* Harriet. It seemed that Samantha's affair hadn't produced a permanent rift in the marriage after all. Or possibly de Courcey had managed to keep it a clandestine romance of which her ladyship still knew nothing. Whatever, it seemed they were still married and obviously pretty well off. As the launch edged nearer, Jack took a closer look at the estate of the man who perhaps knew more than anyone of what had happened to Samantha Waites.

Broad View, proclaimed the name painted in bold black lettering on the life-ring hung by the mooring. An apt, if not particularly imaginative, name for this impressive property built of wooden lapboard with picturesque eyebrow windows peeping out from beneath their thatch of Norfolk reed. The adjoining boathouse, with a guest-studio above, was similarly thatched, its doors left open to reveal the low lines of a traditional Broads marsh punt lying inside. Presumably, in winter, this boathouse was the home of Cantuta 3, but now the big cruiser lay moored to the quay-heading, her gloss-white hull gleaming despite the gloomy day, as she shifted uneasily in the still-gusting wind and rain. Jack looked at the name, picked out in gold leaf on the bow and beside it, the skilfully painted purple, pink and white flower that was doubtless the Peruvian emblem after which she was named. Hadn't Harry Bentley said there was a flower painted beside the name on the cruiser Samantha was staying on all those years ago? That had to be the first boat bearing this name which the Waveney ranger couldn't quite recall. As they glided past the substantial frontage and wide sweeping lawn, Jack knew another piece of this strange jigsaw was clicking into place.

'All right for some, eh?' said Brantley.

But Jack could only manage a nod in return. His attention now was fixed on Broad View's large bay window, a feature of the house that looked right out across the water. Behind that window, a figure was talking on his telephone.

Without pausing, the launch continued on towards the inner broad.

*   *   *

Standing by the picture window of his lounge, Sir Charles de Courcey, put down the phone and looked out across the broad where little white horses rolled across its rain-swept surface. Cutting through them was the sleek form of a ranger's launch just disappearing into the inner broad, the first boat he'd seen all day.

In spite of being in his sixties, Sir Charles was still an imposing figure, tall, straight-backed and with thick grey hair that he'd let grow a little longer in retirement. His working days were well behind him now, giving him the time for such absent gazing at a view that constantly fascinated, delighting as he did in the diversity of wildlife that inhabited the broad and frequented his garden.

One of his favourites was the magnificent heron, several of which lived solitary lives on the surrounding banks. Each morning, one of these large distinctive-looking birds could be found staring expectantly through the de Courcey's French windows, standing motionless, waiting to be fed bacon offcuts bought especially from the local butcher.

Other far less bold, but much loved visitors to the de Courcey's garden were otters, but disappointingly, sightings of these timid, elusive creatures out of the water were very rare. They were far more likely to be spotted frolicking in the broad, especially early morning or at dusk. Sir Charles never tired of watching their playful antics.

During the summer months, of course, the mood of the broad changed as holidaymakers in their hire boats arrived to drop their mudweights and soak up the beauty and serenity of the surroundings. Many cast envious eyes at the beautiful waterside homes and Sir Charles and his wife were always happy to give a friendly wave, well aware how lucky they were to be living in such an idyll.

They had bought Broad View in 1985 after selling the London townhouse, spent a fortune restoring and improving it and had never regretted a single penny. That had been the year Sir Charles had started easing out of mainstream business, his money made and all the cut and thrust of international finance left as far behind as his urban lifestyle. In the years since, he'd worked from home, giving financial advice to animal charities, so he and Harriet could enjoy a quiet, self-contained life in the heart of Broadland with ample free time to cruise the waterways at will. After all the anguish and upset of the previous years, this had been the perfect way to put the past behind them and live their life anew. On a personal level, he couldn't have been happier – until yesterday. As black thoughts once more threatened, Sir Charles felt a presence at his side. 'Harriet, you made me start!'

'You looked miles away.' His wife smiled and handed him his afternoon tea. 'Did I hear the phone go just now?'

'Yes, it was Lorenzo, calling to say he's in Norwich.'

'Shouldn't you be off to pick him up then? He must have been travelling for days.'

Sir Charles shook his head. 'No rush. He's been enjoying looking around St John's Cathedral and is about to have another coffee. He said to pick him up in about an hour.'

'Oh, that's good. Did he sound well?'

'Somewhat tired, I thought.'

'Understandable after all those train connections, but a few days here with us, breathing in fresh Norfolk air, will soon put new life in him.'

'Only *one* day actually,' corrected Sir Charles. 'He's going on to Cambridge tomorrow.'

'Really. What for?'

'He didn't say, but I got the impression there was something special he wanted to discuss with us.'

'Any idea what about?'

'None at all, but I'm sure he'll be glad to have some down to earth conversation instead of all the deep theological erudition he has to constantly spout at that seminary of his.'

'Now, you mustn't be so disparaging, Charles,' reproached Harriet mildly. 'We were only too glad of his spiritual guidance when we went through our own bad patch all those years ago.'

'No, I'll always be grateful for his friendship,' acknowledged Sir Charles, 'but in those days he was still pretty worldly himself. Immersing himself in religious academia since then might have lost him some of his common sense.'

'I doubt it, and it will be good for *you* to be able to talk over old times and anything else that's bothering you.' Harriet glanced again at the worry lines on her husband's face. 'Because there *is* something troubling you, isn't there Charles?'

'Yes there is, actually.' He sank onto the window seat, marvelling as always at how his wife could seemingly read his mind. 'But nothing for you to worry your head about.'

She sat down beside him with her tea. 'If it worries you, darling, then it's something I need to know about.' She placed a warm hand on his. 'Tell me.'

He gave the hand a squeeze back and a shrug of resignation. 'All right. It's probably nothing, but I had an email early yesterday from you know who. It's just that there's been some police enquiry about what happened in 1984.'

His wife put down her cup. 'Police. What police?'

'The Norfolk Constabulary.'

'Why? And why now?'

'I don't know, but don't worry, they've had strict orders to back off and forget it,' he reassured her.

'Oh, Charles.' Harriet shook her head, 'I thought all that business was over and done with. I thought Samantha Waites would never be mentioned again.'

'She won't be, I promise.' Charles gave his wife's hand an extra squeeze. 'I know how painful the memory of all that is to you.'

'It's just that we've found such happiness since. I wouldn't want anything to spoil that.'

'Don't worry, I won't let it.'

'I know you'll do what you can, Charles.' She finished her tea and stood up.

'Where are you going?'

'Just for a row while you're fetching Lorenzo.'

'You're not going to dwell on what I've just told you, are you?'

She smiled reassuringly. 'I'll try not to, but I think some exercise and fresh air will do me good.'

He nodded out to the flume-streaked waters and smiled. 'It'll be fresh all right.' Then his brow once more creased with concern. 'You're not upset are you, darling?'

'Only a little, but don't worry my love.' She stroked the side of his face. 'A good thrash up to the river and back will soon clear away any bad thoughts.'

He nodded. 'All right, but be careful.'

She left him by the window, went and changed into her rowing kit and made her way through the rain to the boatshed.

The marsh punt lay against the boarded side decks, a much lighter GRP reproduction of the old working boat of the marshmen. When the cruiser was in for the winter, the punt was hoisted up into roof space but, with the arrival of spring, the cruiser could lay outside and the punt in the water. Harriet took the long oars off their racks and climbed down into her boat.

It was an exercise she did almost every day when the river was quiet. Not only was it a satisfying way to keep fit, but being alone and at one with nature in such a unique peaceful environment was often a means of clearing her head of life's troubles, which was her intention now. She pushed off and out into the broad, slid the oars into their rowlocks and pulled away.

Harriet was a skilful oarsperson and soon the punt was churning across the broad as she pulled and feathered against wind and wave. She was getting soaked in the process, but didn't mind because the exercise was having the desired effect of putting the news of this confounded police enquiry to the back of her mind. How she hoped that dear Charles was right and that the whole thing had been nipped in the bud. They were so happy now. She glanced over her shoulder to check she was not conflicting with any other boat.

On such a grotty day she expected the waterways to be deserted, so was surprised to see a ranger's launch with two crew just exiting the broad. Harriet continued to pull towards the dyke, just keeping pace with the launch, which was scrupulously keeping to the 4mph limit. She remained a short distance behind all the way up the dyke and it was only when they reached the main river that she noticed the launch stopping and one of the rangers leaving the enclosed wheelhouse and coming into the aft cockpit. It was obvious he wanted to talk to her. She slowed her stroke and manoeuvred alongside, wondering the reason.

But the ranger was smiling, a burly man with a confident air. 'Good afternoon,' he greeted, taking hold of the punt's bow as it nudged the launch's transom, 'my name's Jack Fellows, and you must be Lady de Courcey?'

'Lady Harriet, actually, but yes, that's me.' Harriet was surprised that this man should know her name, but was reassured when the other ranger, Brantley, who she knew, stuck his head out of the wheelhouse window and gave a cheerful wave. So why was she worrying? 'What can I do for you, Mr. Fellows?'

'I'd like to come and have a word with Sir Charles.'

'What about? Is it official business?'

'No, not at all,' emphasised the ranger. 'This is purely a personal enquiry about something that happened many years ago.' He smiled. 'Tomorrow would be good for me.'

Harriet felt a little shiver as old ghosts walked over her grave. 'Well, we've got a house guest tomorrow, so I'm not sure if it will be convenient.'

'It won't take long,' he persisted. 'Would ten o'clock be okay?'

There was something about this man that made his request hard to refuse. 'Well, if it's that important, I suppose it'll be all right.'

'Good, I'll look forward to seeing you then, Lady Harriet. Enjoy the rest of your row. You must be very dedicated, being out in this awful weather. Bye for now.'

And then the ranger was joining his colleague back in his wheelhouse as the launch drew away downriver and past St Benet's.

Harriet watched it fade into the misty drizzle with a heart just as downcast. After what Charles had just told her, the ranger's impending visit surely had to be connected. The only comfort she could glean from the encounter was that this Jack Fellows had assured her it wasn't official. Official or not though, somehow she felt it didn't bode well for her and Charles' future happiness. But Harriet was determined not to dwell on what might be. She took a fresh grip on the oars, more resolute than ever to banish doubt by vigorous exercise.

With swift strokes, she once more powered the marsh punt downriver in the wake of the ranger's launch. She always went this way, past St Benet's, and never upriver. That would take her past… Harriet deliberately froze her thoughts right there. It didn't do to even think about such a dark period of her life, and especially now. Instead, she put all her energy into the strokes, telling herself that the whole business was such a long time ago and that the past was where it must stay.

She pulled away, the kiss of her blades in the water sending the punt ever faster through the rolling wavelets.

*   *   *

'All these look so beautiful Jack, but for now I'm favouring Lake Como.' Audrey put aside the travel brochures she'd just been studying and sat back in her chair. 'So, from what you tell me, this de Courcey, who Samantha had an affair with in Peru, really is now living on the Broads?'

'He is indeed,' replied Jack, across the kitchen table, pleased to avoid further discussion on the Fellows' travel plans. 'It has to have been his first Cantuta that Samantha was staying on when she was researching that monster.'

'*Supposedly* researching that monster you mean,' corrected Audrey. 'But it can't have been de Courcey she was scared of because, if someone's frightening you, you don't escape by hiding on *their* boat.'

Jack nodded. 'Yes, you're right but, hopefully, I'll know more after I've spoken to him tomorrow.'

'Well, if he did play a part in Samantha's disappearance, it obviously didn't tarnish his reputation, seeing as he picked up a knighthood sometime afterwards. Do you think his wife was actually aware he'd had a little fling, Jack?'

'Goodness knows. He was a wealthy man, remember, and any divorce settlement could well have ruined him, so I imagine he went to great lengths to keep the affair a secret from her.'

'Which certainly gave him a motive to ditch Samantha, especially if she was demanding more from the relationship once she returned from Peru,' said Audrey, before considering her words and shaking her head. 'My goodness, Jack, I'm becoming almost as cynical as you.'

He smiled. 'That's the way you have to be when you're investigating suspicious events.'

'Yes, well, enough of that sort of thinking. For now, I'm just thankful that the de Courceys saved their marriage and had a delightful daughter as a result.'

'What I can't understand though,' replied Jack, thoughtfully, 'is why he cheated on his wife in the first place. She's an attractive woman and gutsy to boot. You ought to have seen her rowing that marsh punt in pretty horrendous conditions.'

Audrey shrugged. 'It takes more than looks and nerve to make a good wife, Jack. Loyalty is a big factor too, and if this Harriet chose not to join him in Peru, then perhaps you can understand him falling for the attentions of an intelligent young thing like Samantha. Not that I'm making excuses for him being unfaithful,' she added as a warning.

'Point taken, love.'

But Audrey was now getting well into her stride as she considered another option. 'Look at it another way, Jack. If Harriet de Courcey really is as gutsy as you say, then doesn't that make *her* a suspect too? Perhaps Samantha was feeling threatened by "a woman scorned".'

'You could be right,' conceded Jack. 'I hope to talk to them both tomorrow, which will give me a better idea.'

'Will it really take you much further though? Okay, you've probably found the man Samantha was having an affair with, and that it was his boat she was staying on when she was last seen, but the de Courceys are hardly likely to admit to any involvement in her disappearance.'

'No, of course not, Aud, but you can learn an awful lot by just talking to people and judging their reactions to questions. If nothing else, it might confirm I'm on the right track. The main thing is, I'm sure I've now located two sides of that "eternal triangle", which might tell us how the third disappeared.'

'Yes, but don't forget the "fourth" side, Jack, the one you ought to try and find out more about.'

'Which is?'

'The young marine of course.'

'But I thought you'd made up your mind that Harriet de Courcey had done it,' laughed Jack.

'Only keeping all my options open, as you're forever pointing out,' protested Audrey.

'And very wise too, but I'm not so sure.'

'Why not?'

'Because it's fanciful to think that a level-headed, intelligent young chap would murder his girlfriend simply because he'd been dumped. There'd have to be more to it than that.' He picked up the evening paper and started reading.

Audrey let out an exasperated sigh. 'Well you won't find any answers in there, Jack Fellows.'

'I thought you wanted me to relax more and investigate less.'

'Well, yes, but you still need to check him out.'

'Already have,' said Jack, finishing his rather tepid tea, without even looking up from his paper.

'You – you have?' Audrey refrained from an actual growl. 'All right, Mr Smugness, how, for goodness' sake?'

'Easy.' Jack finally put down his paper. 'I did consider starting with the Navy List for 1982.'

' "Navy List"? What's that? '

'Something that's been published every year for centuries. It gives the name of every serving commissioned officer in the Royal Navy and Royal Marines. Back in 1982 though, the list was a lot longer than it is now and going through that lot for a name with a royal connection, would have been pretty daunting.'

' "Royal connection"? You mean that tenuous lead Jean Henricks gave when she was trying to remember his name?'

'Right, but she also said that this ex-boyfriend of Samantha's had rowed for Cambridge, so all I had to do was bring up the names of the race crews for that period on the internet and look for one with some sort of royal correlation. I wasn't sure what form it would take, but there was one lad by the name of Gregory Kingsbourne. That sounded promising, so I double-checked by forking out ten quid for an online version of the 1982 Navy List, looked for that name and found Lieutenant G S Kingsbourne RM.'

'Which must be him.' Audrey gave her husband a playful pat on the back. 'Well done, Jack, that has to be your man, but what next? That was thirty years ago, so goodness knows where this Lieutenant Kingsbourne is now or whether he's even still alive.'

'I don't know about "goodness" knowing, but I do,' said Jack with a cheeky wink. 'I can assure you he *is* alive,' he nodded towards the study and shrugged, 'but, whether or not he replies to the email I've just sent him is something else again. We shall see.'

*   *   *

From his office window, Major General Gregory Kingsbourne DSO, OBE, RM, looked out across the expanse of Portsmouth Harbour. It was a view he could well be savouring for the last time, but one which gave him at least short relief from the tedious task of clearing out his desk. Promotion was all very well, he mentally conceded, but not something you always wanted.

Certainly, his next office at the MOD in Whitehall wouldn't have such a pleasing aspect, and did he really want to be tied to a desk in the Big City? Here at COMUKAMPHIBFOR, he'd been dealing with men, ships and the sea. In London it would be civil servants, budgets and never ending meetings. He groaned inwardly and scanned again the scene before him.

It was a black night but, on the tidal waters of the harbour, lights betrayed the constant coming and going of assorted vessels. Just passing was the fast-moving silhouette of a patrolling MOD police launch, its probing searchlight sweeping the grey hulls of warships moored in the naval dockyard, several of which were decommissioned and waiting to be towed to Turkey for scrapping. Further seaward, slower steaming lights showed the Gosport ferry making another of its endless transits between the two harbours. Its course would take it well clear of the gliding bulk of a Brittany Ferry, now departing in a blaze of decklights.

Kingsbourne sighed. It was a sad reflection on the country's current defence policy that, in this once mighty naval port, merchant ship movements now seemed to outnumber warships. He only had to cast his own mind back thirty years and the start of the Falklands campaign when things were much different. Back then, the Royal Navy was still a force to be reckoned with, but now… He glanced again at the black water and conceded that whatever ways the forces of man had changed, the forces of nature had not. The sea was still the dominant factor and you disregarded that at your peril.

But something else that would never change was his love for that element. He had served in the Royal Marines for thirty-three of his fifty-four years, many of those at sea and now he only had to look across the harbour to the lights of Gosport on the other side, to know that that was where his heart really lay.

For there, in a private marina at Hardway, was Tumbledown, his own ketch-rigged motor-sailer. Tomorrow, with his desk cleared and four weeks leave before his new appointment, he would sail her out of Portsmouth for some extended cruising away from all the frustrations of life ashore. Out there he would feel fresh sea air on his face again, free to make his own decisions and be answerable to no one. Tumbledown was ready to go, fuelled and stowed, the rig and engine checked, the charts updated. A few weeks of blissful small boat voyaging awaited. And then had come the email, received late that very afternoon.

Dozens passed through his secretary's computer each day, and most she dealt with on his behalf. But this one had hinted at a personal slant and she'd taken the decision, as one of her last duties for him, to hand him the printout personally. It was short, but pertinent enough to cause him some unease.

> *Dear General Kingsbourne,*
>
> *I would like to talk to you about Samantha Waites who I believe you once knew.*
> *A reply by return would be appreciated.*
>
> *Regards*
> *Jack Fellows*

The sender had added a contact number, but who was this stranger bringing up a name that still haunted his thoughts and memories? How could Samantha still be casting her shadow after all those years? What could possibly have triggered this strange resurrection? He knew he had to have the answers to those questions, if only to protect his career and the lives of others, against something they had always feared.

Kingsbourne went back to his desk, opened his laptop, and started keying his reply.

*   *   *

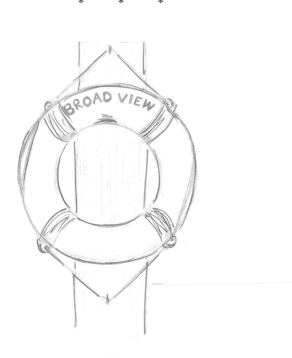

Chapter Six

Next morning found Jack driving towards the de Courcey home in weather directly contrasting to the previous day. Instead of rain, it was now sun that beamed down from a sky, clear and crisp. It gave a heart-warming aspect to the narrow country lanes he was traversing, but also a touch of guilt. He should be out enjoying a day with Audrey instead of pursuing answers to a long-forgotten mystery. Not for the first time did he wonder why he set himself these challenges.

The answer, of course, was truth and justice. They were the ideals that had governed his whole working life and ones he knew he would never surrender. Besides, this investigation was beginning to show results. Driving along, he recalled again the brief email reply he'd received that morning.

> *Dear Mr Fellows,*
>
> *I'm quite prepared to talk to you in confidence
> about the subject raised. I plan to visit the Broads
> in a few days time and will contact you then.*
>
> *Regards*
>
> *G Kingsbourne.*

That should be an interesting chat, he thought, and very soon he hoped to have one as equally enlightening with the de Courceys. Having turned off the main road, he drove slowly down a rough track and through impressive wooden gates, left open to reveal a landscaped garden with a well-tended gravel drive. Parking beside a black Range Rover, he climbed out as the front door of the house opened and a distinguished-looking man came out to meet him. On the corner of the house was a security camera. Clearly the urbane figure now offering a hand but no smile, had monitored his arrival on CCTV.

'Mr Fellows.' There was undisguised coolness in the greeting. 'Sir Charles de Courcey.'

'Good to meet you, Sir Charles. And thank you for seeing me.'

'Quite, but not the best timing, Fellows, as I have an old friend staying for just today.'

'Then I'll try and keep it short.'

'Good. Then you'd better come inside.'

de Courcey led him to what was obviously his study which, like the lounge, enjoyed a picture-window view of the broad. More interesting to Jack though were the densely-stacked bookshelves, where he noticed that volumes entitled *Latin American Economics* and *International Banking Yearbook* rubbed shoulders with *Catholicism in the Modern World* and *The Life of Pope Paul*. Squeezed between the bookcases, ethnic wooden face masks and native weapons shared some wall-space with a TV monitor simultaneously showing four different outside aspects of Broad View. It faced an elaborately carved desk, behind which de Courcey took his seat, at the same time ushering Jack into a leather-padded chair opposite.

'You obviously take security very seriously, Sir Charles?'

'What? Oh yes, the cameras. Installed a long time ago on the advice of the police, seeing as we live in such a remote location.' de Courcey gave a dismissive shrug. 'Useful for checking who's at the door, but we haven't put a tape in for years. But, to get on with the matter at hand – you wanted to talk to me about Samantha Waites?'

'That's correct. I believe that for a time you were quite close.'

'You realise this isn't easy for me, Fellows.' de Courcey lowered his voice slightly as he glanced towards the unseen lounge. 'I wanted to talk to you privately first because…' he looked around, as though searching for words, '… because this is a subject particularly distressing to my wife. It all happened years ago, but women don't forget these things.'

'So your wife does know about Samantha then, Sir Charles.' Jack smiled, sympathetically. 'Don't worry, I won't touch any exposed nerves, but I would like to talk to Lady Harriet later. I promise though not to raise any delicate, personal issues.'

de Courcey seemed only moderately reassured. 'Very well. So, what is it you particularly want to know?'

'Simply, what happened to Samantha Waites,' Jack nodded towards the broad and the marshes stretching out beyond the de Courcey home, 'because, as I expect you're aware, she's not been heard of since she visited the Broads in 1984.'

'Is this an official enquiry, Fellows?'

'Certainly not by me, Sir Charles, and, as I understand it, the police have already been warned off further investigation.' Jack was only assuming his host knew of the restraining order, but the lack of any comment from the other side of the desk served to confirm it. 'No, at this stage this is only informal on my part, but I suggest you be frank with me and that way I might help you if things take a different course.'

de Courcey sat in silence for at least a minute and when he did speak, his manner was slightly less assured. 'You obviously know that Samantha and I had a brief affair, but one which I had to end.' He gave a dismissive shrug. 'It'd been fun while it lasted, but I had a wife and other responsibilities to think of.

Samantha took it badly and said she was dropping out to get over it. I got the impression she was returning to Peru.'

'I'm sorry if I find that difficult to believe, Sir Charles.' Jack leaned forward slightly in his chair. 'Samantha had friends in Cambridge, was close to completing her doctorate and had a promising career ahead of her. Heartbroken she might have been, but I don't think she would have taken quite such drastic action as giving it all up and returning to South America alone. Added to that, no one has heard from her since. The fact is, I have witnesses stating that while she was in Norfolk, rather than heartbroken, she was actually scared.' Jack paused for a few tense seconds. 'I also have in my possession some personal items of hers that indicate she never left the Broads.'

de Courcey frowned. 'Items? What sort of items?'

'I'm not prepared to explain further at this stage,' answered Jack. 'Perhaps it would be better if *you* did the explaining, and from the beginning.'

Studying his desk, de Courcey was obviously indulging in some hard, if very fast, thinking. Finally he shook his head and looked up. 'All right.' There was just a sliver of relief in his acquiescence. 'But I think we could both do with a drink first.' He turned to a well-stocked cocktail cabinet and took out a bottle of Napoleon Brandy and two glasses. 'Will you…?'

Jack shook his head. 'Not before the sun's below the yardarm, thanks, but a cup of coffee would be nice.'

As if on cue, there was a knock on the study door and Lady Harriet came in bearing a tray with two cups, a coffee pot and milk and sugar.

'I'll leave you to help yourselves, Mr Fellows,' she said, placing the tray on her husband's desk.

'That's very kind of you, Lady Harriet.'

'Yes, thank you my dear.' de Courcey indicated the door. 'And now if you'd…'

Lady Harriet left as swiftly as she'd entered, but Jack hadn't failed to spot the slight shadow of disapproval that crossed her face at the sight of the brandy. But it seemed to have been lost on her husband who now raised his tumbler in a mock toast before taking a healthy gulp. 'That's better. Right, the full story, and make yourself comfortable, Fellows, because it's a long one.'

'I've got plenty of time.' Jack poured himself a coffee, left it black and took a sip. 'The main thing is to leave nothing out.'

*   *   *

'We met in Lima, in 1982,' began de Courcey. 'I was there, helping the Peruvian government establish lines of finance for British exports to the country. Harriet wasn't with me because she didn't like travel and was content for me to spend long periods unaccompanied. So, it was a financially rewarding, but personally lonely time. Until, that is, I met Samantha Waites.'

'Who was out there researching the capybara for her PhD thesis,' completed Jack, keen not to waste time on facts he already knew.

'Exactly.' Sir Charles rolled his eyes. 'Bloody rodents. Why a bright girl like that should want to…' He stopped mid-grumble and instead continued, 'We met at a party for British expats hosted by our embassy. I was well-known there of course, but Sam was a newcomer, a little nervous and obviously short of money, living as she was on some meagre student grant.' He turned the cut glass in his hand, dreamily looking through the amber liquid. 'In fact, loneliness was the one thing we really had in common.'

'You away from your wife and she from her boyfriend?'

'That's right: Lieutenant Gregory Kingsbourne of the Royal Marines,' confirmed de Courcey with just a hint of bitterness. 'But he was off soldiering in the Falklands and Samantha was in a strange country, so our friendship soon blossomed into an affair and it was the happiest I'd ever been in my life.'

'So, there you were,' summarised Jack, 'cheating on your wife with a young student somewhat your junior.'

'Cradle-snatching, you mean, and taking advantage of a vulnerable girl away from home?' de Courcey gave a humourless laugh. 'Not exactly, Fellows. Samantha was almost twenty-five and very mature for her age and anyway, Harriet wasn't much older. But I suppose it was like a holiday romance where we saw everything through rose-coloured glasses making life at home seem humdrum and dull. I can assure you I had no intention of continuing the affair once I returned to England.'

'Which probably eased your conscience, if nothing else,' added Jack, unsparingly. 'But how about Samantha with a fella fighting in the Falklands? Surely she felt some guilt at two-timing young Kingsbourne?'

'Obviously, a little at first, but it was his doing. She felt pretty used.'

'Used? How?'

'Oh, him thinking more of his career than her, that sort of thing.'

'Presumably, with the Falklands war in full swing, they weren't in touch anyway,' reasoned Jack.

But de Courcey was quick to correct this with a little snort. 'Oh, they were in touch all right. He somehow managed contact through the embassy, which started the whole messy business in the first place.'

'In what way?'

de Courcey paused, as though realising he'd perhaps said too much. 'Oh, by just being demanding and putting her under undue stress.'

'So, did Kingsbourne know you two were having an affair?'

'He knew we were involved.'

'So, when did he first know it was serious?'

'When Samantha told him we'd fallen in love and she wanted to end their relationship.'

'An honest girl in that respect then, but not the sort of news you want to receive while on active service,' said Jack. 'Presumably, he wasn't best pleased.'

'He certainly had his pride dented. But he deserved it.'

'Oh really. In what way?'

'Perhaps I'm being unfair, considering the circumstances,' backtracked de Courcey, 'but let me just say that any grief Kingsbourne suffered, he brought upon himself.'

'But, the man couldn't help being deeply involved in a war,' protested Jack on the marine's behalf, while feeling he might just be beginning to at least scratch the surface of this mystery. 'What had he done that was so terrible as to lose Sam's affections?'

But, de Courcey merely shook his head. 'I'm afraid that's one aspect of this story that I can't discuss with you.'

'Why not?'

'Please don't ask. Let's just say it had a bearing on all that happened later.'

'All right. So, what did happen later?'

'Our return from Peru. We left, almost at the same time, later in 1982, me to my London base with Harriet, and Samantha to her studies.'

'Were you still continuing your affair back here in England?'

'I hadn't planned to, but yes, with all the restrictions of separation and heavy hearts.' de Courcey glanced beyond the closed study door. 'By this time my wife had found out about us and made it quite clear there could be no question of a divorce. You see, we're both devout Catholics, as is Samantha, so, she knew from the start that there could be no future in our relationship, which cast a deepening shadow on the times we did manage to spend together.'

'Which, I assume, was on your boat on the Norfolk Broads,' chanced Jack.

'How did you know that? But, yes, the first Cantuta.' de Courcey took another swig of his brandy. 'Although my family home was in London, I'd always had a boat here, moored up the Ant.'

'Is that her?' asked Jack, nodding to a framed black and white print on the study wall. It showed a traditional wooden broads motor cruiser, about forty-five feet overall and with sturdy lines.

'Yes, a lovely boat, built by a local yard in the nineteen-fifties when they were still crafting in wood.'

'Was that the boat Samantha was staying on when she disappeared in '84?'

'Yes. She rang me to say she wanted to come and research some strange river monster sighting and asked if she could take Cantuta.' de Courcey gave a humourless smile. 'River monsters. All a load of piffle, of course, but I was glad to help her in any way I could. You see, Fellows, I was still deeply in love with that girl.'

'But you realised the river monster business was just an excuse to lose herself afloat on the Broads?'

'I think her professional interest was genuinely stirred by the possibility of one of those rodent things actually turning up in this country, but, yes, it was obvious she was actually frightened of something.'

'Of what?'

'I don't know.' de Courcey finished off his brandy. 'There could have been several factors.'

'Such as?'

'A jealous boyfriend for one, perhaps.'

It was Jack's turn to nod towards the unseen lounge. 'Or perhaps a jealous wife?'

de Courcey shook his head vigorously. 'No, not that. I admit Harriet was beside herself with anguish over the affair, but she would never have gone to those lengths to end it. That's a ludicrous suggestion.'

'Really,' replied Jack, unconvinced.

'Absolutely. As I said before, like me, Harriet's a devout Catholic and would never have even considered murder.'

Jack deliberately raised his eyebrows. 'I'm glad you offered that word first, Sir Charles. So, you do think Samantha was murdered then?'

de Courcey wavered before nodding. 'Yes, I'm sure she was, because, from that day, I haven't heard another word from her.'

'And who do you suspect? Kingsbourne?'

'No, not him.'

'Then who?'

'I'd rather not say.'

'Okay,' said Jack slowly. 'In that case, can you please tell me all you know of Samantha's disappearance.'

'She'd just returned from that weird trip to the southern rivers and we were due to meet up for the weekend.'

'On the boat?'

'Yes. She called me from Horning to say she was back and to meet her there.'

Jack frowned. 'Did she still sound frightened?'

'Yes, more than ever, so I came straight down from London.'

'Didn't your wife raise objections to that?'

'It didn't arise, because she was away at the time.'

'Really. Where, exactly?'

'Er, staying with friends, I think.'

'Where?'

'I can't remember.'

'Then hopefully *she* can when I talk to her, but for now just tell me what you found when you arrived at Horning.'

'Nothing. I found nothing,' replied de Courcey. 'There was no Cantuta and no Samantha at Horning Staithe and no message either. Knowing her state of anxiety, I was pretty desperate, so I hired a boat from a local yard and went looking for her. I found Cantuta a few miles downstream...'

'... at a bend in the river not far from here,' completed Jack.

de Courcey jerked a little in his chair. 'Yes, that's right. But how did you know that?'

'Because that's where Sam's handbag was fished out just a week ago.'

'My goodness,' gasped de Courcey. He ran a hand through his hair and Jack noticed it was shaking slightly. It was time to bring this interview back on track.

'So, what state was Cantuta in when you found her? Any sign of a struggle?'

'No, none.'

'Were her things still onboard?'

'No, all her clothes and possessions were gone as well.'

'Hmm.' Jack took another sip of his coffee before leaning a little closer. 'So, having found your boat empty and your very frightened girlfriend gone, what action did you take?'

'I informed the authorities.'

'Really, which ones, because the Norfolk Constabulary doesn't seem to have any file on the incident?'

de Courcey shrugged. 'Friends – in high places – who helped, but please don't ask me to name them.'

'I don't think it would do me much good if I did,' shrugged Jack. 'But what about you? Here you were with the girl you loved missing with no explanation and, by your own admission, probably murdered. Surely, you must have been distraught.'

de Courcey nodded as he poured himself another brandy. 'Damn sure I was, but I couldn't make waves, as I was trying hard to patch up my marriage and earn Harriet's trust again. She'd suffered enough heartache, so we decided to make a new start by selling up in London and moving to Norfolk. That's when we bought Broad View and, shortly after, we were thrilled to discover Harriet was pregnant.'

'Rosemary?'

'Yes, that's right, but how...?'

'It doesn't matter,' cut in Jack. 'But what does concern me is that Samantha Waites' disappearance back then resulted in one less complication in your life.'

'What are you implying?' snapped de Courcey. 'You surely don't think I would have harmed her?'

'I'm prepared to think anything at this stage.' Jack paused. It was time to change the tack of his questioning. 'So, what was jilted-lover Kingsbourne's reaction to his ex-girlfriend disappearing?'

'I've no idea, because I never discussed it with him, but he must have felt some guilt himself.'

'Guilt!' threw back Jack. 'He was the aggrieved party, so why would he feel guilt unless he actually murdered her?'

'By asking her to…' Once again, the financier stopped short of further explanation and instead took a gulp of his brandy. 'I'm sorry, I didn't phrase that very well. What I probably meant was *regret* at allowing her to slip out of his hands.'

'Yes, I'm sure that's what you meant,' said Jack with deliberate scepticism. He got up. 'Well, thank you for telling me what you have, Sir Charles. I've got a clearer picture of the situation now, even if it has brought me no nearer to what actually happened to Samantha.'

'I'm sorry I couldn't be more helpful.' de Courcey came around from behind his desk, obviously relieved this difficult conversation was finally over. 'It's pretty obvious, isn't it, that we'll never find the whole truth?'

'What's obvious to *me*,' said Jack, moving to the door, 'is that no one was ever meant to find it. But, "the truth wins out" goes the old saying, and it surely will, Sir Charles, be it thirty years late.'

de Courcey scowled. 'Do you have any idea just what you're getting into here, Fellows?' The voice changed to one sounding almost benevolent. 'Take my advice, old chap, forget the whole business, get yourself a life and go back to patrolling the rivers.'

'This "business" *was* my life before I started patrolling rivers, Sir Charles. It might seem old-fashioned, but I still believe in justice.' Jack opened the door and stood back to allow his host to lead the way. 'Let's go and see if your wife can help me find it, shall we?'

*　　*　　*

Lady Harriet was sitting in the lounge when they entered, but she wasn't alone. Beside her on the window seat was a sallow-skinned man wearing black trousers, a dark grey cardigan and a priest's collar. She stood up to make introductions. 'Mr Fellows, this is an old friend of ours, Monsignor Lorenzo Coletti from Rome, who is staying with us before travelling on to Cambridge.'

'Pleased to meet you, Monsignor,' replied Jack, taking the priest's hand. 'When are you going to Cambridge?'

'This afternoon.' His broad face beamed a kindly, if somewhat forced, smile and his English was only slightly halting.

'Just a short visit here then.' Jack smiled back. 'Are you mixing business with pleasure?'

'In a way.' The priest gestured towards the de Courceys. 'It is good to talk over old times with my dear friends. But please excuse me if I go and have a little rest, prepare for my journey and leave you good people to talk in private.'

'Of course,' said Jack. 'I hope you enjoy your time in Cambridge.'

'If God wills,' returned the priest, and left the room.

de Courcey obviously felt some explanation was necessary. 'The monsignor was a good friend of mine in Peru. He was on missionary work there at the time, but now he's rector of a seminary.'

'Obviously a devoted man,' observed Jack, 'but he looks very tired.'

'He travelled overland from Rome, which has left him pretty exhausted,' explained Lady Harriet. She glanced at her watch. 'I don't want to hurry you, Mr Fellows, but we're driving Lorenzo on to Cambridge later this afternoon. I'm not sure why you're here asking questions, but time is short, so please make them brief.'

'I'll try,' promised Jack. 'It's not my intention to open up any old wounds, Lady Harriet, but you know I'm investigating the disappearance of Samantha Waites.'

'Yes.' She brushed some crumbs from her cashmere jumper. 'Though I don't really see how I can help you there.'

'Well, for a start, by possibly giving me your opinion as to what happened to that girl.'

'I have no idea.' Lady Harriet's tone was suddenly sharp. 'She wasn't someone I had any desire to have anything to do with. In fact, I was more than glad when she disappeared from the scene.'

'Yes, I can understand that,' said Jack with a kindly half-smile. 'You were staying with friends when she vanished, I believe. Where, exactly?'

Lady Harriet cast a quick questioning glance towards her husband, who merely nodded, before answering, 'Not far from here, actually. Up on the North Norfolk coast.'

'Could your friends verify that?'

'I'm afraid not. They were an elderly couple who've been dead themselves for several years now.'

'You used the word "themselves" as though you're sure Samantha Waites is also dead.' Jack's expression hardened slightly. 'What makes you so certain Lady Harriet?'

'Only that no one has heard hide nor hair from her since and, frankly, that suits me just fine.'

'Yes, but she disappeared off your boat,' pressed Jack. Doesn't that at least make you curious?'

'I have *no* interest in what went on in that boat.' Harriet paused to wipe her eye with a tissue. 'The less it's mentioned now, the better. I couldn't bear to set foot on that Cantuta again anyway, after all that happened, so we sold her and bought Cantuta 2.'

'And now you have Cantuta 3 and the past is well behind you,' said Jack.

'Which seems a good time to bring this interview to a close,' declared de Courcey, standing up. 'I think it's time for you to go, Fellows.'

'Yes, I think you're right,' agreed Jack, allowing himself to be shown to the door. But before it was opened, he turned back to the couple. 'Oh, by the way, I met your lovely daughter yesterday morning.'

'What, Rosemary?' said a surprised Harriet.

'Yes, at the vets.' Jack explained the circumstances.

'So, you met McQuaid as well then.' de Courcey said the name with little warmth.

'Yes, nice young chap and seems a good vet too.'

de Courcey shrugged. 'So everyone says, but I'd be happier if he made an honest woman of our daughter.'

Harriet, at least, seemed grateful for this diversion from the subject of Samantha Waites. 'Now, come on Charles, don't be such an old fuddy-duddy. You know how happy Rosemary is with Gordon, and they're really making a go of that practice together.'

'In which case they should get married,' grumbled her husband. 'Perhaps I'm old fashioned, but I don't go along with this "partner" thing. I've made it quite clear to him that if he truly loves Rosemary, he should convert to our faith and marry the girl.'

'Well, at least he likes boats,' chipped in Jack, keen to put in a good word for the vet. 'I saw a photo of the sailing cruiser they've bought.'

de Courcey merely gave a grunt. 'What, Foxglove? Hmm, load of work and expense, especially as they chose not to moor it here, but in the marina up the way.'

'What, the one just by the entrance to the broad?'

'Yes, that's right,' answered Harriet. 'I know it costs money, but I don't blame them. Young people need their privacy.'

'Don't we all,' agreed Jack, 'and now I must respect yours and get out of your hair.'

The de Courceys didn't argue with that and had closed the front door before Jack even reached his car. The quicker they want you gone, the more they have to hide, he thought to himself as he drove back down the lane. Perhaps he was no further toward a solution, but he now knew he was at least on the right track.

*   *   *

70

Chapter Seven

At the end of the track leading from Broad View, Jack didn't turn right for home but instead turned left towards the small marina nestling at the entrance to the broad. His mission now was to see Foxglove. There was no particular reason why he should wish to do this other than a vague interest in following the latest thread in this strange trail. The few hundred yards of narrow track ended at the marina gates, where he parked the car and continued on foot to search the berths.

It was a pleasant location for the few boats moored there, the tree-lined banks offering happy refuge for the numerous birds singing joyfully in the spring sunshine. On the east side of the embankment, the marshes stretched away in perpetuity, their flat expanse broken only by the leaning relics of long-disused windpumps and the slow movement of cattle grazing the lush meadows. On the other, the dyke flowed lazily by, undisturbed this morning by river traffic or holidaymakers. Of the boats moored stern-on in their berths, several were sailing cruisers, but only one was of traditional design, wooden built and with *Foxglove* picked out in fading gold leaf on the varnished transom.

That varnish was certainly in need of some attention, as was much of the white paint on the hull. A canvas cover protected the cabin but, above this, the tall mast rose amidst stays and shrouds. Aloft, these ran through spreaders which, together with the bowsprit for'ard, only accentuated the impression of bygone sail. It would take a lot of work to restore this boat to pristine shine, but the result would be worth it.

Jack stood back to further admire this river cruiser's lines. The canvas cover stopped him getting a true perspective, but he noticed for the first time that the access panel leading into the cockpit was unzipped. Not only that, but the boat suddenly began to rock slightly and a girl with her hair tied back emerged into the cockpit to empty a bowl of dirty water. Although dressed in scruffy, faded blue jeans and an old sweatshirt, she was easily recognisable as the young lady from the vets.

'Rosemary de Courcey?'

'That's right.' At first she seemed a little startled and slightly confused by this unexpected visitor, but in a second had recovered enough to recall the face before her. 'Oh, you're Spike's owner, Mr...'

'Fellows, but call me Jack, like everyone else.'

'And everyone knows me as Rose, but the important thing is, how's dear Spike?'

'Doing really well. The infection's almost gone.'

'Good, well make sure he finishes the full course of antibiotics.'

'We will.' Jack nodded towards Rose's empty bowl and the cabin interior. 'You seem to have quite a job on your hands.'

She nodded and looked around her in mock despair. 'Haven't I just. No appointments at the surgery this morning though, and Gordon's off on a farm visit so, being such a lovely day, I decided to come here and spend a bit of time on the old girl.' She swept her hand over the neglected boat. 'As you can see, plenty of scope for improvement.'

'Yes, but it'll all be worth it in the end.' Jack glanced again at the boat's hull. 'What is she? Thirty foot?'

'Thirty-three if you include the bowsprit. Want to see below?'

Jack eagerly climbed aboard and was soon seated on one of the cushioned berths in the aft cabin. Foxglove's interior was roomy, smelling fresh from her clean, and varnished throughout. 'Some hot water and vinegar will soon restore this,' he said, running a wetted finger down the adjacent bulkhead.

'Yes, new curtains and cushion covers and she'll be really cosy.' Rose was obviously very proud of their boat. 'I know they're a lot of work, but I do love wooden boats.' She gave one of the little brass cabin lamps a rock in its gimble. 'Such a tangible connection to our old sailing past.' She nodded in the direction of the broad. 'My parents' boat is pretty luxurious, but doesn't have anywhere near the character of this one. A pity really, because their first cruiser was wooden and I know Dad still thinks that was the best boat he ever owned.'

Jack took advantage of the lead. 'Actually, I've just spent some time with your parents at Broad View.'

'Really. I had no idea you knew them.' She sounded genuinely surprised. 'For what reason, Jack?'

'Oh, just to talk over some boat related things. Do you get to see them much, Rose?'

'Probably not as much as I should. We're still close, but Dad doesn't exactly approve of my present lifestyle. Both my parents are devout Catholics and don't think people should live together unless they're married.'

'They're a different generation, Rose. If they see you're happy, I'm sure they'll come around to your point of view.' Jack gave an encouraging smile. 'And, who knows, you might decide to marry young McQuaid anyway.'

But it failed to cheer her. 'I'm not sure if that would make Dad much happier. You see, Gordon's not Catholic – or anything else actually – which makes that an added complication.'

'The main thing is that you love each other and that you're doing something really worthwhile together.' Jack looked towards Broad View, just visible through the entrance to the broad. 'Are you going to see your folks today?'

'I would have done, but they have a house guest, so I thought best to leave them in peace.'

'Ah yes, Monsignor Lorenzo Coletti. I was introduced to him. I gather he's a very old friend of your parents.'

'Oh yes, from way back in Peru where Lorenzo was a missionary. Dad never explained fully, but I always got the impression that it was a very stressful time for him and Mum and that Father Lorenzo was someone who helped them a lot.'

'We all need someone to confide in at stressful times,' said Jack, 'so it's nice that they've remained friends since.'

'Yes, even after my parents settled down again in England and Lorenzo went back to Rome where he's now rector of a seminary.'

'So I understand, but here en route to Cambridge, apparently. I wonder what for?'

'I've no idea,' admitted Rose, 'but probably some theological conference or something. From what I gather, he's going to be there a while, but coming back here to spend a few more days with Mum and Dad before returning to Rome. I'll see him then, because he's actually my godfather.'

'Really? Well, I'm sure you couldn't wish for a better one,' said Jack, filing away this additional information. 'He seems the sort of man who can inject his spirituality with a good dose of practical common sense.'

'Yes, I wish I could see him more often.'

'I'm sure you do.' Jack glanced out of the open deadlights as a small dayboat passed, heading for the broad and rocking them in its wake. 'This is a delightful spot to keep your boat.'

Rose nodded. 'Yes, we love it here.' She gave a slight sigh. 'Of course, Dad can't understand why we don't just moor at Broad View and save ourselves some money, but the truth is that this boat is our little bolt-hole and we want to keep it that way. If Foxglove was there, every visit would be a family inquisition.'

'I can see you've got your priorities well worked out.' Jack glanced at his watch. 'Time for me to be on my way and let you get on with your cleaning.' He climbed back out into the cockpit. 'It's been nice talking to you, Rose.'

'And you, Jack.' She frowned. 'I hope I haven't gone on too much about personal affairs.'

'Not at all.' He brought a card out of his pocket. 'Here's my number. Whether it's about boats or any other problem and you think I can help, just call me.'

'Thanks, I will.'

Driving homeward, Jack considered all he had heard and learned that morning. If he'd established only one thing, it was that the vet, Gordon McQuaid, was a very lucky man.

*   *   *

The man himself would probably have been the first to agree with Jack that fine spring morning, as he swung his battered Land Rover into the long drive leading to Grange Farm, some thirteen miles from home and close by the village of Stoke Holy Cross, to the south of Norwich. The farm specialised in breeding pedigree livestock and, at the request of Mr Knights, the owner, he was calling in to check on lambs delivered only the previous week from his prize-winning flock of Romney Marshes.

'Thanks for coming, Gordon,' greeted the farmer outside his rambling Elizabethan farmhouse. The building was representative of the whole farm, an extensive six hundred and fifty acres that had been in the Knights' family for generations. Even in these difficult times, it was obviously still turning over a healthy income and, although not afraid of getting his hands dirty, Mr Knights could perhaps now be classed as a gentleman farmer. Certainly, locally, he was regarded, in standing if not in name, as the squire and this morning he certainly looked the part in well-worn Harris Tweed jacket, cavalry-twill trousers and slightly muddied brogues.

This was one of the reasons the vet always enjoyed a visit to Grange Farm, not only for the civility shown by the owner, but also in the knowledge that his bills would be paid promptly without hardship or complaint. 'Not at all,' he responded grabbing his bag from the Rover, 'but no problems with the lambs I hope?'

Mr Knights shook his head with a smile. 'No, they all look fine, but the wife and I are off abroad for a week's holiday in a day or so and leaving Carol to hold the fort. So, I just want to make doubly sure they're all in good shape before we go away.'

'Makes sense.' Carol was the farmer's daughter, hale and hearty, almost twenty-one and an only child. Why they'd had no more children, McQuaid didn't know, but any disappointment they might have felt in not producing a son, was obviously more than compensated by a daughter enthusiastically willing to throw herself into farm life. 'This must be the first time she's had that responsibility?'

'Yes, but she's well up to it.' A flicker of pride crossed Knights' ruddy face. 'A confident girl is our Carol. Only finished at agricultural college a few months ago, but in three day's time she's off to give a talk about her time there to the local Young Farmers. I have to say, she can't wait to get her hands on the controls, so to speak.'

'You've got a great girl there, Mr Knights.' McQuaid picked up his case. 'Right, let's have a look at these lambs.'

For convenience, Knights had had the sheep brought into an adjacent field, and so it was only a short walk before the vet was surveying the large flock with their characteristic long dense fleeces. Happily, one look at their offspring, gambolling in the lush meadow and spring sunshine, told him there would be few problems with this healthy breed, but the farmer obviously wanted to be reassured and so the vet went around checking them all in turn. 'As far I can tell, they're all fit and healthy, Mr Knights,' he was glad to report, though he did have one area of concern. 'I just hope no one will try and take some off your hands while you're away.'

'Rustlers, you mean.' There had recently been several cases of livestock theft in the area, and this pedigree flock of Romney Marshes were worth a lot of money. But, as Knights led them out of the pasture and back towards the yard, he seemed confident no such deed would blight Grange Farm. 'Not much chance of them coming here I think.' He gave a contemptuous laugh. 'In fact, I think we'd be the last ones those blighters would target. Did you see the security cameras as you drove in?'

'Yes, I did actually. When did you have those installed?'

'Last one was put in a week ago,' explained the farmer smugly. 'Had them as added security for when Carol's here on her own. They cover the sheds, paddocks, house and stables so our midnight johnnies can expect swift arrest if they ever try bringing their damned stock wagons up my drive.'

'A worthwhile investment I should think,' agreed the vet. They were back in the yard now and, as he put his bag back into the Land Rover, he could see the camera covering them. 'Well, I'm glad you didn't need me for anything more than reassurance, Mr Knights. I almost feel guilty having to charge you for this callout.'

The farmer gave him an appreciative slap on the back. 'Not at all, only grateful you could come so promptly.' He hesitated. 'But, while you're here, there is something else I'd be glad of your opinion on.'

'Sure.' McQuaid glanced at his watch. 'I've still got some time before my next call. What's the problem?'

'Well, it's Sindbad, actually.'

'Sindbad?'

'Yes, Carol's horse. She took him for a gallop yesterday, but noticed when they got back that he'd become a bit lame. Would you have a look at him?'

'Of course, I'll see him straight away.'

Knights led them across the yard to the stable block, a well-constructed building in black lapboard that faced away from the yard. When they turned its corner, they came across a fine looking steed being groomed by a jovial girl in jodhpurs and wax jacket. She looked around as they approached and smiled when she recognised the vet. 'Carol, Gordon's going to have a quick look at Sindbad for you.'

'Oh, that's great.' She looked relieved. 'I was hoping his lameness might have sorted itself by this morning, but I'm afraid it's still there.'

'Right, walk him up and down a bit so I can have a look.' Carol complied, leading Sindbad by a loose rope around the paved area of the stable-yard. The horse was certainly moving awkwardly with some definite lameness in one of his hind legs. 'Try and get him to trot, Carol.'

With a few words of encouragement from his mistress, Sindbad duly complied, but it was obvious he was suffering some discomfort.

'Okay, let me have a closer look.' With Sindbad back by his stall, McQuaid bent down and, while talking quietly to the horse, ran probing hands up and down the offending leg. It was Carol though who seemed to be in more distress.

'Will he be alright, Mr McQuaid? I've had him since I was a little girl and dread anything happening to him. Do you think it's serious?'

The vet straightened up, thoughtfully. 'No, I don't think so. For starters, let's just give him a box-rest for a few days and see how he does.'

'Does this mean he can't be ridden?'

'Not until I've seen him again.' McQuaid pulled a diary from his bag and flicked forward through a few page-filled entries. 'I'm actually passing here in three days time, so I'll pop back in then and see how he's doing.'

'Oh, thank you so much,' said a comforted Carol.

'We'll be gone by then,' reminded her father, 'but it's good to know the problem is in your capable hands, Gordon.'

The vet said his goodbyes and was soon gunning the Land Rover down Grange Farm's driveway towards the next call on his rounds. Exiting the brick-lined gateway, he noticed the security camera wink its own goodbye.

*   *   *

'Well, I still think it was Lady de Courcey,' said Audrey, tipping a bowl of potatoes into the kitchen sink.

Jack took up the peeler and set to work. 'I'm not so sure, Aud. After all, Sir Charles chose to stand by her and not go off with Samantha.'

'But she's admitted she was in Norfolk at the time, and how convenient that her alibis have both died since.'

'Yes, I know but we *are* talking about thirty years ago. Any of us would be hard-pressed to produce witnesses for our defence after all that time.'

'I suppose you're right.' Audrey paused in selecting some other vegetables from the fridge. 'But why do you think Sir Charles didn't insist on a full-blown investigation to find out what happened to Sam?'

'Perhaps he didn't want his dirty washing hitting the headlines unless…'

'… he suspected his wife had murdered Sam and was covering up for her? I bet that's what happened, Jack. Unless of course he killed her himself. Did he actually go to the police and explain his fear she'd been murdered?'

'According to him, he did, but, whoever it was, then decided to let the matter drop.'

'Poppycock. You know as well as I do, that no police force in the country, then or now, would have chosen to turn a blind eye to such an incident, regardless of how influential the persons concerned. It seems to me that the only decent member of that family is the daughter.'

'Yes, they made a good job of bringing Rose up and I'm sure she's enjoyed a perfectly normal, happy home life, totally unaware of what went on during the early part of her parents' marriage.'

'I'm sure her arrival helped to cement their reconciliation, and bringing up a daughter has obviously given them both something to focus on.'

'Unfortunately, the father is still focussing on her,' said Jack as he peeled potatoes.

'In what way?'

'Oh, by being so negative about her relationship with young McQuaid. It seems as though Sir Charles' strict Catholic principles make it hard to condone them sharing a house without being married.'

Audrey placed a bowl of carrots, parsnips and broccoli beside the potatoes. 'I'm all for morals, Jack, but how hypocritical can you get? Here he is, a confessed adulterer, daring to criticise his own daughter just because she hasn't walked up the aisle before living with her partner.'

'And, apparently, even tying the knot wouldn't appease Sir Charles, because it seems he's dead against her marrying a non-Catholic anyway.'

'Poor girl,' sympathised Audrey. 'Surely the main thing is that she and Gordon are good, honest people who love being together. I thought needing to be the same denomination as your partner went out years ago. Which brings me to that enigmatic priest you told me about.'

'Monsignor Coletti?'

'Yes, him. He sounds a bit strange too. Very vague about why he's off to Cambridge, a city we know has already played a significant part in this drama.'

Jack tossed a peeled potato into the colander and picked up another, 'I'm sure he knows more than he'd ever let on, seeing as he was Charles' spiritual advisor in Peru and probably took all his confessions.'

'Well, *that* must have made pretty interesting listening,' said Audrey, grinning.

'Priests probably hear far worse than that, Aud, and I agree Sir Charles was wrong in playing away, but one thing that did interest me was when he hinted strongly that young Kingsbourne had somehow upset Samantha.'

'How on earth could that be, seeing as he was thousands of miles away at the time?'

'I don't know, but...' Further discussion was ended by the ringing of the study phone. Jack wiped his hands and went off to answer. When he came back he wore a smug expression. 'As I said, Audrey, I don't know, but I soon will. That was the man himself, Major General Kingsbourne as he now is, calling from his boat just off the Thames Estuary. Reckons he'll be in Lowestoft the day after tomorrow and wants me to meet him in the marina there.'

'My goodness, what next?' Audrey started to cut up some of the few potatoes that Jack had peeled. 'A pity it's not sooner, because that's another conversation I can't wait to hear related.'

'A day between will suit me fine,' said Jack, resuming his peeling. 'It'll give me time to do a little more research.'

'On what?'

'Oh, just a theory on what might lie behind all this.'

'A good job you've not started your summer duties yet then.'

'Only just.' Jack put the peeler on one side and once more wiped his hands. 'The chief ranger called me first thing and asked if I can start earlier. Apparently one of the regulars is off on a management course.'

'How much earlier?'

'First thing next week. But I plan to be on the river tomorrow, actually.'

'What, patrolling?'

'No, purely a private little operation this one, Aud.'

'Oh no, Jack. Just what scheme are you hatching now?' asked an ever-fearful Audrey.

'Just one that will hopefully set the cat amongst the pigeons. I'll tell you more, love, once I've made a phone call.'

And with that, Jack disappeared again into his study leaving his long-suffering wife to finish off the potatoes.

*　　*　　*

'Charles, what are we going to do?'

Audrey wasn't the only wife with worries that evening. Returning from dropping Lorenzo at Cambridge, the de Courceys were now speeding homeward with their own ever-deepening problems foremost in the conversation. Their interviews with Mr Fellows, the ranger, had been upsetting enough, but that had turned to pure anguish with a telephone call received within seconds of shutting the front door on him.

'Don't worry, darling. Things will work out. They always do.' Even as he tried to give his wife a crumb of comfort, de Courcey was well aware he was failing to convince even himself. 'Perhaps Lorenzo can sort something.'

'It's not fair to involve him, Charles.'

Despite Lady Harriet's initial reservations, discussing the problem with the priest had seemed the best thing to do. After all, Lorenzo Coletti had been such a strength and comfort in past bad times, when his reasoning mind and keen perception had pierced the enveloping dilemmas and replaced them with advice and hope. So, once again, after this morning's distressing call, he had sat down with them and tried to soothe their worries and allay their fears, assuring them he would take the matter in hand just as soon as his own business in Cambridge was complete.

'But he wants to, Harriet. Somehow, I think, it helps ease his own conscience.'

'He shouldn't even be carrying *that* on *his* conscience, Charles. It was none of his doing.' Lady Harriet looked out at the darkening forests of Breckland speeding past the Range Rover's windows. 'And anyway, it might be weeks yet before he can do anything.'

'Let's hope it is, for his sake.'

'Yes, of course.' She couldn't help feeling some guilt of her own. 'But that other party isn't going to wait, Charles. Something has to be done immediately.'

'Yes, you're right,' agreed de Courcey, wishing with all his heart that he knew just what.

*　　*　　*

Chapter Eight

'I like the boat, Jack. Where'd you get her?'

'A yard upriver that owed me a favour.' At the open wheel position amidships, Jack brought the wooden workboat to a standstill alongside the quay-heading and tossed a rope to the stocky figure waiting on the staithe. 'Here, catch this.' Once the boat was secure, he climbed ashore. 'Thanks for coming, Jeff, especially at such short notice.'

It was early the next morning at Ranworth Staithe, the air still undisturbed by convection, and the water only by wild-life just stirring in the dyke.

'No problem. I didn't have any other job today, so I'm pleased to help.'

Jeff Barker ran a small diving business on the Broads, a somewhat shallower and certainly less rigorous environment than the North Sea, where he'd spent years on oil-production support. It had been marriage and children that had prompted the move to less demanding climes and, having been born and brought up in Broadland, he'd decided to offer his unique skill and knowledge to the boating community there. Everyone predicted failure, but what most hadn't realised was the great number of boats that every year managed to get a rope around their propeller or a discarded plastic bag in their bow-thruster. Getting those boats back to their yard for slipping was a time consuming business, whereas a quick call to Barker Diving Services brought an immediate fix. Now he was on regular contract to several yards, and the rangers, often coming across boats with underwater snags, also knew who to call for quick service. Jack's call of the evening before, however, had been a purely personal request.

'Well, I appreciate you giving me your time anyway,' Jack replied, before nodding towards the diver's pickup truck positioned nearby. 'Right, let me help you get your gear on board.'

Together, the two men humped across bags of diving kit, including a small portable compressor. When all was safely stowed, Jack restarted the boat's engine, cast off and they were on their way.

'Not far from here then?' Barker enquired as they motored across the broad, up Ranworth Dyke and onto the main river.

'No, a quarter mile at most.' Jack pointed ahead. 'Just around the next corner, in fact.'

'This watch of yours must be pretty precious, Jack, to go to all this trouble.'

'Sentimental value. You know how it is.'

They were soon there, the workboat secured to the bank with rhond anchors and a rigid blue and white Alpha flag to indicate "Diver Down", hoisted in good view. 'You sure you're quite happy about operating the gear?' Barker asked as Jack helped him into his diving suit.

'Yep, no problem. I've done it often here and with the Met when I was in Thames Division.' He nodded towards the grey water. 'I just hope it's worthwhile.'

'Well, don't build your hopes up too much,' warned Barker as he prepared to pull on his helmet and attached airline. 'A watch is a pretty small thing to find in the bottom mud.'

'I won't, but I suppose there's just a chance it could have got hung up on the roots of that dead alder.' Jack, pointed to the stump of the offending tree. 'Worth having a good look anyway. Who knows what you might find down there?'

'What do you think I might find?' asked Barker with just a hint of suspicion.

'Perhaps something significant.'

'Well, if I do, I'll let you know.'

'Thanks.' Jack went and started the compressor. This kept a supply cylinder topped with air, which in turn fed a constant supply to the diver. After testing the system, Barker climbed over the side and down the ladder hung on the gunwale. Jack paid out the airline, watching the diver descend in a vortex of bubbles. He was very soon lost to sight, only the stream of bubbles very close to the bank showing just where he was searching. There was little river traffic so early and the few boats that passed, slowed down, possibly observing the Alpha dive flag but, more probably, just to have a good look at what was going on.

It wasn't long before Barker's head once more broke surface. He made his way back to the side and took hold of the ladder. 'Sorry, Jack, it's like thick chocolate down there. I really think your watch is a gonna, but there is something rather odd hanging on that root.'

'What?'

'I'm not sure. I just hope it's not what I think.'

'Go and have another look, Jeff. Bring it up, whatever it is.'

'Your shout, Jack,' acknowledged the diver, pulling down his helmet and once more descending into the murk. More bubbles, more mud churning and then he surfaced again, but this time holding something aloft. Jack went to the side and collected the object in the scoop net. He had little doubt what it was. He'd seen enough of them in his working life.

Lying there in the net was the unmistakable form of a human femur.

*   *   *

It was a revelation of an altogether different kind, however, that Rose de Courcey was now trying to come to terms with. Having just nipped up to their small flat above the practice to make her and Gordon's morning coffee, she'd answered the telephone and, by so doing, changed her life forever.

Now she sat in disbelief, the shock of it all gradually creeping over her. Somehow, this one call, out of the blue from some hideous unknown, had neutralised all the joy she'd previously known in life. Never in her wildest dreams had Rose ever imagined that she would be the victim of blackmail, but now it had happened and she couldn't come to terms with it.

It wasn't the demand for some impossible amount of money that was causing her immediate grief. That was a seemingly insurmountable problem that would have to be faced later. No, it was the agony of being told things which she found hard to believe, but which the caller had assured her he could prove, that was causing her this unbearable distress. Suddenly, all the things she'd cherished in her life - the love of her parents, her life with Gordon, the future they'd planned together - seemed to have been devoured in a sea of evil intent. What was she to do? Would she ever know happiness again?

As Rose wrestled with her feelings and the biggest problem she'd ever had to deal with in her life, she heard Gordon's footfall on the stairs and knew he was about to join her for his coffee. Quickly dabbing her eyes with a tissue, she went into the small galley kitchen and put the kettle on.

'Are you okay, Rose?' McQuaid had caught just a fleeting glimpse of her red eyes. 'You look upset.'

'No, I'm fine. Perhaps a cold coming on.'

The rot had started already she thought, as she made the coffee. For the first time ever, she was lying to Gordon. How could she resolve this awful situation without resorting to further deception?

*   *   *

'Detective Inspector Bailey wants to talk to you, Jack,' said the constable, holding out his mobile phone.

It was mid-morning now, and the dive site on the River Bure, a much busier place since Jack's call to the police. He'd reported finding the remains by going through the normal channels, rather than direct to the detective with whom, over the years, he'd formed such a good working relationship. Part of this was his knowledge of Bailey's already heavy workload, but the main reason was the DI's previous strict order to drop anything connected to Samantha Waites.

And so a small armada had eventually gathered on this normally quiet little spot on the river, starting with the swift arrival of BroadsBeat in their high-speed launch. After a quick examination of Jack's find, a return call to headquarters had brought in the diving team from Norfolk Fire and Rescue Service for a more comprehensive search. Now their open dive-boat was over the site while a RIB lay stationed upriver, stopping the passage of all boats once the diving operation commenced. Fulfilling the same duty downriver was the ranger's launch in whose patrol area this flurry of activity was now occurring. Jack's workboat lay just to one side now, he and Barker having already given their first brief statement to BroadsBeat and then, like the rest, watching as the brigade team went to work.

There were two divers down, while a third remained in the dive-boat, keeping an eye on his colleagues under the water. Also in the dive boat were three other crew handling the succession of grim relics being brought from the river bed. Sad as this was, Jack couldn't help feeling some relief that his hunch and this expensive response had indeed been worthwhile. Of course, not everyone would be happy with the finds, starting with the man at the other end of this phone.

'Bailey. Good morning. What can I do for you?'

'You can start by telling me what the hell's going on,' growled the voice of a far from happy DI.

'Bones, Bailey. Human ones if I'm not much mistaken.'

'I know that, Jack. The crew on the spot have told me. What I'm asking is, what are you doing sending a diver down there in the first place?'

'Trying to recover the watch I lost the other day, but while he was down there he found these remains. You know the form, Bailey. We have to report anything like this immediately.'

'I know the form, thank you Jack.' There was an audible sigh. 'This wouldn't, by any remote chance, be at the spot the handbag was found?'

'Who knows? It could be.'

'Thanks, Jack.' Bailey sounded like he had lost much of his usual good-humour this busy morning. 'Now you've really dropped us all in it.'

'Or perhaps triggered some action that should have been taken decades ago.'

'We'll see about that. I should have read you the Riot Act first time, Jack, instead of just giving you a friendly warning. You said you'd find a way to pursue this one way or the other, and it looks like you have.'

'Something had to be done, Bailey, and you did owe me this one.'

'Right, well consider us quits. You've caused enough chaos for one morning, so get your man out of there and go home to that lovely wife of yours and have some breakfast.'

'Sounds a good plan,' Jack agreed before pushing his luck that little bit further, 'but I would like to know what the pathologist thinks when he's had a look.'

'Jack, if this is what I think it is, it'll be me on the slab when the Chief Constable's finished with me.'

And with that, the DI rang off.

*   *   *

'So, now you've even gone and got the wrong side of Bailey,' scolded Audrey as she and Jack walked together with Spike along a lane near their home. 'Getting your own diver like that. Goodness knows what it cost.'

'If I hadn't, those remains would never have been discovered, Aud.' Jack paused to throw a stick for Spike while at the same time neatly avoiding the last part of his wife's admonition. 'As it is, we've found Samantha Waites.'

'And doubtless stirred up a real old hornet's nest in the bargain, which, I suspect, was probably your real intention all along.'

'Well, at least this way she'll get a coroner's inquest.'

'And, eventually, a Christian burial, but the thing that worries me, Jack, is that someone was powerful enough to stop Bailey proceeding with this in the first place. Now you've forced the issue, that person, whoever it was, is going to be far from happy.'

'I don't doubt it.' Spike had just come bounding back with the stick, which Jack immediately threw again. As the border collie went tearing off in pursuit he nodded after him. 'Now that infection's cleared up, he's his old self again.'

'Thank goodness, but don't change the subject, Jack, and instead consider the fact that some things are best left alone.'

'Every murder victim deserves to be avenged, Aud. That's what justice is all about, regardless of how influential the people involved may be.'

'And just who do you think those "people" are? The de Courceys?'

'Could be. Sir Charles actually said that at the time of Samantha's disappearance, he had enough clout to report it to some "higher authority" without going through the local police. Who, I don't know, but remember his main home was then in London and he probably mixed in influential circles. He could well have been buddies with someone at the top who used his or her position to keep what might have been just a missing person enquiry, nicely under wraps.'

'What, like someone at Scotland Yard?'

'Not then. I was there at that time, and they came down heavily in those days on anything even hinting at sleaze.'

'But, whoever it was, must still be around and important enough to have the stoppers put on poor Bailey and now you've dropped him in it even further with the discovery of poor Samantha's remains. Surely the powers that be will stop him taking this development any further as well.'

'I can't see how.' Jack whistled to Spike and turned for home. 'As far as Bailey is concerned, he can regard this latest development as just a plain case of human remains being discovered. As yet, no one except us has put a name to them.'

'But the coroner will want to know, surely?'

'Undoubtedly, and I'll be called as a witness and tell them all I know.'

'Oh, Jack.' Audrey gave a little shudder. 'I think you're venturing into dangerous territory here. Why not drop it now while everything is still nice and vague?'

'I've already explained why, Aud.' Spike had caught them up with his stick and Jack paused to throw it yet again. 'But let's wait and see what General Kingsbourne has to say tomorrow before we think any further ahead.'

'I can't see him telling you anything, Jack, if the openness of the others is anything to go by.'

'No, but I might be able to tell *him* something.'

'What, for instance?'

'Well, the finding of Samantha's remains for a start. That might shock him into a bit of candour. And, on top of that, I have my own theory as to the background of this whole mess, which I'll also run up the flagpole and see if it gets a flutter.'

'You and your theories. What's this one?'

Jack gave his wife a conspiratorial wink. 'I'll tell you tomorrow if it proves correct.' They were back at their cottage now, kicking off boots in the porch and Spike ready for his rubdown. Jack grabbed the towel and nodded inside. 'But a bit more research yet this evening. If I'm going to take on a war hero, I'll need all the ammo I can get.'

*   *   *

Chapter Nine

As the morning train to Lowestoft trundled across swing-bridges and over the Yare and then the Waveney, Jack blinked through the spring sunshine and picked out the spot where, only a few days previously, Harry Bentley had shown him the location of that strange monster sighting. Now he was back in Suffolk and on his way to meet Gregory Kingsbourne, who had sent him a text the night before confirming his arrival in the port and giving details of where he was berthed. The general had also explained his intention of spending time on the Broads and asking if Jack would help him negotiate the lock into Oulton Broad.

So, knowing where he'd be boarding, but not where he'd be disembarking, Jack had taken the more flexible and pleasurable option of travelling by rail. Now, in the short final run from Oulton Broad, the landscape changed, becoming more industrial with tantalising glimpses of Lake Lothing and big ships alongside quays, before pulling into Lowestoft itself. Outside the station, Jack sniffed air that carried the unmistakable tang of the sea and the shrieking of seagulls, reminders that this was indeed an old seaport. He crossed the road to where the masts and funnels of large vessels rose from the docks, and headed seawards, passing the old trawl basins where, on long ago childhood holidays, he'd looked in awe at the big deep sea trawlers in from the North Sea and Icelandic fishing grounds.

Sadly, those days were long gone now and the trawlers replaced by offshore wind farm support vessels that lay beside what had been the old packing sheds. He continued around the biggest of these until the road turned right towards the last basin known as Hamilton Dock. This was now one of Lowestoft's largest marinas and, even before Jack arrived at its gates, he could see an assortment of private and commercial craft moored to lines of floating pontoons. He checked his watch and was relieved to see he was within a minute of the scheduled ten-thirty time.

Someone else who obviously believed in punctuality was the tall, straight-backed figure waiting by the gate. Spotting the ranger, he fingered some numbers on a nearby keypad and slowly but surely, the big gates swung open. Jack walked through and was greeted with a smile and an outstretched hand. 'You must be Jack Fellows. I'm Kingsbourne.'

'Good to meet you, General.' As he took the firm grip of this ex-boyfriend of Samantha Waites, Jack took in the still blond close cropped hair, the weathered chiselled features and bull neck. Kingsbourne was wearing tan sailing trousers and a floppy dark blue jumper, but they failed to disguise the broad, athletic frame beneath. 'Thank you for seeing me today.'

'I think we both know I had no option,' Kingsbourne replied. He nodded to the marina below. 'Let's go onboard. I'm booked in for the eleven-twenty bridge lift, so we'll get under way and chat as we go along.'

'Sounds good.' The tide was obviously low and the gangway down to the finger pontoons, quite steep. As they descended, Jack was glad to see that, as well as pleasure craft, a fair number of inshore fishing boats still used the dock.

They were half way along the first long pontoon when the general paused beside a ketch-rigged motor sailer with rugged, almost trawler-like lines. *Tumbledown*, proclaimed the name on the blue hull. 'Here she is.'

'And very nice too.' Jack followed Kingsbourne on board and into the varnished wheelhouse. 'You're obviously a dedicated sailor, General.'

'Dedicated to anything to do with the water, but Tumbledown's certainly the perfect escape from military commitments.'

'But those must be exciting enough in their own right. Royal Marine Commandos don't exactly live a sedentary life.'

'It was a brilliant life while I was still working with marines, but I've been desk bound these last five years.' Kingsbourne was at the steering console now, turning the ignition and bringing a powerful diesel, somewhere below, to immediate life. 'And it's going to get worse, unfortunately. My next appointment is at the MOD, so I'm making the most of this joining leave to catch up on sea time.' The engine was settling into a steady rumble now and the flick of a few switches brought other services on-line, including the VHF, from which the voices of Lowestoft Port Control and other boats and shipping now joined them in the wheelhouse. 'I disconnected the shore-power just before you arrived,' he explained, 'so all we need to do is cast off.'

'Which I can take care of,' offered Jack.

'That would be great.' Kingsbourne paused. 'Now, let's dispense with formalities shall we, Jack. The name's Greg.' He eased the single lever forward and Tumbledown moved slowly ahead to the limit of her back-spring. 'This will hold her alongside until you've cleared the head and stern lines. Then I'll take off power while you get the spring in.'

'Aye aye, Greg.' Jack left the wheelhouse and headed for'ard. All the ropes were doubled back to the boat, so there was no need to leave the deck. When only the back-spring remained, he unhitched that rope from its midships cleat, leaving just two turns around for instant slipping. A nod to the wheelhouse, a thumbs-up in return, and then the power came off and Tumbledown eased against the spring. Jack let go the remaining turns and hauled the rope through its ring and onto the sidedeck. 'All clear.'

A nod back, the feel of the engine going astern and Tumbledown was backing out of her berth. By the time Jack had returned to the wheelhouse, Kingsbourne was already on the VHF making his call.

'Lowestoft Port, Lowestoft Port, this is yacht Tumbledown, yacht Tumbledown.'

'Yacht Tumbledown, Lowestoft Port Control, go ahead,' came back the friendly feminine voice at the other end.

'Good morning, ma'am, we've just let go in Hamilton Dock for the eleven-twenty bridge lift.'

'Roger, you're clear to proceed, with no conflicting traffic.'

By this time, they'd cleared Hamilton Dock and were passing Waveney Dock before continuing on towards the harbour entrance lying to port with its pagoda-like light towers on each side. Through the gap, the limitless expanse of the North Sea beckoned enticingly, but Kingsbourne turned to starboard, idling towards the still closed bascule bridge ahead. Through its lowered spans, Jack could see two other yachts, obviously waiting for passage outbound. Spot on time, against the background wail of a warning siren, barriers started lowering across the road and all traffic passing through Lowestoft centre ground to a stop. Then the two big spans of the bridge began to smoothly and silently rise. When they were pointing skywards, the signal lights, close to harbour control, turned green and Kingsbourne once again eased the engine ahead. Soon they were sliding between the bridge columns, exchanging cheerful waves with the two passing sea bound craft. Then they were through and into the inner harbour with the bascules already closing behind them.

Jack sat back and relaxed, taking in the view of some large tugs moored to starboard and, just a little further on to port, the somewhat incongruous site of a large supermarket. Kingsbourne nodded further ahead. 'I radioed through to Mutford Lock earlier, so the keepers are expecting us. The rail bridge should be open for us, but I'll need to give him a call when we're a bit closer.'

Impressed by Kingsbourne's competence, Jack glanced at the chart spread out beside the steering consol. It was small scale with pencilled tracks coming all the way from Portsmouth. 'A long passage on your own, Greg. Didn't you want a mate?'

'Not really. I prefer single-handing and anyway, it's much easier these days, what with sat-navs, autopilots and the like. And this boat's a dream to handle.' He stood back and indicated the wheel. 'You take her, Jack, while I go and brew us a coffee. Standard NATO?'

'Yep, with just one sugar, please,' answered Jack, taking the spokes of the varnished wooden wheel and amused, as always, at the quaint expressions so relished by the military.

With Kingsbourne below, he took the opportunity to enjoy again a part of the river system rarely used by Broads boaters, but fascinating in its variety and links with the area's maritime past. Such a link was passing now to port – the old Brooke Marine yard where commercial boats and minor warships had been built throughout the nineteen-hundreds. Perhaps they'd even built the two military-looking vessels moored to starboard and now passing abeam, their grey sides still carrying the title ARMY.

'Tank Landing Ships,' explained Kingsbourne, emerging from the cabin with steaming mugs and nodding towards the large open tank decks and closed bow doors. 'Obviously laid up for disposal.' He handed Jack his mug and took a swig of his own. 'They bring back memories of when I skippered a smaller version during my time with the Landing Craft Unit.'

'Which accounts for your sea-going knowledge,' replied Jack, taking a mouthful of coffee and easing Tumbledown's throttle back slightly as they came to more small boat moorings. 'Was that in the Falklands?'

'No, I was 42 Commando in those days.' He broke open a packet of biscuits and offered them across.

'No thanks.' Jack patted his stomach. 'Trying to give them up.' Instead he nodded towards a brass plate mounted just above the windscreen. It showed Tumbledown as having been built in the late nineteen-eighties at an Isle of Wight yard. 'I like your choice of boat name. Was that one of the battles you were in on the Falklands?'

Kingsbourne shook his head. 'Not really. The Battle for Mount Tumbledown was mainly an army show by the Scots Guards and Gurkhas. The Marines only supplied some mortar support, and I didn't even get my hands on those, having been shoved into our intelligence section early on in the war. However, I like to think the info I supplied played some part in the planning and made a contribution towards its success.'

'I'm sure it did,' acknowledged Jack, mentally reappraising his impression that the young Kingsbourne had emerged from the Falklands War as something of a hero. 'Were you in intelligence for the whole campaign then?'

'Unfortunately yes, but it wasn't my choice, I can assure you. I'd joined the Royal Marines to see some action and the Argentinean invasion promised to provide plenty. It did, but not for me. The problem was I'd studied modern languages at Cambridge, including Spanish, so that suddenly made me a prime candidate for secondment to intelligence.' He shook his head, sadly. 'I was pulled out of the line and sent to their field detachment so quick my feet didn't even touch.'

'Doing what, exactly?'

'Mainly monitoring enemy radio traffic or interrogating prisoners. Just listening to the Argentine soldiers chatting amongst themselves gave us a lot of information as to the state of enemy morale.'

'It must have been at this time that the navy started to take serious losses from Argentinean Exocet missiles?'

'Yes. Bloody things.' Kingsbourne joined Jack back at the wheel. 'They were the biggest thorn in our fleet's side for the whole campaign.'

'And stopping Argentina getting their hands on more must have been a top priority.'

'It certainly was.' Kingsbourne turned to fix Jack with a perceptive frown. 'You seem unduly interested in Exocets, Jack. Any specific reason?'

'Oh, very much so.' Jack returned the glance and smiled. 'You see, Greg, I think those missiles were the reason you drove Samantha Waites into the arms of another man.'

For a second, the general paused as if considering his options. Then he turned away and indicated the swing bridge just coming into view at the head of Lake Lothing. 'Time to give the lock a call, Jack.' He took the wheel and nodded for'ard. 'Get up there and be ready to hold a line.'

Up ahead, the swing bridge was slowly opening.

* * *

'You're the only boat going through, Tumbledown,' said the voice of the lockmaster on VHF, 'so proceed up to the holding pontoon.'

'Many thanks, Mutford.' As the old railway bridge swung fully open, Kingsbourne eased the throttle ahead and the motor sailer into the next small basin. Here they idled once more until another warning horn signalled the closure of the busy road bridge joining both ends of Oulton town. Smoothly and silently, the bridge rose before them, followed by the footbridge just beyond. Then a further clearance on VHF saw them into the dank interior of the lock itself where high walls rose above the wheelhouse and friendly keepers came out to take their lines and a small passage fee. The lines were passed through rings and doubled back to the boat, Kingsbourne leaving his wheelhouse to take the aft, and Jack the for'ard. Like some mythical monster devouring its prey, the seaward gates slowly rumbled shut behind them, and then Tumbledown, her engine still idling, slowly and surely started to rise. Taking in the slack on his line, Jack smiled at the folk watching from behind the barrier as they waited for the pedestrian bridge to lower once more. Gradually the water level in the lock came level with that on the landward side and the lock gates ahead opened. Lines were let go and hauled on board and then Tumbledown was easing slowly forward into the picturesque, tranquil waters of Oulton Broad, seemingly a world away from the working harbour they'd just left. Astern now, the road bridge descended as smoothly as it had risen, traffic flowed again and Tumbledown was in the broads system.

'Are you going on from here?' shouted Jack, still on the foredeck and coiling the headrope.

'Yes, but we'll have a break first,' called back Kingsbourne, indicating ahead. 'It looks as if there's a free buoy over there. Standby to pick up.'

Jack grabbed the boathook as they came slowly up to the buoy. The engine went to stop and then astern in perfect time for him to hook the mooring ring, haul it up and slip through the head rope. He secured it to the samson post and gave Kingsbourne a thumbs-up. The engine stopped and stillness descended. They were made fast.

Jack rejoined Kingsbourne in the wheelhouse. 'What are your onward plans, Greg?'

'Spend a few days on the Yare reliving old memories.' He gazed beyond the houses, old maltings and boatsheds surrounding the broad, westwards towards the dyke leading to the unseen expanse of Broadland beyond. 'It's been thirty-odd years since I was here last. Sam and I hired a sailing cruiser when we were students and spent a wonderful week exploring these magic waters.'

'A lot's certainly happened since then, Greg.' Jack hadn't failed to notice the catch in the general's voice as he recalled that time. 'Any regrets?'

'Of course, but that's life.' He nodded down below. 'Let's have a spot of lunch and then we can chat afterwards.'

*   *   *

Twenty miles away, Rose de Courcey was trying to sort her own more imminent dilemma. With Gordon off on a farm visit and no one else in the surgery, she was desperately reconciling the practice accounts and calculating just how much cash she could get her hands on.

The result made depressing reading. On a day to day basis the practice was holding its own but, with loans to be repaid, pharmaceutical bills to meet and their own meagre salaries, there was precious little spare cash. With the hopelessness of the situation more apparent than ever, Rose felt despair and anguish rising like a dark tide about to engulf her. She would do anything to preserve the happy memories she treasured so dearly, but how? It was a problem that seemed almost insurmountable.

Making an effort, she once again shook away self-pity and pulled herself together. There had to be something she could do other than sitting feeling sorry for herself. She picked up the telephone and rang the number that despicable man had given her.

Ten minutes later and she was feeling more wretched than ever.

*   *   *

Chapter Ten

Seated either side of Tumbledown's polished saloon table, Jack and Greg drank soup from mugs as they exchanged anecdotes from their nautical lives. It was only afterwards, over coffee, that the general's good humour subsided slightly into a distracted tapping of his cup with the spoon. It was as though he was going through some inner anguish while deciding what further direction their conversation should take. Then he looked up, blinked and said, 'A while ago, Jack, you were asking about Exocet missiles. Somehow, you seemed to think they'd had a bearing on why my relationship with Sam ended.'

'Yes, and I still think that.'

'On what basis?'

'Only on a bit of internet research concerning the Falklands campaign.' Jack leaned a little closer across the table. 'What did become very obvious reading those accounts, is that those missiles could very easily have cost us the war.'

Kingsbourne nodded. 'I think we all knew that, Jack. The Royal Navy had centuries of experience behind it, but it only took one pilot able to program a weapons system and press a button and a warship could be taken out...' he clicked his fingers, '...like that.'

'Pretty scary,' agreed Jack, 'but the problem for Argentina became one of supply, didn't it, because pressure by Britain had seen a complete embargo on the sale of *any* arms? That stopped the French manufacturer Aerospatiale selling them any more Exocets which, at seven hundred thousand dollars per missile, was a big loss of business.'

Kingsbourne nodded. 'Especially as the *junta*, in desperation, were offering to pay *four million* U.S. dollars per Exocet for a minimum order of twenty.'

'No wonder international arms dealers were falling over themselves to find a back door. All they needed was a way of getting around the embargo. But, of course, to you, working in intelligence, all this must have been common knowledge.'

'You flatter me, Jack.' Kingsbourne smiled. 'Remember, I was only in a field detachment, not MI6. Of course, we knew something of the work going on to stop the Argies getting their hands on more Exocets, including some pretty shady work by the French.'

'Who were still keen to supply the missiles,' Jack continued, 'and one way was by supplying them to other countries willing to help Argentina. But even that was risky, with British Intelligence well able to follow any money trail back to France. So, Aerospatiale needed a South American state where they could do a bit of money-laundering and for that, they chose Peru.'

Kingsbourne poured them both another coffee from the pot on the stove. 'Isn't all this just a bit fanciful, Jack?'

'Not at all. So far I've stated nothing that can't be found on the internet, but now I'm going to use my imagination and give you my best shot at just how you and Samantha got involved in this whole murky business.'

The general's eyes narrowed slightly. 'What makes you think I would tell you whether your theory was right or wrong?'

'The fact that all this might be coming out in the near future anyway.' Jack took a sip of his coffee. 'But me knowing the full facts could still work a bit of damage limitation.'

'Hmm,' said Kingsbourne, sitting back. 'All right, Jack. Go ahead.'

*   *   *

In the flat above the practice, Rose wished she had someone to talk to. She'd retreated there for sanctuary, a coffee and to get a grip of her fast eroding emotions. But shock was still there and suddenly the tears came, making little rings as they dropped into the mug cradled in her shaking hands. Only twenty-four hours ago, she'd known complete contentment. Now, everything suddenly looked so black.

But this session of soul searching was destined to be short lived as she heard the sound of the Land Rover arriving back and, a minute later, the clump of Gordon's boots running up the stairs. Before she even had time to grab a tissue and wipe away the worst of the tears, he was sweeping into the small lounge, obviously well pleased with his morning's work. 'Gosh, that calf took some delivering. I'm all in and famished. Any chance of...' He suddenly noticed that Rose's normally happy countenance was now one of tear stained dejection. 'My love.' He knelt beside her. 'What on earth's the matter? What's happened?'

Rose gulped back a sob. 'Something terrible, Gordon.'

'What? Tell me about it.'

'I had a telephone call. An awful call.'

'When? Who from?'

'Yesterday, when I came up to make coffee. From a man. I don't know his name. A dreadful man I've never met.' She sniffed back more tears. 'But he knew of me and my family and he told me some terrible things about Mum and Dad.'

'Your parents?' He put a comforting arm around her. 'What sort of terrible things, Rose?'

'You'll find it hard to believe when I tell you, Gordon.' She sniffed. 'I couldn't believe what he said myself, but the awful thing is that he wants me to give him money to keep quiet about it.'

'A blackmailer? How do you know this man's accusations carry even a shred of truth?'

'I don't,' admitted Rose, shaking her head, 'but he says he can back them all up with proof.'

'Well, whether he can or not, the police will know how to deal with him.' McQuaid reached for the telephone, but even as his finger touched the first 9, Rose's hand stopped him.

'No, darling, we can't take that chance. If the police come into this and it's true, Mum and Dad could go to prison and I couldn't bear to see that just because we handled it badly.'

'Prison! For God's sake, Rose, what have your parents done?'

'I'll tell you later. The critical thing now is that this horrible man is demanding money.'

'How much?'

'Ten thousand pounds.'

'Phew!' McQuaid blinked twice. 'That's a lot of money, Rose, but not an impossible amount, surely?'

'It is if you haven't got it, and we haven't.' Rose gave her eyes another wipe.

'We could sell Foxglove.'

'No,' she said, laying a tender hand on his and feeling better already at being able to share this dilemma, painful as it was. 'Once I realised the money was out of the question, I decided to put up a fight, rang him on the mobile number he'd given me, and told him that I simply couldn't pay.'

'And...'

'... and the hideous little man came back with an alternative plan.'

'Which is?'

The answer, though, stuck in Rose's throat, drowned by the repugnance of this whole situation. Instead, she simply dissolved into another fit of uncontrollable sobbing.

*   *   *

On Oulton Broad, Tumbledown swung to her mooring, slightly more now in the freshening breeze. Through the saloon portholes, some local sailing dinghies could be seen skimming across the dappled water, their young crews obviously delighting in this happy meeting of wind and sail. In the yacht station, hard by the pleasant setting of Carlton Park, a few early cruisers were snug in their mooring while two more were approaching down the broad itself. It was all a common enough scene in this corner of Broadland, but a world away from South America where Jack's thoughts now returned.

'Peru, Greg. Word must have come to you, via the intelligence grapevine, that this was where some shenanigans were going on regarding the purchase of Exocets.' Kingsbourne didn't contradict this, so Jack continued, 'But, my guess is that British intelligence surely needed more data and that's where you knew you could help by using someone near and dear to you. Here was an opportunity to really make your mark, because fate had handed you the gift of Samantha. Here she was, an innocent young student, already in Peru conducting some minor research for her PhD, but someone who might just be persuaded to include a bit of nosing on behalf of her country.'

Kingsbourne nodded. 'Intelligence already knew of the proposed sale of Exocets through Peru, but they needed the start of that money trail back to Aerospatiale. So, through our military channels and the embassy there, Sam was contacted and asked to help.'

'And she agreed?'

'After a bit of soul-searching and appeals to her patriotic instincts, yes. I think she felt it was one way she could do her bit.'

'Presumably, at this stage, she didn't know that it was you who'd suggested her in the first place?'

'No. Back then she just assumed it was the embassy's own intelligence section doing its job. The plan was simply to infiltrate the Peruvian banking system. The embassy already knew another Brit in Lima who could do just that, someone with just the right contacts to glean the information they needed.'

'Charles de Courcey?'

'Yes, a man known to be deeply involved in financial dealings in the country and who we could profitably use.'

'And here's one aspect I don't quite understand,' interjected Jack, frowning, 'which is why intelligence didn't just use him in the first place without ever involving Samantha?'

'Simply because our people there weren't sure that de Courcey wasn't actually part of the deal. Like you said yourself, he was known to be well in with the Peruvian government and had already set up many trade agreements between the two countries and we had to be sure *he* wasn't involved in that missile dealing. Okay, he held a British passport, but he also had a name French enough to raise a few eyebrows. So, Sam's first job was to vet de Courcey.'

'By getting close enough to suss him out with a bit of pillow talk?'

'That's about it.'

'How did you feel about that?'

'I chose not to think about it too much. We were at war, Jack, and things were desperate so the embassy simply made sure Sam attended a small reception to which de Courcey was also invited, the two could meet...'

'... and she could strike up a relationship?'

'Exactly,' admitted Kingsbourne, quietly and almost to himself. 'It all seemed straight forward enough at the time, except...'

'Except it worked too well, didn't it? What you hadn't allowed for, Greg, was that they'd both fall deeply in love.'

'No, that was something I hadn't reckoned on.' He shook his head. 'It came as a bit of a blow when I found out.'

'But, from what I know of her, Sam didn't seem the sort to be unfaithful and fall so readily for someone else unless she'd worked out that it was you who'd put her name forward and were willing to let her prostitute herself for information.' Jack shook his head, sadly. 'Not the behaviour of a man in love, even if it was for the good of the country. It serves you right that she fell head over heels in love with de Courcey.'

'I don't deny it,' said Kingsbourne, 'but you have to put it in the context of the time, Jack. Strategically speaking, we had our backs to the wall down there. Just a few more Exocets could have spelt disaster for the fleet and any hope of retaking the islands. Enough of our chaps had already made the ultimate sacrifice, so mine wasn't that big on the scale of things.'

'It was big enough, Greg, but was it worth it?'

'Very much so, from an intelligence-data viewpoint.'

'But from a personal?'

'Pretty painful.' He shook away what were obviously tormenting thoughts. 'But it did produce the goods. One thing that Sam quickly established was that de Courcey was indeed innocent of any involvement in the deal himself. So, now we could use him and his contacts to find out how these Exocets would be paid for. He'd obviously fallen for Sam in a big way and, when he found out the true nature of her mission, he was only too willing to use all his know-how and help.'

'A little clandestine work in a foreign land doubtless added to the romance of the whole thing,' reasoned Jack, before adding, 'but hard to think that they both didn't feel a little used.'

'Yes. When it was over, Sam told me in no uncertain terms what a heartless, manipulating bastard I'd been and that it served me right that our relationship was finished and that she'd fallen in love with de Courcey.' Kingsbourne shrugged. 'Our government, on the other hand, was very grateful for my contribution which undoubtedly saved a lot of British lives and helped secure the final victory.'

'And gained you a lot of kudos.'

'Yes. I received a commendation and my career never looked back from that point on.'

'Even if your love life suffered. How about Sam?' Jack asked. 'What did she get out of it?'

'From the government, not much, apart from a small monetary reward and the sincere thanks of MI6. But she had found a lover more than willing to put his considerable wealth into furthering her zoological research.'

'He could afford to,' pointed out Jack. 'Presumably, he got the knighthood in recognition of his own secret service?'

'Oh yes. He was rich anyway, so I guess the government felt that a title would be far more useful to his international finance work than a bit of extra cash.' Kingsbourne shrugged again. 'He had, after all, sacrificed his South American business, because the Peruvians soon found out who'd been snooping into their financial affairs, with the result that he and Sam were asked to leave the country soon after the war ended.'

'So, when Sam vanished, rumours that she and de Courcey had returned to Peru to live, couldn't have had any substance whatsoever?'

'None at all. The Peruvians wouldn't have let them back that soon and I can't think they would have wanted to anyway, with Sam on the verge of completing her studies at Darwin and de Courcey based in London rebuilding his business and marriage.'

'It must have been a time of very mixed emotions for everyone?'

'It was for me. I was pretty cut up at losing Sam and knew I'd take a long time to get over it.'

'You didn't try for a reconciliation?' asked Jack.

'Oh yes, I made overtures and suggested we take up where we'd left off, but she was having none of it. All her love, she made plain, was now for Charles de Courcey, regardless of whether he still wanted her or not.'

'You mean, by this time, he was trying to cool off the relationship?'

'I think so. After the fling in Peru, he soon realised on which side his bread was buttered and that any divorce would cost him everything.' Kingsbourne shook his head. 'I tried to tell Sam that, but she wouldn't listen.'

'Which must've made you somewhat bitter?'

'Very much so.'

'Bitter enough to kill her?'

Kingsbourne leaned forwards across the table. 'Now you *are* off track, Jack. I'm a marine, remember. We're trained to handle our emotions and control aggression. And, besides, two years had passed and I'd come to terms with what had happened by then.' His broad shoulders seemed to sag slightly. 'Anyway, as you pointed out, it was all my fault, so...'

'So, if you didn't kill her, who did?'

'I don't know.'

'Where were you on the night she was murdered?'

'Are we sure she was murdered, Jack? All I know was that she disappeared. Could be that she was still running from whatever was scaring her.'

'Any idea what that was?'

'No, but she called me to say she feared for her life and that's why I came up to Norfolk.'

'You mean you too were near the scene at the time of the incident?' asked Jack, taken completely by surprise at this new revelation.

'Yes, at the Stanford battle area near Thetford, making preparations for an exercise. I still felt some guilt at the way I'd used Sam, so being there when she needed me was the least I could do. It took a day or two to arrange leave, and then I came straight up.'

'With what arrangement?'

'That I'd join her on de Courcey's boat. I suppose I still had the vague hope that she might want us to get back together again. However, when I arrived at the rendezvous at Horning Staithe, it was only to find Sam and the boat gone.'

'But de Courcey himself there and equally confused?'

Kingsbourne nodded. 'Yep, a bit of a bummer all round. Apparently, he'd been down in London and was worried about Sam's state of mind, so he also set off for Norfolk to be with her.'

'Not exactly the action of a man who'd cooled off his relationship with her,' observed Jack. 'Meeting up together must've been a bit awkward but, presumably, Sam's disappearance was enough to override any animosity you probably felt towards each other?'

'It certainly was, because she'd been quite specific about being at Horning Staithe. de Courcey didn't waste any time chartering a boat to go searching for her, and I went with him. We found Cantuta moored a few miles downriver, but no sign of Sam.'

'Yes, I know exactly where you found the boat, but what I don't understand is the way you just accepted the situation.' Across the saloon table, Jack fixed Kingsbourne through narrowed eyes. 'Here's a girl who had pleaded for you to join her because she was scared stiff of something, who had now mysteriously vanished, leaving the two chaps who professed to love her seemingly just shrugging their shoulders and writing her off as if she never existed. I don't get it.'

'It wasn't that simple, Jack. There were other implications involved there.'

'What sort of implications?'

'Security ones, national security.' Kingsbourne looked down at his coffee. He seemed almost penitent. 'I can't say any more than that.'

'It's enough for me to get the picture, though,' said Jack. 'What's obvious is that de Courcey had clout enough with someone to hush the whole thing up and I've already worked out that that must be either MI5 or MI6. Presumably, they wanted it kept under wraps as well?'

'Yes, I was told in no uncertain terms to simply let the matter drop and get on with my life.'

'Which you did?'

'What else could I do? The points I'd scored in the Falklands got me early promotion and my own command, but I often wondered what happened to Sam and where she ended up.'

'Not far away, as it turned out,' said Jack quietly. 'They brought human remains up yesterday from the very spot where you found Cantuta.'

'Remains. They can't be Sam's.'

'Why can't they?'

'Because...' Kingsbourne hesitated for just seconds, '... because, whoever would want to murder her?'

'Or why?' added Jack. He took a final sip of his coffee. 'The answers to both those questions probably lie in the reason Sam Waites was scared out of her wits. Didn't she give you any clue what it was?'

Kingsbourne merely shook his head again. 'I'm sorry, I've said too much already.'

'And I appreciate what you have told me,' said Jack, 'but that won't stop me pursuing further enquiries and suspects. de Courcey for instance. If he was trying to reconcile with his wife, then Sam's disappearance must have been a blessing in disguise.'

'I don't know. He seemed upset enough at the time, though it's true, after Sam left the scene, his marriage went from strength to strength.'

'Even being blessed with a daughter,' added Jack.

Kingsbourne nodded. 'Yes, Rose. A lovely girl.'

'You've met her then?'

'Only briefly a few years back, when I diverted through Norfolk on the way to an exercise in Scotland.' Kingsbourne smiled. 'I got the impression she was a girl who knew her own mind.'

'And still does,' agreed Jack, before going on to explain Rose's current work and domestic arrangements. 'And, like you, a keen sailor. She and young McQuaid have got an old river cruiser called Foxglove which they're doing up together.'

'Good for her,' said Kingsbourne with genuine admiration. 'Growing up in Norfolk seems to have worked well for her.'

'Indeed. So, when exactly did the de Courceys move up here permanently?'

'Very soon after Sam's disappearance.'

'A strange thing to do in the circumstances.'

'Not really. de Courcey had always had a boat here and a great love for the county. From what I gather, he retired from public life completely after Sam's disappearance.'

'But kept in touch with you, hence your visit and meeting Rose?'

'Yes, in a strange way, in our loss of Samantha, we had something in common.'

'And he also kept in touch with other acquaintances from that period. Like an Italian priest I met when I was with the de Courceys, one Monsignor Lorenzo Coletti. Do you know of him?'

'Only vaguely from what I've been told. Apparently, he was a close friend of Charles in Peru and has remained so ever since. I think he went on to become rector of a seminary in Rome.'

'And still is, although, right now, he's in this country visiting Cambridge.'

'Really. For what reason?'

'I wish I knew. I was hoping you might.'

'Sorry, can't help you there,' replied Kingsbourne, 'but I expect he'll try and see Rose while he's here, seeing as he's her godfather.'

'Yes, I know.' Jack glanced at his watch. 'Time for me to be going. Can you drop me at the yacht station?'

'No problem.'

Ten minutes later and they were at the outer pontoon. With a short backspring and the engine running slow ahead to hold Tumbledown secure alongside, Kingsbourne jumped down to shake hands. 'In spite of it all, it's been good to meet you, Jack. Sorry I couldn't have been more helpful.'

'That's okay, Greg. Sorry I had to stir up some painful memories.'

'Just a few, but I learned how to handle them a long time ago.' He looked Jack in the eye. 'Can I give you some advice though?'

'Which is?'

'To realise that there are people in high positions out there who want all this forgotten. The best thing for you is to do likewise.'

'That could almost be construed as a threat.'

'No, just advice, which you'd do well to accept.'

'We'll see,' said Jack, picking up his bag. 'Have a good trip Greg, and perhaps we'll see each other again along the way. I'm back on ranger duties tomorrow.'

'Good. Then perhaps we will.'

As Jack crossed the footbridge en route to the station, he glanced across the broad to see Tumbledown and her distinguished owner already motoring west for Oulton Dyke and the river.

Somehow, he sensed that meeting might be sooner rather than later.

*   *   *

Another boat out that afternoon was Cantuta 3. News of the discovery of human remains had come as an unpleasant shock for the de Courceys, and just idling along the river, heading nowhere in particular, had seemed as good a way as any to put some distance between their life and reality.

From the wheelhouse of this big cruiser, high above the water, it was possible to see for endless miles across the surrounding marshes where, other than the odd farmhouse and a few stunted windpumps, there seemed little between them and the unseen North Sea. But it was a prospect not uninviting to Charles de Courcey. Standing at the wheel, he looked eastward. 'Makes you feel like keeping on going.'

'Yes, but where to?' Beside him, Lady Harriet knew what he was thinking, even if she didn't share his outlook. 'I know things look bleak, darling, but you mustn't despair. Try and relax and just enjoy being afloat again.' She paused to take in for herself the empty river and all encompassing sky. 'It's so peaceful here at this time of year, before the holiday season gets under way.'

de Courcey nodded. 'Yes, a bit like our own life right now. Calm tranquillity, but surely only a prelude to what's to come.'

'Actually, I love to see lots of boats and a bit of life on the river again,' returned Lady Harriet, trying to put a more positive slant on things, 'and, by the same token, we mustn't allow ourselves to get pessimistic about the future.'

'Difficult not to.' de Courcey eased back the throttle. It was time to start heading home. 'The trouble these days is that once the media get their teeth into something, your life's blighted for ever.'

'Well, they haven't yet and I can't allow myself to dwell on what *might* happen.' However, the sadness in Harriet's face belied the optimism she was attempting. 'Life is so lovely with you, Charles. I couldn't bear the thought of you being taken away.'

Even as her husband struggled for words of comfort in reply, his dilemma was eased by the ringing of Harriet's mobile. She checked the number calling and straightway answered it. 'Oh, hello darling – are you all right? – yes of course, but I'll have to get it off your dad and text you back.' She paused again. 'Are you *sure* you're all right, darling? – no, it's just that you sounded a bit subdued – okay, I'll get back to you – bye.'

'Rose?' asked Charles.

'Yes, she was calling to ask for Lorenzo's number.'

'Lorenzo! What does she need to call him for?'

'I don't know.' Lady Harriet took her husband's mobile, checked the cleric's number and texted it back. 'There, she's got it now, for whatever reason.'

Charles gave a brief snort. 'We shouldn't be bothering Lorenzo, now of all times.'

'He might be glad of the diversion,' his wife suggested, 'and I'm sure he's always glad to hear from his god-daughter.'

'She hasn't spoken to him for years, so why now?'

'I don't know and she didn't say. Perhaps she wants to ask his advice on something.'

'Then why can't she ask us?'

'Presumably, it's a personal problem she doesn't want us to know about. You know Rose. If she and Gordon are having problems, she certainly won't want to admit it to us, and Lorenzo's her godfather, after all. With him conveniently in the country, it's only natural that she may want to turn to him for some words of wisdom.'

'Or it could be the other business. Do you think she knows?'

'How can she? I'm sure local gossip has already spread about the bones being discovered, but surely she won't have connected that to us.'

'But, she sounded upset?'

'Yes, not our usual bubbly Rose at all.'

de Courcey shook his head again. 'Poor Lorenzo's got his own business to sort out in Cambridge and won't want bothering with Rose's problems. I feel guilty that we even bothered him with ours.'

'He needed to know that, Charles. Don't forget, he was involved at the time.'

'I suppose so.' The boat had slowed enough now for de Courcey to put the helm hard over and turn Cantuta through a hundred and eighty degrees. As they headed back upriver, he turned again to his wife. 'We all seem to be having more than our share of anguish right now, don't we?'

Lady Harriet moved across and put her arm around him. 'Yes, but at least we're still together.'

'You're right,' he agreed, responding, as always, to the warmth of his wife's touch, ' but we've had a grim time of late and I think we're due a bit of pleasure.' He nodded to the copy of the Eastern Daily Press lying on one of the wheelhouse couches. 'I see the Light Dragoons are holding a band concert in St. Andrew's Hall in a couple of days. Shall I try and get us tickets?'

'Oh, that would be lovely. Some good rousing music might be just the thing to help us forget all these problems for at least one evening.' She turned to descend to Cantuta's galley. 'You've definitely earned your afternoon cuppa for that, Sir Charles.'

He grinned back, always glad to see his wife smiling. 'Forget the tea, Lady Harriet. Double whiskeys all round right now might be more appropriate.'

*   *   *

'So, what was he like, this distinguished officer?'

The Fellows were experiencing a togetherness of a different sort as Audrey probed her husband for a full account of his day with General Kingsbourne.

'Very personable, on the face of it.' Jack poured himself a lager and sat back in the kitchen chair. 'He certainly has that indefinable quality that marks out natural leaders.'

'But not enough to stop Samantha Waites looking elsewhere all those years ago?'

'Someone who shows leadership and someone you want to spend your life with might be two different things, Aud. And anyway, she had good reason to be more than a little cheesed off with Lieutenant Kingsbourne back then.' Jack went on to explain all that had been disclosed.

Audrey listened with mounting distaste. 'Good heavens, what a story! No wonder Sam had no qualms about falling for de Courcey. I don't blame her, poor girl, being used like that.'

'I know it sounds pretty cold-blooded,' agreed Jack, 'but Kingsbourne saw it as a means to saving the Falklands campaign and, put in that context, it might just be pardonable.'

But Audrey was having none of it. 'Well, it just confirms to me what a dirty world espionage really is. I'm amazed he even admitted it. In fact, the whole story is something of a revelation.' She fixed Jack with a quizzical look. 'Just how did you manage to wheedle all that out of him?'

'By half-guessing the truth in the first place.' Jack gave one of his disarming smiles. 'The internet's a wonderful thing, Aud. I simply took the locations of the key players in our drama, Falklands war and Peru, and fed them into the search engine to see what came up. It disclosed the whole business of the Exocet deal. You know me, I don't believe in coincidence and I knew right there that Greg and Sam somehow came into the story. I admit, until I met Kingsbourne, I'd assumed he'd just been a line officer in the marines and simply passed Sam's name on to his superiors as a useful contact. However, once he told me he'd actually been serving in intelligence himself at the time, I knew the involvement must be even deeper.'

Audrey pushed across a bowl of peanuts. 'Another triumph for the master inquisitor. Well done, Jack, but poor Sam – as far as I'm concerned, Kingsbourne deserved to lose her.'

'Actually, in retrospect, I think he'd agree with you, especially as that might have had some bearing on her murder. He didn't seem unduly shocked when I told him they'd recovered some human remains and his words were a bit strange as well.'

'Perhaps for more personal reasons than he'd like to admit.'

Jack shook his head. 'I know what you're thinking, love, but having met him, I'm more convinced than ever that he'd never do a thing like murdering a girl, especially one he'd loved.'

'But you've always told me that love and jealousy lie behind the majority of murders.'

'Not usually two years after the event, but yes, I agree, General Kingsbourne does have to stay on our list of suspects, if only because we now know he was right there at the time of Sam's disappearance.'

'And, if he didn't do it, then it's hard to imagine he doesn't know who did,' reasoned Audrey.

'I think perhaps he does have an idea, but doesn't want to say.'

'And how about you, Jack? Do you have any theories yet?'

'Nothing I can be specific about, though certain thoughts are beginning to offer themselves as pieces of the jigsaw.'

'Such as?'

'Too soon to say. This whole business is more complex than I ever imagined. What is frustrating though is that there's some very relevant factor at the back of my brain, just yelling to be included in the equation.'

'What sort of factor?'

'That's it, I don't know, but I somehow have the feeling it came into my time at Scotland Yard. I've been racking my brains to think what, but I just haven't managed to tease it out.'

'It'll come when you're least expecting it,' said Audrey, 'but just stop the "teasing" for one evening, Jack, and put your feet up. You're back patrolling again tomorrow, don't forget, and tonight you deserve a bit of relaxation.'

Not for the first time, Jack could only agree his wife was right.

*   *   *

Chapter Eleven

'Well, how about that missing piece of the jigsaw?' asked Audrey at breakfast the next morning. 'Any revelations during the night?'

Jack dunked yet another toast soldier into his boiled egg and shook his head. 'Afraid not, Aud. I went to sleep racking my brains for a clue and woke up still none the wiser.'

'Does it relate to something you were actually involved in yourself or just something you knew of?'

'I'm not sure and I won't be able to give it much thought today, being back on river duty.'

'Which is the best thing that can happen,' said Audrey. 'Having too much spare time on your hands is what's got you back into this detecting lark and I don't think it's that healthy, Jack. So, I for one am only too glad to see you back at work with other things to occupy your mind.'

'I can't drop the "other thing" that easily.' Jack poured himself another coffee. 'I know I'll be turning this over and over until I put my finger on it.'

'Well, do you need to put *your* finger on it Jack? Finding those remains has effectively put this whole sordid business in the hands of the police, which is exactly what you wanted, isn't it?' Audrey glanced at the kitchen clock. 'And the river is where they want you, so you'd better get a move on if you're not going to be late.' She got up and took her husband's lunchbox and flask from the worktop. 'Here, feed your braincells with this, but just for today at least, forget about missing students and international espionage.'

'Okay, love, but I can't help wondering…' Further discussion was suspended by the phone ringing. Jack went off to answer it and was away only a minute before returning. 'That was Bailey wanting to meet for a drink and chat sometime today.'

'For what reason?'

'He didn't say.'

'But, you're going to be patrolling all day.'

'Yes, which is why I promised I'd meet him this evening.' Jack grabbed his bag off the back of his chair and stuffed his lunch inside. 'Sorry love, but I'll be late home.'

'On your first day back,' called Audrey after him as he disappeared out of the door. She slumped onto a kitchen chair. So much for my dear husband keeping out of it all, she thought, but hoping at the same time that DI Bailey was going to order him to do just that.

*   *   *

Certainly, the River Bure seemed a million miles from international intrigue that morning, as Jack followed the familiar meanders of his assigned beat and got on with the job he loved. Strange how, when taking out his own launch again for the first time in many months, it had seemed as though the dark days of winter had never been and that he'd come off this same duty only the evening before.

The weather helped to foster this sense of well being, the morning feeling fresh with only a slight edge to the gusting winds, a day for turned-up collars and vigorous pursuits in the bracing outdoors. And definitely one for sailing, as evidenced by the several gaff rigs gliding swiftly over the reedbeds like disembodied ghost boats, sheeted hard in for those clawing to windward and well out for those lucky enough to be heading downwind.

There were two of the latter running goose-winged towards him now, their jibs and mainsails spread either side as they rode the south-west wind towards Thurne Mouth. Seconds later, they were passing, their crews calling cheerful greetings above the clatter of running blocks and the sluice of their bow and quarter-waves. They had good reason to be cheerful, thought Jack, with a fair wind in their sails and the flood tide beneath, all speeding them upriver. His own launch pitched only slightly through their wash as he continued on towards Acle against a flood tide now running at its mid-flow strongest.

Tidal flow was always a factor to be reckoned with, here on the lower Bure. Though a good ten miles from the sea at Yarmouth, it was already strong enough to have his launch passing fields, marshes and riverbank much slower than he was churning through the water. What matter, thought Jack, as Upton Mill passed by to starboard and the gaunt remains of Oby Mill rose up ahead to port, warm as he was in his wheelhouse, the diesel purring contentedly and the Authority ensign fluttering over the transom. He was back in the world he loved and the river was never a place to be in a hurry anyway. Much of his work as a ranger was spent convincing other boaters to think likewise. Perhaps it was understandable that folk leading lives spent on fast roads and motorways should at first find crawling along at the same sedate pace as other river users something of a trial, but that was what a Broads holiday was all about. Forget speed and time when you're on the river, was Jack's simple philosophy.

And forget your worries too. Purring down the last long reach after Upton Dyke, Jack realised dear Audrey was right, as he hadn't given one thought to poor Samantha Waites and her sinister disappearance since casting off over an hour ago. Perhaps it really was time to forget this whole business completely. What was the point anyway except to prove to himself that he could still crack cases and right wrongs? Instead, he should listen to his wife's wisdom, concentrate on the more pleasurable things in life and leave the abject world of crime to younger, brighter heads than his. He was in the reach to Acle Bridge now, slowing down to the limit and espying a boat moored on the south bank that seemed vaguely familiar. Then he recognised her and realised he wouldn't be consigning Sam's case to the dead-file just yet.

*   *   *

'Ahoy, Tumbledown,' called Jack through the open wheelhouse window, after easing to dead slow and bringing his launch to a relative stop alongside the tall figure coiling ropes on the foredeck.

'Jack!' Gregory Kingsbourne turned and came to the rail. 'I didn't think we'd be meeting again this soon.'

'Me neither,' replied Jack, coming into the aft cockpit and making fast a line on one of Tumbledown's midship cleats. 'How on earth did you get here so soon?'

'Come on board and have a coffee and I'll tell you.'

Jack glanced at his watch. 'Yeah, time for my break anyway. Don't mind if I do, Greg.'

As Kingsbourne secured lines fore and aft, Jack clambered on board. Minutes later, and they were down below with the kettle on.

'The last time I saw you, was only twenty hours ago and you were departing Oulton Broad,' said Jack, making himself comfortable on a saloon couch. 'I got the impression you were staying on the southern rivers, so why here?'

'Oh, just impulse really,' replied Kingsbourne, while busying himself with mugs. 'After I left you, I cruised straight up to St Olaves and had another look at the tide tables. They showed low water at Yarmouth for early this morning and I realised that, by making an early start, I could go through and be on my old stomping grounds by mid-morning. So, I rigged-down for the bridges that evening, set off at first light, and here I am.'

'Well, it's good to see you.' Jack took his proffered mug of steaming coffee. 'What plans now?'

'Not sure. Just a bit of aimless pottering probably.' Kingsbourne sat down opposite with his own mug. 'First job though is to get rigged-up which takes a bit of ingenuity on your own.' He gave a questioning raise of the brows. 'Any chance of a hand with that, Jack? I'll do all the sorting in my own time, but someone to take up the slack on the stays as I heave the masts would certainly help.'

Jack glanced at the bulkhead clock. 'Yep, shouldn't be a problem if we get straight on.'

'Great.' They swigged back their coffees and returned to the deck where a cat's cradle of stays, shrouds and other assorted rigging seemed to envelope the boat. 'It all looks a bit of a jumble, but it sorts itself as the masts go up,' assured Kingsbourne, tapping the mainmast which lay horizontally in its tabernacle with the truck resting on the wheelhouse roof. He nodded towards the forestay, running through blocks at the stemhead. 'I'll heave the mast, and you just take up the slack.'

Jack did as ordered while Kingsbourne went to the fore part of the wheelhouse, took hold of the heavy wooden mast and heaved away as though bench-pressing a two-hundred pound weight. As it rose above his head, he steadily moved for'ard, all the time elevating the mast until it was vertical in its tabernacle. Jack had been continually tensioning the forestay during the raising, and now he cleated it off. Kingsbourne flexed his shoulders. 'Phew, is it my imagination, or is that mast getting heavier?'

'Or are we getting older?' suggested Jack. 'That was quite a lift you had there.'

'Yes, but about the only weight-training I get these desk bound days. I should go to the gym more.' He nodded aft. 'Just the mizzen now, Jack, but that's smaller and not quite so heavy.'

It was indeed and minutes had that mast vertical also. 'Good, a bit of sorting and then I can sail again,' Kingsbourne smiled. 'I hate using the engine when all that wind is out there for free.'

'And a fair one for running up the Bure,' confirmed Jack. 'So, where are you bound, captain?'

'Oh, just a few miles on for now.'

'Going to see the de Courceys while you're here?'

'Perhaps.'

'Well, give them my regards,' said Jack, climbing down into the launch, squeezing back into his wheelhouse and restarting the engine. He leaned out of the window. 'Thanks for the coffee, Greg, and enjoy your stay.'

Kingsbourne dropped the lines into the launch. 'I will, and thanks for helping me rig up.'

After turning at the bridge, Jack headed back upriver himself. As he passed Tumbledown, her skipper was already rigging booms and gaffs back onto the masts, but looked up in time to exchange Jack's wave.

So much for leaving well alone, thought Jack, intrigued by the fact that ever since the discovery of Samantha Waites' bag and the disclosures it triggered, personalities from the de Courcey's past seemed to have been regathering around them. First the strange shadowy figure of Monsignor Lorenzo Coletti and now Gregory Kingsbourne.

As he sped upriver on the fast-flooding tide, thoughts of Monsignor Coletti caused Jack to wonder just where that enigmatic cleric was right now.

*   *   *

In fact, Lorenzo Coletti was still in Cambridge, taking a taxi to the city centre after having just spent an hour of silent solitude in the church of Our Lady and the English Martyrs. Here, in yet another Gothic revival place of worship, he had prayed deep and earnestly, asking again forgiveness for the sins of the past and for God's strength and guidance in the days to come.

How should he spend these days? He knew the answer only too well. By assisting his dearest of friends, the de Courceys as best he could. Even before coming to Cambridge, he had pledged to Charles and Harriet his help in this latest of dilemmas, but now that need was all the more urgent after last night's call from his god-daughter, Rose. Her obvious distress and plea for his help and advice had made this morning's mission all the more essential.

The taxi dropped him just outside the grandeur of King's College, from where he made his slow and unsteady way towards the market square and the small alleyway he sought. Here, between a travel agent and a bistro, he found the shop he was looking for, a very run-down little establishment bearing the name of Boffin Books. He pushed open the paint-peeling door and walked inside to the accompaniment of a jangling bell.

From behind the dusty counter, a round-shouldered figure looked up and perused the clerical collar with apparent disinterest. 'Can I help you, Reverend?'

'Er, Monsignor, actually. Monsignor Lorenzo Coletti. I wondered if you could help me find a book.'

'What sort of book?' Over the half-moon spectacles, the look was far from amiable. 'Is it a work on science?'

'Oh no,' explained Coletti with a half-smile. 'It is a – how do you say – a reader – a collection of fiction, drama and poetry written by the Irish autore – author, Samuel Beckett.'

'Then, I can't help you,' said the shopkeeper, brusquely, 'you'll need to go to some bookseller dealing in that sort of thing.'

'Ah, but to do that I need to know the titolo – the title,' persisted Coletti. 'I was wondering, do you have a catalogo – a catalogue of books by famous authors.'

'What's his name again?' asked the shopkeeper wearily, turning to a flickering computer screen at his side.

'Beckett. Samuel Beckett.'

There was the clicking of keys and soon a list of titles appeared on the screen. 'He's written a lot. Can you recognise it from any of these?'

'Let me see,' said Coletti, putting on his own ancient reading specs and peering at the display. 'Yes, this one!' he exclaimed triumphantly, pointing to one line on the screen. He felt for a pen and paper and realised just as quickly he had neither. 'Mi scusi, can you please write that for me?'

With a grunt of impatience, the shopkeeper snatched a piece of headed notepaper and scribbled down the title.

'My thanks for all your kind help, Signore… ?'

'Odell. Doctor Bruce Odell.'

'Ah. Will you write that down for me also, please?'

Odell scribbled his name below the book title.

'Grazie. Grazie, Doctor,' thanked Coletti, pocketing the note and making his way to the door. 'May you reap all that you deserve.'

*   *   *

That wasn't a sentiment uppermost in Detective Inspector Bailey's mind that evening as he sat at his desk in North Walsham Police Headquarters, wading his way through a backlog of files, reports and returns. Somehow, the prefix to his rank seemed an anomaly these bureaucracy obsessed days. "Administrative Inspector" might be more appropriate. He glanced again at his watch. It wasn't like Jack Fellows to be late.

In spite of the fact that any meeting with this avuncular character invariably produced more work than it saved, Bailey, strangely enough, still looked forward to it. Well aware that the ranger's previous years at Scotland Yard covered a wealth of experience light-years from his own, he didn't shy from drawing on it whenever the circumstances allowed. Neither did he fail to secretly acknowledge that his own advancement had been somewhat aided by success in cases in which Jack Fellows had played no small part. Of course, he always went through the motions of telling the retired policeman to leave crime to those still paid to fight it, but that didn't stop him bouncing ideas and theories off him at every opportunity, which he'd do tonight when... Bailey's thoughts were suddenly interrupted by a uniformed constable at his door showing in the man himself.

'Sorry I'm late, Bailey.' Jack came bustling in, a temporary station pass clipped to his shirt. 'Had a bit of a confrontation between a motor cruiser and sailing yacht to deal with just at the end of my stint.'

'No prob, Jack, only ten minutes.' Bailey motioned him into a chair opposite. 'I hope you managed to sort them out.'

'Oh yes, just as soon as we'd managed to get the yacht's bowsprit out of the cruiser's saloon window,' explained Jack with a grin. 'But how are things with you?' He glanced at the pile of files. 'I thought computers would see the end of all this bumph, but it seems worse than ever.'

'Tell me about it,' groaned Bailey before turning to the lingering PC. 'Get us a cuppa, please Jones. Coffee all right for you, Jack?'

'Something wetter and stronger would be better, but I'll settle for caffeine.' Once the PC had departed Jack's eyes settled on Bailey's paper-strewn desk. 'Sorry if I've added to all this with my discovered remains.'

'That's what we're here for. And I should have known better anyway than to think Jack Fellows would drop any case, once he'd got his teeth into it.'

'Especially if I'm convinced there's one to answer.'

'Then you'll be interested in this.' Bailey tossed across a file. 'The initial pathology report on your bones.'

Jack opened the beige cover and scanned the lines of medical jargon. 'Just give me a summary, Bailey.'

'They're those of a young woman in her twenties.'

'Any evidence of cause of death?'

'None.'

'But they could be Samantha Waites'?'

'I'm sure they are,' acknowledged Bailey, 'but, with no relations to check DNA, we can't be certain. We'll leave that to the coroner to decide.'

'When's the hearing?'

'The day after tomorrow.'

'Not wasting any time are you.' The PC came back with two plastic cups of coffee and Jack waited until he'd departed before continuing, 'Presumably, you'll need me as a witness?'

'Not immediately, no.'

'Oh. Why not?'

'Because I'm going to ask for an immediate adjournment while we make further enquiries.' Bailey leaned across his desk. 'Jack, let me level with you. So far, I haven't even mentioned the name Samantha Waites in relation to these remains being found.'

'The reason being…?'

'The immediate gagging order I had the last time I tried. So, this time I'm going to be a bit canny. So far, no one has made a connection between the remains and that girl's disappearance and the longer it stays that way, the better for us. An adjournment will let me conduct an enquiry just as I would with any such discovery and, by the time it's complete, what's disclosed might well have taken things too far for anyone to stop the wheels of justice turning.'

'Yep, I can see that,' agreed Jack, 'but it's a pity we can't go further now, because all the key players in the original drama have suddenly reappeared on the scene.'

'Really. For what reason?'

'I'm not sure, but it may be a reaction to my stirring things up in the first place. That and the fact that I've already spoken to them.'

'Crikey, you don't waste time do you,' said Bailey, somewhat taken aback. 'Just who have you spoken to exactly?'

'All of them.' Jack glanced around the DI's office. 'Bailey, if we're going to keep this informal, why don't we go and talk about it somewhere more convivial.'

'Good idea.' Bailey stood up and put on his coat. 'After I've heard what you have to tell, I'll probably need a drink anyway.'

*   *   *

'Strewth, what a hornet's nest,' groaned Bailey, knocking back the remains of his shandy after listening to Jack's narration of events. The ranger had left out nothing of his discoveries to date, much of it complete news to the young DI. 'So, what do you make of it all, Jack?'

'Difficult to say.' They were seated at a table in the saloon bar of a country pub, quiet enough to allow discussion without fear of eavesdroppers and far enough from North Walsham for no one to recognise the head of CID. It served good beer too, as appreciated by Jack as he took another swig of his own half-pint. 'There are so many permutations and it's so long after the event, that every theory has to be mere conjecture.'

'Well let's apply the good old police dictums of "means, motive and opportunity",' suggested Bailey, 'starting with this Sir Charles de Courcey. It was his boat, so he certainly had the means. He probably wanted to get shot of his bit on the side and, knowing she was alone in the remoteness of the Broads, had the perfect opportunity. The same could also apply to this marine, Kingsbourne, except in his case the motive would be jealousy and bitterness at being dumped.'

'Jealousy as a motive could equally apply to the wife,' pointed out Jack.

'Yep, and by her own admission, so you tell me, she was up in Norfolk at the time as well.' Bailey sat back and looked at his remaining drink. 'And she's the one I'd put my money on right now, knowing as she did that her husband was continuing to see Sam and that he'd let her use their boat on this whacky monster searching thing.' The detective leaned forward. 'Okay, try this for starters, Jack. Let's assume Lady Harriet got wind of the fact that her husband was going up to Norfolk to meet Samantha at Horning. So, she dashes up there first and murders the girl. She'd certainly know how to handle the boat single-handed, so she then takes Cantuta to that remote spot and deep-sixes the body.'

Jack considered the theory before answering. 'I'm not sure, Bailey. It doesn't ring true that a woman would commit a crime like that. For a start, it takes some strength to tip a dead body overboard. And, also, how could she have got back?'

'You said she's a keen rower, so perhaps she took the tender in tow and rowed back or even walked over the fields to the road and called up a taxi. There was no investigation at the time, so she never had to explain her movements anyway.'

'Which leads us to one of the mysteries of this case, which is how Sir Charles got the thing hushed up,' continued Jack. 'If it was for any of the motives you've just suggested, it's hard to see the police being prepared to cover it up.'

'Not if Sir Charles de Courcey was calling in his own big favour from the country,' argued Bailey. 'According to what you found out from Kingsbourne, the powers that be owed him big time.'

'And they also "owed" Samantha,' countered Jack, 'justice, if nothing else.'

'Good point.' Bailey stood up. 'My round. Same again?'

'Better not. Get them to just top up with lemonade.'

Bailey took the glasses to the bar, had them refilled and returned to the table. 'You're right, Jack, the more we go through this, the more we go round in circles.'

'And, you're forgetting the other participant in the drama, this priest, Monsignor Lorenzo Coletti.'

'Who, you say, is also here. Where do you think he fits in?'

'Perhaps, only that, as Sir Charles' old spiritual advisor and, presumably, his confessor, he's the one man who knows all the truth.'

'Well, I wish we did,' sighed Bailey. 'But if this Coletti really did travel here overland from Rome, he must have set off days before this whole thing came up. So, presumably, he'd planned to come anyway and, if so, what for?'

'Perhaps some Cambridge theological meeting or whatever, related to his seminary. I'd dearly like to know though. Any chance of someone doing a bit of sniffing there, Bailey?'

'I'll see what I can do, but I'm going to have to rely on you to keep your finger on the pulse regarding the family, Jack. You say there's a daughter also on the scene?'

'Yes, Rose. Nice girl in a relationship with a vet called McQuaid and also god-daughter of Coletti.'

'A real spider's web.' Bailey shook his head. 'So, have *you* got a theory, Jack?'

'Just a small one beginning to form, though nothing to go on yet, other than things said in casual conversation.'

'Really. Anything you'd like to share?'

Jack gave a chuckle. 'You know me, Bailey. I never commit myself until I have firm evidence and I'm still struggling to come up with a motive.'

'I thought we decided that in Lady Harriet or Kingsbourne's case it might be jealousy, or the plain shaking-off of inconvenient loose ends by Sir Charles himself?'

'They certainly fit the facts and simplify things generally,' acknowledged Jack, 'but I have a feeling this whole mystery is somewhat more complex than that. Somewhere, at the back of my mind, is another factor, something that happened way back and which could account for why the whole thing was covered up like it was.' Jack tapped a beer mat on the table and shook his head. 'I've been trying to recall what the heck it is for a day now, and I'm still no nearer.'

'Well, if it comes to you, let me know,' said Bailey, finishing off his drink. 'In the meantime, remember the rule regarding spider's webs – don't get ensnared.'

'Too late for that,' declared Jack, standing up, 'but the good thing is that I've no career to risk any more, which is why it's better for me to be in the front line rather than you.'

'Yes, well keep watching your back, Jack. Remember, any sleuthing you do on this one is strictly on the QT.'

'I will, but right now the biggest hazard in this whole business is me arriving home late to Audrey.' Jack glanced at his watch. 'Strewth, almost ten. And I never even got my pass signed.'

* * *

Chapter Twelve

Such restrictions were not something worrying General Kingsbourne early the next morning, as he cast off from Thurne Mouth.

The previous evening spent at this popular but remote mooring had been a pleasurable one after days of solo voyaging. After a brisk walk along the riverbank, he'd enjoyed a drink at the local followed by a good night's sleep. It was only during an early breakfast that he'd received the call on his mobile, in response to which he was now motoring up the Bure.

Heading westward in the fine spring sunshine, Kingsbourne listened to the rumble of the diesel beneath his feet with some frustration. His Broads cruising so far had been made under power and today he'd promised himself some sailing, but this summons meant passage against the prevailing wind, and along the narrow Bure was no place to be tacking a large motor sailer like Tumbledown. Besides, he'd promised to be there by mid-morning.

And so he rumbled on, the spokes of the varnished wheel slipping through his fingers as he negotiated the bends between each reach, his eyes on the river ahead and the flat Broadland scene stretching out on either side. His thoughts though were very much on where he was going and, even more significantly, who he was going to see when he got there.

*   *   *

'We should be in the surgery earning some money, Rose. We've enough problems to deal with without having to rush off to some obscure meeting with your parents,' grumbled McQuaid as he gunned the old Land Rover towards South Walsham, the narrow country lanes mercifully quiet at this time in the morning.

Beside him, his partner in both life and business gave a half-smile and nodded. 'I think you'll find it's about the same thing, Gordon, and, anyway, you only had three appointments before ten, which I've managed to reschedule.'

'Well let's hope that whatever your parents have to say won't take long, because I've got a couple of farm visits in the second half of the morning and farmers aren't quite so accommodating when it comes to being messed about.'

'The first is a sick calf, isn't it?' recalled Rose, trying to remember the appointments. 'Where's the second?'

'The Knights at Grange Farm.'

'Ah yes, Carol Knights' lame horse.' They were turning off the road now into the lane towards the broad. 'Not exactly a life and death case, Gordon.'

'No, but it's what my profession is all about, Rose. Caring for sick animals, not attending family conferences suddenly called to presumably discuss what's to be done about some shady character from your parent's past, who's now trying to take us all to the cleaners.' A tractor ahead, ambling its way to the next field, had added to McQuaid's frustrations. 'And, anyway, how about that priest godfather of yours?' He ground into a lower gear and ran the Rover's offside wheels onto the verge to overtake the lumbering obstruction. 'I thought he was going to try and sort things.'

'Lorenzo only promised to try, Gordon, though I don't know what he can do, seeing as how that awful man only gave us a phone number to contact. No doubt he'll tell us if he achieved anything.'

'Why, is he going to be there as well?'

'Yes, apparently Mum and Dad collected him last night.'

'I thought he was going to be in Cambridge a while yet?'

'That's what my parents thought, but it seems he got things out of the way quicker than expected.' Rose shook her head sadly. 'I really felt bad asking for his help and advice. The poor man sounded really tired when I spoke to him.'

'Which means he's probably been unable to help at all.' They were turning now into the de Courcey's lane. 'Not that he'll take very kindly to me anyway, an unashamed agnostic living in sin with his god-daughter.'

'I'm sure he'll take you as he finds you,' assured Rose as they drew into her parents' driveway. She had long ago realised that Gordon, forced to deal daily with the grim reality of life and death, had cultivated a somewhat jaundiced view of religion, regardless of denomination. 'I know he was a great support to Mum and Dad a long time ago and it's been my experience that many clerics are far more broad-minded than we think.'

McQuaid shrugged and switched off the engine. 'Well, we'll soon see.' He climbed out and glanced along the side of the de Courcey home to where the early morning sun was shimmering off the waters of the broad. He never felt comfortable visiting what might be termed his in-laws and, to delay the dreaded moment, he first wandered around to the waterside.

Rose, well aware of her partner's discomfort, joined him. 'Look, you can see Foxglove's mast just beyond the entrance,' she said, in an effort to brighten his outlook.

'Perhaps we'll have time to enjoy her again once this rotten business is sorted.' He indicated towards a boat anchored close to Broad View, a largish ketch-rigged motor sailer with blue hull and varnished wheelhouse. 'It would be nice to have her looking as smart as that one some day. I wonder who owns her?'

'I'm not sure, but it might be…' Rose's voice trailed off as she recognised the well-built man, she'd met only briefly years before, rowing an inflatable dinghy towards her parents' home.

*　　　*　　　*

Unlike the de Courcey family, Jack was in a reasonably contented state of mind as, sometime later, he once more patrolled the Bure upriver towards St Benet's. It hadn't been a particularly arduous patrol so far, with all the boats he'd encountered scrupulously obeying river speed limits, river tolls displayed and, thankfully, managing to avoid any sort of emergency.

One thing he had noticed though on passing Thurne Mouth, was the absence of Tumbledown. Clearly, General Kingsbourne had made an early departure for his intended day's sailing which, considering the steady westerly wind, Jack presumed had involved either a reach back down the Bure towards Acle or up the Thurne to Potter Heigham. So he was surprised as he approached the abbey, to see the motor sailer moored there in solitary isolation, and the general coming on deck to check if it was the ranger he knew.

Jack came out of the wheelhouse to the cockpit's open steering position. The tide was on the ebb now, so it was no problem bringing the launch to dead slow and holding position alongside.

'We meet again, Greg, though I thought you intended some sailing today.' Jack sniffed the fresh westerly breeze. 'You must have had to motor against this.'

'Yes, but I decided I needed a bit of exercise instead, so I came here and went for a good run over the abbey grounds. A fascinating place.'

'Yes, and with quite a history, though not all of it good.'

'In what way?'

'Oh, the usual tales of jealousy, treachery and deceit.'

'That's a thread that runs through history, Jack. Things don't change much over the years.'

'More's the pity,' said Jack, 'but I suppose it's all a matter of perspective really. What's loyalty to one side is treachery to the other.'

Kingsbourne shrugged. 'You're probably right, but that doesn't mean that those who sell out to the other side shouldn't be punished for it.'

'Like all wrong-doers,' agreed Jack, before looking back to the river and changing what was fast becoming a rather loaded conversation. 'Where to from here?'

Kingsbourne pointed westward. 'Not far. Ranworth. Somewhere I've never been before.'

'Interesting place with a fine old church to explore and a floating Conservation Centre full of displays and information relating to the Broads.' Jack's expression became a little more serious as he indicated the nearby Fleet Dyke. 'But not far to South Walsham from here, Greg, if you want to see the de Courceys. I'm patrolling down there myself shortly.'

'Thanks, but I'd prefer to get going. The pilot book says the moorings at Ranworth can get pretty full if you're not there in good time.'

'Yes, they always fill up whatever the time of year,' agreed Jack, before pointing at the inflatable hanging in davits from the ketch's stern. 'There is a dinghy dyke though, so you can anchor on the broad and run ashore in your tender.'

'I'll do that, because I need to get some provisions before the evening.'

'Sounds like you have something planned tonight,' said Jack, detecting just a hint of design.

'Only a bit of personal business.' Kingsbourne smiled. 'We all need to relax sometimes.'

'Well, enjoy yourself, whatever you do,' said Jack, preparing to get under way himself.

'Thanks, I will, and I'm sure our paths will cross again before I move on.'

But under what circumstances, thought Jack as he swung the launch around and turned off for South Walsham He couldn't help wondering just what "personal business" General Kingsbourne had in mind.

*   *   *

After purring at reduced speed down the Fleet Dyke, Jack was once again at the small marina where he could already see Foxglove lying on her usual mooring, the yacht's cabin roof raised and Rose just emerging into the cockpit. Spotting Jack's launch, she waved him into an adjacent berth and was soon securing lines and giving her natural smile.

'Jack. Nice to see you.' She transferred a cleaning cloth into another hand and shook his with the other. 'Good timing too. I was ready for a breath of fresh air. Come on board.'

Jack followed and was soon making himself comfortable on a cushioned cockpit seat. 'So, what are you doing now?'

'Oh, just a bit of internal titivating.' She wiped away a smudge of dirt from her cheek. 'But that's as much cleaning as I'm going to do. I don't think my guest is too worried about her being spic and span as long as she sails okay.' As if in answer to Jack's unspoken question, another figure emerged from the cabin. 'You've met already I believe?'

'Yes, we have. Good to see you again, Monsignor Coletti,' said Jack, hiding his surprise as the seminary rector climbed awkwardly up into the cockpit to join them. 'How was Cambridge?'

'It was – how do you say – enlightening.' The cleric sank down onto the other side bench next to Rose.

'Well, I hope you achieved all that you went there to do,' said Jack. 'I had it in my mind that you were intending to stay there longer.'

'Quite so, but God decided otherwise,' was all the priest would admit.

'And now Lorenzo's enjoying some well-deserved rest,' said Rosemary, affectionately putting her arm around her godfather's shoulders. 'Unfortunately, not realising he would be returning so early, my parents had arranged to go to a musical event at St Andrew's Hall in Norwich this evening. They wanted to cancel, of course, but then I had an idea.' She glanced up to where the gaff and boom lay in their crutch above the cockpit, tan sails bent on and sheets attached. 'Why not take Lorenzo for a sail in Foxglove. He jumped at the idea.'

'I can understand that.' Jack turned towards the cleric. 'Have you sailed before, Monsignor?'

'Indeed yes, for I grew up in Sardinia where my father was a beach fisherman.' Coletti gave a smile of happy recollection. 'I think as much of my youth was spent on the water as on the land. It is therefore so nice to be afloat once again.' He turned towards Rose. 'Especially with dear Rose, who has kindly agreed to let me take this boat on a little trip.'

'What, alone?'

'Yes indeed.'

'Are you sure you feel up to it, Lorenzo?' asked Rose with tender sympathy. 'How is the head now?'

'Much better,' said the cleric. He turned to Jack. 'Just a headache, but I'm sure your river air will soon clear it away.'

'I'm sure it will, but wouldn't it be wise for either Rose or Gordon to be with you?' Jack glanced towards the broad. 'Or at least until you're familiar with the boat and these waters.'

'Unfortunately, Gordon's off on a farm visit and I need to spend some time with my parents,' explained Rose, 'but I'm going to have a quick sail with Lorenzo on the broad first to make sure he's happy with the boat before letting him loose in her.'

'To where?'

'Ranworth actually. Another of my Mum and Dad's old friends is going to be there with his boat and Lorenzo thought it would be nice to go and meet him in Foxglove.'

'Major General Gregory Kingsbourne?'

'That's right.' Rosemary's eyebrows rose. 'How did you know that?'

'Oh, he's just someone I've met on my patrols,' explained Jack with economy of truth. He turned back to Coletti. 'Ranworth's not far, but perhaps a bit challenging for a first trip in a strange boat, Monsignor. Are you sure you're up to it?'

'Si, si. It will be nice to sail on the lake, the broad you call it. But I intend to travel the river using the motore, the engine, rather than God's free wind.'

'Very sensible. Sunset's just after six o'clock this evening and the weather's due to deteriorate, so you won't have time to dawdle,' cautioned Jack, standing up, taking out one of his cards and handing it over. 'I won't be going that way myself, but give me a call if you need any assistance.'

'Grazie, grazie. But I hope that won't be necessary,' replied the cleric shaking Jack's hand in farewell.

'Thanks anyway,' added Rose, walking back with Jack to his launch. 'He's so determined to make this trip that I haven't the heart to say "no", so I'm just going along with it.'

'Well, it's your boat,' conceded Jack, 'but a big cruiser like Foxglove could be a bit of a handful for someone who hasn't sailed in a while and he does look pretty exhausted, Rose.'

'I know, but I'll make sure he's completely happy with handling her before he launches off on his own.' Rose glanced back to the old cruiser and the priest busying himself sorting ropes in the cockpit. 'Bless him, this trip seems so important to him, so who am I to put the damper on things?'

'Well, he shouldn't get into too much trouble on the river if he just uses the engine.' Jack glanced back to the old boat. 'But how about Foxglove? Is she ok?'

'Oh yes. Of course, she's still a bit shabby cosmetically, but structurally she's fine and Gordon checked the rig and bent on the sails himself this morning.'

'Gordon was here as well, earlier?'

'Yes, we came to meet Lorenzo at my parents. Once we'd decided on a sail, Gordon just had time to give her the once over before dashing off on some animal visits. I'd just finished clearing up in the cabin when you appeared.'

'And now I must disappear,' said Jack, climbing back aboard his launch and restarting the engine, while Rose cast off the lines. 'Take care then, and make sure our dear cleric's up to scratch if you want your boat back in one piece.'

'Don't worry, I will,' she promised as Jack's launch pulled away and slipped into the outer broad.

*   *   *

'Well, he's certainly a lot better than the last time I saw him, Carol, so I don't think it's anything serious.' Gordon McQuaid pushed his cap to the back of his head and smiled. He was back at Grange Farm, observing Sindbad being led by a somewhat cheered Carol Knights around the open area in front of his stable and noting with satisfaction that the previous lameness had all but disappeared.

'Yes, thank goodness,' agreed Carol. 'I've only walked him out for grazing since you saw him last, but it seems to have almost done the trick.' She gave a look of expectation. 'Does this mean I can ride him again now?'

But McQuaid shook his head. 'No give him a few more days rest yet, to lose the lameness completely. We'll also add some bute to his diet which will act as a pain killer and anti-inflammatory and speed the healing process.' He opened his bag and gave an exasperated groan. 'Damn!'

'Problems?' asked Carol.

'Only my own forgetfulness. I meant to put some sachets in here just in case, and now I realise I left them on the surgery table. I don't suppose you have any?'

It was Carol's turn to shake her head. 'No, sorry.'

McQuaid straightened up and glanced at his watch. 'I've got a full afternoon of visits, but I've nothing on later this evening and it's my fault, so I'll come back then and drop some off. The sooner we get them in Sindbad's diet, the better.'

'That's really kind of you, Mr McQuaid, but what time would you be here?'

'I'm afraid it probably won't be until about tenish.'

'Oh blast, I won't be here,' said Carol, dismayed. 'I've agreed to give a talk on my college experience at the Young Farmers' meeting and I'll be leaving soon after six and won't be back until after eleven.'

'That's okay. I'll give Sindbad one to be going on with when I arrive and then leave a week's supply just outside the stable door here for you to add to his feed.'

'That would be great, if you're sure you don't mind,' said Carol appreciatively, before hesitating and asking, 'but will this cost a lot?'

Clearly the girl was worried about running up vet bills during this, her first time in charge of Grange Farm, but McQuaid was quick to reassure her. 'Don't worry about that, Carol. I'd like to check on him anyway and it's due to my own stupid fault, so no charge for tonight's visit.'

'Gosh, thanks.' She gave the vet a big kiss on the cheek before asking, 'But are you sure Rose hasn't made plans for tonight?'

'Yes, but they don't include me.' For a second, a shadow of anxiety flitted across McQuaid's fresh features before being replaced by a hastily enforced smile. 'So I'll be glad to have something else to occupy me.' He closed the medical bag and put on his wax jacket. 'You'll be doing me a favour actually.'

'I think you're just trying to make me feel better.' Carol smiled and nodded towards the stable door. 'I'll leave all this unlocked for you. Don't worry about the dog barking when you drive in. He always does when the security lights go on.'

'A good guard dog then. I really must push on,' said McQuaid, picking up his bag, 'but good luck with your talk tonight. I'm sure the Young Farmers will enjoy it.'

As the old Land Rover disappeared down the farm road, Carol Knights couldn't help thinking that if Gordon McQuaid were her partner, she wouldn't be off out on some evening jaunt alone. 'Lucky old Rose,' she said out loud as she gave Sindbad a final pat, before shutting the stable door behind her.

*   *   *

Several miles away, Gregory Kingsborne was enjoying an early afternoon glass of wine on the afterdeck of Tumbledown, when a traditional sailing cruiser came motoring onto Malthouse Broad.

He'd arrived there himself soon after lunch and, seeing the Ranworth moorings full as Jack had predicted, had followed the ranger's advice, anchored mid-broad and launched his inflatable. Although the tender had a small outboard motor, he'd rowed in, downed a quick pint at the Maltsters and then enjoyed a brisk walk on a circular route around the adjoining lanes. After stopping to admire St Helen's church atop the hill, he'd re-entered the village, pausing only to buy some provisions from the general store alongside the staithe.

Now, as he watched the wooden sailing cruiser come puttering in on its outboard, he could see it had certainly known better days. But, in spite of being in need of a lot of restoration, this boat still had definite character, something Kingsbourne liked with his own leanings towards traditional boats. He collected his binoculars from the wheelhouse, returned to the afterdeck and trained them on the boat which seemed to have come to a stop in the centre of the broad. Focussing on the lettering on her bow, he recalled that Foxglove was the name of the boat belonging to Rose de Courcey and her vet partner. But it certainly wasn't Rose or even what looked like a vet at the helm of the boat now. Incongruously, hoisting the main sail, was a man in black shirt and trousers and clerical collar.

Although early in the season, there were a couple of other boats at anchor on the broad and from them, holidaymakers watched with some amusement and then admiration as this lone cleric heaved away at the main halyard and slowly hoisted the big gaff on his own. Eventually, both mains'l and then jib were luffing in the fresh breeze before being sheeted in, causing Foxglove to heel slightly as she got under way.

What now became apparent to all watching the old cruiser reaching backwards and forwards across the narrow broad in the increasingly fresh breeze, was that this clergyman was an experienced sailor. And a good thing too, thought Kingsbourne, remembering that the evening forecast predicted a deep low moving through, bringing cloud, rain and some squally conditions soon after sunset. But that was still some hours away and, in the meantime, holidaymakers were making the most of the remaining daylight.

One, a middle-aged man, was helming a small lugsail dinghy that Kingsbourne had seen earlier towed astern of a hire cruiser. Pottering back and forth between the anchored boats, Kingsbourne guessed he was probably trying his first hand at sailing and not making a bad job of it either, considering the gusty conditions. He seemed to be having some good fun, but Foxglove was also tacking back and forth in the same patch of water. It wasn't long before they narrowly missed each other with only a swift and skilful change of course by the helming priest avoiding a collision. 'Sorry,' called out the apologetic and rather shaken dinghy sailor, 'but I'm new to this game.'

But the priest only laughed and shouted back, 'Non preoccuparti, fratello, there is plenty of God's water for us all.' And then he was helming Foxglove about on the far side of the broad, a tack that would bring him past Tumbledown's stern. 'Buon pomeriggio,' he shouted to Greg on the afterdeck, as he went churning by with a weight of wind in his sail.

It was close enough for Greg to shout back, 'Lorenzo Coletti?'

'Si, si, Generale Kingsbourne,' shouted back the priest who, without continuing to the other side, now instantly came about, bringing the cruiser up into the wind and stopping expertly right alongside Tumbledown. 'It is good to meet you again, fratello.'

'And you too. Come aboard and have a drink,' invited Kingsbourne, holding up the bottle of Spanish plonk.

'Grazie. I will. The wind now is – how do you say – very gusty.'

With sails dropped and her lines passed over, Foxglove was soon made fast to the ketch. The holidaymaker in his little lugsail dinghy was also finding it just a little too squally for comfort. Having listened to this exchange between the two skippers, he dropped his lugsail and rowed back to his own cruiser, seeing as he did so, the yachtsman in holy orders already being helped aboard the larger boat.

*   *   *

If Carol Knights thought Rose de Courcey lucky, the veterinary nurse herself was feeling anything but, that afternoon, as she shared a cup of tea with her parents in Broad View's lounge.

Perhaps it was only a desire to avoid meeting their eyes that caused her to continually gaze out absently over the scene outside. It was two hours now since she'd hopped ashore from Foxglove and then watched with mixed emotions as the old cruiser set off without her, bound for Ranworth. There had been just one other boat on the water at the time and the crew onboard seemed visibly surprised as they watched the strange sight of a cleric helming his way up the Fleet Dyke.

Now, as the afternoon wore on, she noted with some concern that the sky to the west was darkening. Clearly, stormy weather was approaching and her thoughts returned to her beloved Foxglove. Already, sudden spasms of disturbed water showed where a gust from aloft had come down to touch the surface of the broad, some of them quite fierce.

Normally, like her father, come rain or shine, Rose never tired of this view. She'd grown up in this house, loved the magic of its outlook whatever the weather's mood, and still thought there could be no nicer place in the world. She knew also how happy her parents had been at Broad View and felt again the despair at events now conspiring to possibly rob them of it forever.

In the past, most childhood and adolescent problems she may have encountered had been appeased by simply sitting at this window and letting the peace of the broad soak into her soul. But now, even this idyllic setting was failing to lift her spirits. She pushed her half-drunk cup aside and ran a distracted hand through long dark hair now freed from its ponytail. Would she ever know that old peace again?

'So, how was Lorenzo's sailing?' asked her father, obviously recognising his daughter's melancholy expression and attempting some sort of diversion.

'Oh, fine,' she answered, forcing a smile. 'Just getting a tiller in his hand again seemed to lift the years away. He was like a small boy with a new toy.'

'That's nice,' joined in her mother, managing a smile of her own. 'The poor man deserves some happiness at a time like this.'

'Don't we all,' returned Rose with an involuntary shudder. 'All I want is for this whole business to be over and done with.'

Her father frowned. 'I don't think Lorenzo will feel quite the same, Rose.'

'No, of course not. Sorry, Dad. I didn't mean it that way.'

'I know you didn't,' reassured her father.

'Rose, are you quite sure you want to go through with this?' asked Lady Harriet, with the perception only a mother can know. 'I mean, to go ahead with this after the demands that man's made of you. If you don't feel able, just say and...'

But Rose cut her short. 'It has to be done, Mother, so let's not dwell on it. All I'm hoping is that if it works, we might perhaps regain some semblance of the lovely life all of us once knew. If that means I have to go through an unpleasant few hours, so be it.'

'No girl should be expected to go through that, let alone our own daughter,' said Lady Harriet, her voice trembling with emotion. She shook her head in despair. 'I can't believe that while you're enduring that, I shall be sitting through a band concert and pretending I'm actually enjoying it.'

'It has to be done, my love,' replied de Courcey compassionately. 'You know how important that will be.'

Lady Harriet nodded forebodingly. 'Yes, I do. I'll try not to break down, but I still don't know how I'll manage to appear normal.'

Rose forced a smile. 'You'll be fine, Mum. Just try and enjoy the music and think that this time tomorrow, your main worry will have been taken care of.'

'If all goes to plan,' cautioned her father, shaking his head. 'A musical evening, tonight of all nights, does seem somewhat bizarre under the circumstances. The fact is though, we arranged it as some sort of escape before we realised that things would be coming to a head sooner than we thought.'

'Sooner than any of us thought,' agreed Rose as a gust of wind slammed against the picture window. 'I just wish you'd told me everything before now, Dad. I'm not a child any more, remember. If I'd known this whole story earlier, it wouldn't have come as such a shock when the truth finally came out.'

'The whole idea of tonight is to make sure the truth doesn't come out,' stressed her father with feeling.

'We didn't tell you, darling, because the time never seemed right,' her mother tried to explain. 'We kidded ourselves the truth would never surface and so we kept it from you for your own good. We loved you so very much that we couldn't bear the thought of our happy home being upset by events that happened before you were even born. Your father and I only wanted you to think the best of us and you'll understand that when you have children of your own.'

'*If* I ever have children,' responded Rose, despondently. 'You and Dad have made it quite clear that you don't approve of Gordon just because he's not a Catholic and I wouldn't want to get married without your blessing, so my chances of domestic bliss seem pretty remote right now.'

'Things change and attitudes change, Rose,' said her father in a voice more understanding than she'd known in a long time. 'Not only you, but young McQuaid too, have had to hear some pretty devastating revelations about us. I thought he took it magnificently and I won't forget his understanding.'

'He's being more than understanding, Dad. I don't think many actual sons-in-law would do what he's prepared to do.'

'You're right,' agreed her father. 'When this business is over, I promise to do some bridge-building with Gordon.'

Well, at least this whole mess might be producing some positive spin-off, thought Rose and was about to say as such when she was distracted by the sound of her mobile's ring tone. 'It's a text from Lorenzo,' she said, before reading out loud: *"Sorry. Lost rope up mast. Need help per favore? Dio ti benedica. L"*

She quickly fingered a reply before turning to her father. 'Right, Dad, I need a lift.'

* * *

Chapter Thirteen

'Well, Jack, this makes a pleasant change. I could get used to a bit of family life.'

That same evening, DI Bailey sat at the Fellows' dining room table, enjoying some welcome domesticity and watching with pleasant anticipation as Audrey served him a generous helping of beef casserole.

'Yeah, well don't get too used to it,' warned Jack as he poured each a generous glassful of Vino de Espana, 'but you're right, it does make a change from always ending up in some pub trying to keep our voices down.'

'Not to mention worrying what your wife's going to say when you roll in at some late hour,' added Audrey. She picked up her husband's plate and spooned a helping before giving the DI a reassuring smile. 'But it's good to see you, Bailey, and Jack's right, we should have had you round before.'

'He wouldn't be here now if he hadn't rung me this afternoon,' admitted Jack, recalling how the call had come as he cruised back to base after his day's patrolling with the thought of a quiet night in, uppermost in his mind. Turning Bailey's suggestion of a get-together at some pub into an invitation to supper at the Fellows' home had, in reality, been purely selfish, and he'd given the long-suffering Audrey very little warning that there'd be an extra mouth to feed that night.

'*I'm* not complaining.' Bailey was already digging into his casserole with the relish of a man obviously unused to good home-cooking. 'Beats a ready-meal from the microwave, any day.'

'Well, make the most of it while you can then and good health.' Jack raised his glass and while the others clinked back, he added, 'but, presumably, there was some reason behind your wanting to see me other than for my inestimable good company?'

'Just to bring you up to date with what's happening.' Bailey cast an enquiring glance towards his hostess.

'Oh, that's all right, talk away,' said Audrey. 'It wouldn't seem like a normal meal in the Fellows' household if some crime or other wasn't raising its ugly head.'

'So, what is happening?' asked Jack, keen for any update.

'More like what's not, actually. Like the activities in Cambridge of your mysterious priest, Monsignor Coletti.'

'How do you mean?'

'That the Cambridgeshire lads made enquiries as you suggested.'

'And?'

'And, nothing. There is no ecclesiastical conference, meeting, seminar, synod or any such religious occasion going on in Cambridge this week, last week or any time this month.'

'Hmm. Perhaps he was attending a university function then?'

'They contacted all the colleges,' replied Bailey, 'and none of them have ever heard of a Monsignor Lorenzo Coletti.'

'How about the Catholic churches in Cambridge?'

'No luck there either.'

'How very strange,' said Jack, 'because, when I spoke to him he was quite adamant that he was going there for a specific purpose.'

'But obviously didn't say what or where?'

'No.' Jack took a sip of wine. 'But, anyway, we can ask him ourselves now, because he's back.'

'What, here?'

'Yep, I saw him myself this afternoon on the old yacht owned by de Courcey's daughter and her partner Gordon McQuaid.'

'But you didn't ask him what he'd been doing in Cambridge?'

Jack shook his head. 'No, I was hoping we'd find out through your enquiries. The less the other side are aware of what you know or don't know, the better. But, whatever, his stay in Cambridge was much shorter than everyone predicted and now he's not only back here, but off sailing on his own.'

'Sailing. Alone. What's that all about?'

Jack explained the proposed sail to Ranworth to meet Greg Kingsbourne.

'The Royal Marine General? How did those two know each other?'

'I'm not sure, but they both figure in the de Courcey's past, and they both love sailing, so they do have that in common.'

'And perhaps something else,' said Bailey, thoughtfully.

'You mean a secret shared by them all.'

'Exactly.'

'You could be right.' Jack finished off his wine and shook his head. 'But, whatever, I just hope Monsignor Coletti gets back okay, because the evening forecast is for pretty filthy weather.'

'Well, surely he knew what the conditions were going to be like before he left,' joined in Audrey. 'He obviously felt he was up to the challenge.' She paused briefly, and then continued with a slightly furrowed brow. 'You know, I'm quite surprised that someone as well travelled as he must be, would chose to journey all the way from Rome by train. Don't you think that strange?'

'Perhaps he just doesn't like flying,' reasoned Bailey.

'Yes, but he used to be a missionary in Peru which means he must have been willing to fly there.'

'Good point,' conceded Jack. 'Of course it might just be that he's a railway enthusiast or flying simply doesn't agree with him now. In fact...'

'In fact what?' asked Bailey, leaning forward eagerly. 'You've thought of something, haven't you, Jack?'

'Oh, just an idea.'

'Well, I wish you'd let me know what it is, Jack, but I suppose I'll have to wait to find out.'

'Until I have something more concrete – yes.'

'But I thought you were supposed to drop this investigation anyway, Bailey?' chipped in Audrey.

'The Samantha Waites disappearance, yes, but the coroner is going to want information about those remains when the inquest is reopened and I'm as sure as your husband is, that the two are connected.'

'And the only way we're going to find out is by our own endeavours,' insisted Jack, pointing his knife, 'because none of those involved are going to tell us anything. I spoke to Kingsbourne, Rose and Coletti this afternoon and I'm certain none of them were being as honest as they might have been.'

'In what way?'

'Well, for starters, Kingsbourne said he hadn't contacted the de Courceys, and yet they knew he was going to be at Ranworth tonight, hence the Coletti sailing mission.'

'And you think there might be some sinister motive behind that?'

'Hard to imagine what, when a priest and senior officer are involved, but, yes, I'm convinced there's something underhand going on.'

'What about the de Courceys themselves?'

'They're going to a musical evening in Norwich.'

'Well, at least they'll be staying out of trouble,' said Bailey while glancing at the left-over casserole.

'How about a second helping?' asked Audrey, not failing to notice the detective's hungry eye.

'Mmm, please.'

'How about you, Jack?'

But her husband's thoughts were now well away from the evening meal. Outside, he could hear the wind moaning through the trees in their garden. It would be a pretty uncomfortable return trip for Monsignor Coletti back to Broad View, especially if the suspicion he'd just formed was correct. But, if he was right, why then had the priest chosen to sail alone to Malthouse Broad?

*　　　*　　　*

Those same thoughts might well have been shared by General Kingsbourne as his inflatable lopped over the increasingly choppy waters of Malthouse Broad towards Ranworth Staithe. Already it was close to sunset and the forecast of deteriorating weather was proving uncomfortably accurate. There was a decided chill in the air now as patches of low stratus scudded in from the west like the scouting party of some advancing army. Kingsbourne turned up the collar of his oilskin and the outboard throttle another notch.

Rowing would certainly have been warmer exercise, but inflatables were tricky things under oar at the best of times and, in squally conditions such as now, seemingly had a mind of their own. Besides, Rose's reply to the cleric had indicated she would be here very soon and so Kingsbourne had simply pulled on an old submarine sweater and his yellow oilskin and used the outboard to speed towards the staithe.

Having secured the tender in the dinghy dyke that lay just to one side of the main moorings, he made his way around the staithe-side buildings in time to see Rose walking from the car park opposite the Maltsters. A quick wave and she joined him by the pub's entrance, Kingsbourne giving her a good hug and a nod towards the public bar inside. 'I thought we could have a quick drink together before going out to the boats.'

Rose glanced up at the ever-darkening sky. 'That rain's not far away, Greg, so I think the sooner I get Lorenzo sorted and heading home, the better.'

But Kingsbourne wasn't to be put off so easily. 'It's going to be a long night, Rose, so enjoy a quick one while you can.'

'Just one then, and it'll be a *very* quick one.'

In the Maltsters it was warm and cheerful and quite busy even though this was early in the season. But Ranworth was always a popular mooring regardless, and the crews of several boats were already in there, enjoying the convivial atmosphere, good ale and fine food of this old watering hole. Kingsbourne was keen to sample at least the ale, but first he smelt his hands and then wrinkled his nose. 'Sorry, put some fuel in the outboard before I came to fetch you. I'll just go and have a wash before ordering.'

'Of course.'

In the mensroom, he was just enjoying the luxury of hot water when he heard the door open once more and saw in the mirror that another man had just entered.

*   *   *

Just two miles downriver, at St Benet's, a lone car was just drawing into the car park, a new hard-standing area laid as part of the old abbey's regeneration programme. Now, with the sun fast setting and all ramblers and visitors long since departed, it was empty save for this one rather battered-looking mini.

It had been a long drive to Norfolk and, for a few minutes, the driver was content to sit and unwind, thinking of the meeting scheduled in an hour's time and the rewards it would surely bring him. But he couldn't sit for long, for it would soon be dark. This was his first time here and he needed to get the lie of the land.

He had no liking for heritage and would personally never have chosen this as a meeting point. But the other party had and, glancing around at the encircling emptiness, he could see why it was a natural choice for furtive encounters. The main road and any signs of habitation were left far behind at the end of what seemed like a never ending track leading to this isolated parking area. But, somewhere near here were public moorings where his meeting would take place and he needed to locate them while there was still some daylight. Rather reluctantly, he climbed from behind the wheel and emerged stiffly into the very fresh Norfolk air. Looking around, he was struck by the desolate expanse of marshland that stretched as far as his eyes could see, made all the more sinister by dark clouds scudding overhead and the moan of rising wind as it blew unhindered over the surrounding reedbeds. Pulling on a shabby raincoat and battered hat, he set off toward a nearby path that led to ancient ruins.

Here, he climbed over a stile and came to a very old flint gatehouse with what looked like the remains of a brick mill built within it. There were signs that these ruins had been recently restored but he paused only long enough to scorn the wasted money such repairs must have cost. Instead he picked out a path in the encroaching gloom and followed it, passing the remains of ancient walls until he reached a large wooden cross standing out on the top of rising ground. He had little time either for faith or religion, but this higher ground did allow him to get his bearings and he turned his attention to the view out over the surrounding landscape.

There, spread before him, languishing under a huge threatening sky, were thousands of acres of uninhabited Broadland. With the oncoming darkness and rain-bearing overcast, this scene served only to deepen his incipient unease. The sole light he could see was from a boat alongside the riverbank, just beyond the gatehouse. These must be the moorings he'd been told about and where his tryst would take place.

He knew little about boats, but enough to know this was not the sailing boat he'd been told to expect. The boat he could see now was obviously a modern motor cruiser, the crew of which had, for some unaccountable reason, chosen to spend the night in this desolate hole. He mentally cursed them, because he would have preferred to have enacted his plan in total secrecy. But by the time his boat arrived it would be dark anyway and the weather filthy, so it was doubtful if the occupants of the other would have any interest in events further down the quay.

He glanced at his watch. Not long now, and she would be here. But already he could feel the first spots of rain. Turning up the collar of his coat and pulling his hat lower to shield his face, he trudged back down the slope towards the moorings. As he did so, a flight of geese went winging ahead of the oncoming storm, their squawking joining his own curses at this stupid choice of place for such an assignation.

*   *   *

When the public moorings at Ranworth are full, another alternative for those boats not wishing to spend a night at anchor on Malthouse, is to moor on the island on the far side of the broad. Boats mooring there, however, need a tender to reach the staithe if they intend to enjoy a run ashore. On this evening, with the oncoming darkness accentuated by lowering cloud and the first spatterings of rain, only one crew decided to brave the crossing by open boat. They were a group of three men, enjoying a bachelor break away and determined not to miss a single evening without a few noggins in the local pub. And so, in spite of the darkness and gusting wind, they made their cheerful way across the rain splashed water, one rowing bravely and the other two, in bow and stern, offering cheerful encouragement and reports of other boats in their path.

There were two lying on their route to the staithe, boats they had seen and commented on earlier. One was a large smart sea-going ketch with the unusual name of Tumbledown and, tied alongside her, an older broads sailing cruiser called Foxglove. The latter had her mast down but, illuminated by the ketch's masthead light, three figures were preparing to re-raise it. All were hauling away, a tallish man in white roll-neck jumper and yellow oilskin, an attractive young woman in waterproofs and, most bizarre of all, a dog-collared priest dressed in black. By the time the shore-party came abeam in their tender, the mast was up but, nevertheless, in the darkness and with the weather so threatening, they felt obliged to check all was well.

'Anything we can do to help?'

It was the girl who answered. 'No. Thanks for offering, but we're almost there now.' Already she was hoisting the mainsail while the taller man climbed back aboard the ketch. 'Lorenzo's determined to sail back to South Walsham tonight as the wind's favourable, so we need to get him going.' She secured the halyard and joined the man on board Tumbledown. Although the mainsail on Foxglove was fully reefed, it was still flapping and cracking in the gusting wind.

'Not the best night for a sail I would have thought,' shouted another of the men in the rowing boat, as a strong gust slammed against them.

The man on the ketch grinned back. 'Or for a row.' The accent was refined with a commanding edge. 'Are you going far?'

'No, only to the pub.' The man rowing paused and leaned on his oars. 'It'll take more than a bit of filthy weather to stop us havin' a few swift ones.'

'Good for you. I wish we could join you.'

'Well, we can squeeze the two of you on board if you want,' offered the oarsman. 'We're coming back ten-ish.'

'Appreciate the offer, old chap, but we've got our own tender, thanks, and in this rising wind, I think we'd better stay on board and keep an anchor watch. The forecast tomorrow is for significant improvement, so I'll give myself a bit of shore leave then.'

'You in the navy then, sir?' asked the man in the dinghy, catching the service expressions.

'Royal Marines, actually. Still am.'

'Leatherneck, heh. I was a pongo myself.'

'Pong...?'

'Pongo. You know, sir. Army. Did my time in Helmand and then took my discharge six months ago.'

'Well, you've certainly earned this break then,' replied the marine, 'but take care rowing back tonight if you've had a few.'

'We will. At least ours is tied alongside, so she shouldn't come to no harm,' said the ex-soldier, pointing towards the only cruiser moored at the island, 'but rather you than me, stuck out here.'

'Right, but if it gets really bad in the night, we might have to up anchor and shift elsewhere.'

'Good luck, anyway,' called the crew as they pulled away and continued towards the staithe. A few minutes later they glanced back to see Foxglove's lines let go and the yacht with the priest at the helm, heeling and surging up the broad. By the time they'd reached the dinghy dyke and secured their tender, rain was falling heavily and the yacht had disappeared down Ranworth Dyke. None of them envied the priest his lonesome trip, but they did envy the owner of Tumbledown. 'Lucky devil, having a cracking looking girl like that on his boat for the night,' said one with a wink to the others.

'Yeah, an' young enough to be his daughter by the look of it,' grinned the other.

'Bloody Marines. Always did know how to pull 'em,' grumbled the ex-soldier.

'Especially with a boat like that.'

They all looked out across the broad to where the marine and the young woman had now disappeared, presumably down into the cabin from which portholed lights blinked through the falling rain.

The men pulled their coats over their heads and ran across the road to the pub. It was nearly eight o'clock, but they still had a good few hours of drinking time before them.

*   *   *

On board the hire cruiser lying on St Benet's solitary moorings, Brenda Morrison turned from scanning the gloom of near night through the for'ard saloon windows and called her husband. 'This could be the boat he's waiting for, Steve.'

The Morrisons were from the Midlands and this was their first holiday on the Broads. So far, it had proved idyllic, loving as they did, nature, peace and solitude. That was why, seeing the old abbey silent and deserted and no other boats on the public moorings, they had chosen St Benet's as that night's place to stop. Keen ramblers, they'd intended a post-supper walk amongst the historic remains but, with darkness descending and the weather turning foul, had decided instead to enjoy the comfort of their boat's cosy saloon for an evening's warmth and telly. The next day forecast was good and they would have their promised walk then.

However, it was just as they were finishing washing the supper things that a strange looking character had arrived and proceeded to pace up and down the quay heading, all the while casting impatient glances up-river. He was clearly expecting another boat, and the old sailing cruiser now dropping its sails and edging in towards the moorings could well be the one.

'A grotty night to be sailing something like that,' Steve observed, reaching for the binoculars hanging from the saloon door and focussing them on the scene. 'It's called Foxglove,' he reported, 'and whoever's helming seems to know what he's doing.' He zoomed in on the skipper, now throwing a line to the figure on the bank. 'Would you believe it – crikey – he looks like a priest, Bren!'

'Really, let me have a look.' Brenda took the binoculars and adjusted them for her own eyes. 'Yes, I think you're right. I can definitely see the dog-collar under his waterproof. Well, vicar or not, that other strange man doesn't seem particularly pleased to see him.'

'Probably fed up at having to wait in this rain,' suggested Steve. Even without the binoculars, he too could see the figure on the bank apparently remonstrating with the priest on the boat. 'Whatever, he's far from happy.'

'Anyway, he's going on board now,' reported Brenda, peering ever intently at the slightly bizarre scene being enacted. Finally, with both men out of sight in the sailing cruiser's cabin, she put down the binoculars. 'Well, I wonder what that was all about?'

'Goodness knows,' answered her husband as he turned away from the window, 'and, in weather like this, I certainly don't intend trying to find out.' He switched on the television. 'I wonder what's on this tonight?'

'The usual old rubbish, as you keep telling me,' replied Brenda as she settled down in front of her favourite soap. 'Funny though, I've always looked forward to watching Corrie at home but, since we've been on the Broads, I'm beginning to realise how much valuable time I've wasted over the years. In fact, I think this will be the last episode I'll bother with.' She took another quick glance out of the saloon windows. 'But I'd dearly love to know what's going on in that boat right now.'

*   *   *

Brenda Morrison wasn't the only one anxious to know of events beyond her sight. At St Andrew's Hall in the heart of Norwich, Lady Harriet was finding it increasingly difficult to concentrate on the night's musical programme. The hall was full and the audience entranced but, in spite of the stirring music being played by the Light Dragoons, she found her thoughts constantly straying to what her daughter was doing at that very moment.

It was the most natural thing in the world for a mother to worry, she told herself, but what did it achieve? To force her thoughts into pleasanter channels, she allowed her eyes to wander over St Andrew's splendid arched columns, hammer-beamed roof and ingrained history that made such a perfect setting for traditional music. She remembered that, back in the thirteenth century, this ancient building had been home to a sect of Dominican Blackfriars, a name given to the smaller adjacent hall that formed part of this unique complex. Then Lady Harriet felt a cold shiver crawl down her spine and knew it was the very association of that name that was returning to haunt her. It was a relief when the band completed a rendition of regimental marches, the lights went up and the first half was over. As she joined in the applause, the lady next to her smiled and enthused, 'Wasn't that wonderful?'

'Oh. Yes. Very stirring.'

'And I believe the band is leaving for Afghanistan with the rest of the regiment in just a week,' added the lady, who then introduced herself as Marjorie Reynolds.

'Nice to meet you. I'm Harriet de Courcey and this is my husband, Charles – Sir Charles.'

'It's an honour to meet you, Sir Charles,' gushed Ms Reynolds, obviously impressed by titles. 'You seemed to really enjoy that first half yourself.'

'Yes indeed,' he answered courteously. 'I really don't think you can beat the British military when it comes to martial music.' He let go of Harriet's hand to check his watch. 'Can I get you both something to drink? It's still only eight thirty-five, so plenty of time before the second half starts.'

Orders taken, he went off on his mission for two gin and tonics, without admitting that a stiff brandy wouldn't go amiss for himself. Like dear Harriet, he couldn't help wondering what was going on right now on the far distant River Bure.

*   *   *

It was Foxglove setting sail again that had once more caught the attention of the Morrisons. They had drawn the saloon curtains and so didn't actually see the yacht cast off, but they heard the sound of an outboard motor start and the raised voices of the two men. Their saloon lights were already turned low to watch the

TV and so it only needed a quick glance between the curtains to catch sight of the old yacht motoring past their cruiser and heading downriver.

'But he's left that strange man on the bank,' noticed Brenda, pointing out the figure once more pacing the quay heading.

By this time, Foxglove was passing right by their window, close enough for the collared priest at the helm, realising he was being watched, to give a friendly wave and a call of 'Buona notte' that carried even above the sound of the running outboard.

'That sounded Italian,' said Steve as they both gave slightly embarrassed feeble waves in return. He glanced at the clock on the cruiser's saloon bulkhead. It was nine o'clock exactly. 'I wonder where he's off to now?'

That question was soon answered by the yacht's almost immediate turn to starboard into the Fleet Dyke.

'South Walsham, by the look of it,' said Brenda. She turned her attention back to the quay heading. 'His friend doesn't look any happier at being left behind though, does he?' Sure enough, the stooped figure in hat and raincoat was still pacing up and down the moorings, stopping occasionally only to shake his head in a distracted manner. 'In fact, he looks positively upset,' she added with some concern. 'Do you think we ought to invite the poor man on board? At least it would get him out of the rain.'

'No, it would only look as though we were being nosey,' decided her husband after only the shortest consideration and before tweaking the curtain and peeping through the gap one last time. There was no sign of the figure in the dark and it could only be assumed he'd gone. Steve nodded to the clock. 'I don't know about you, but I'm ready for bed.'

In fact, the effect of days spent on the river, breathing in the fresh country air and enjoying long walks, meant they were both healthily tired in the evening. Neither could remember sleeping as soundly as they had since being afloat and tonight, though still a good two hours before their normal time, their eyelids were already beginning to droop.

Brenda agreed. 'Me too. I want to be up early tomorrow anyway to explore the abbey.' And so, just a few more minutes found them both in bed, a snuggle made all the cosier by the drumbeat of heavy rain on the deckhead and the creak and groan of the mooring lines, as the boat moved and shifted in the rising wind.

Perhaps it was the awful weather outside that caused Brenda's sleepy mind to continue thinking about the strange scenes they'd witnessed that evening. 'I hope that man's home and dry by now,' she murmured, dreamily.

'He'll be fine, so stop worrying,' replied her more phlegmatic husband as he kissed her goodnight and turned out the light. Sure enough, the Bure was still working its magic and within a few minutes, both of them were fast asleep.

*   *   *

In a village hall, well to the south of Norwich, Carol Knights was another whose thoughts were straying elsewhere. Her talk to the young farmers on her years at agricultural college had gone off well enough and prompted a whole host of pertinent questions. But now, with that part of the evening over and the young people enjoying a bit of good natured socialising, Carol's own thoughts had turned to her beloved Sindbad. Had Mr McQuaid dropped off the sachets of bute as he'd promised? As if in answer, Carol heard her mobile's ring tone and saw it was a text from the vet himself. She edged into a quieter corner of the hall and read:

Hi Carol. Have dropt off bute & givn Sindbad 1st dose. Seems fine. Hav gd meetng. Wil b in tuch latr. Gordon

Carol smiled with relief and glanced at the clock on the wall of the hall. It was ten o'clock. She texted a quick reply of thanks and, knowing all was well, set herself to enjoying what was left of the evening.

*   *   *

In Norwich, the band concert was playing its last piece, an arrangement of Sousa marches that had the whole audience clapping in time. Finally, after a rousing encore, the concert was brought to a close.

'Well that's the best played music I've enjoyed in a long time,' announced a rather flushed Marjorie Reynolds.

The de Courceys nodded their own agreement. 'Yes, really stirring stuff.'

The audience were putting on their coats now and slowly filtering out of the hall, but some were hovering around the stage, taking the opportunity to meet the bandsmen. Marjorie nodded towards them. 'Come on, let's just go and tell them how much we've enjoyed their performance.'

'Well, we really should be getting home,' protested Lady Harriet with a glance at the clock showing nigh-on ten-thirty.

But Marjorie Reynolds was in full-flow by now. 'Oh, come on. We'll only be a few minutes,' she insisted.

And so they made their way to the stage where the scarlet-coated bandsmen were only too happy to discuss the technicalities of their music and the lot of army life. Marjorie managed to latch on to one of the cornet players, a slim young corporal, modest in his acceptance of her praise and kind enough to answer the continuous questions that Ms Reynolds was throwing at him. In the end, in an effort to break free without offending this somewhat pushy woman, he turned to the upright gentleman beside her. 'I hope you enjoyed it too, Sir.'

'Yes indeed. That last compilation was quite something. I don't think I've heard The Liberty Bell played with quite such gusto.'

'Well, it's hard not to give a Sousa march all you've got,' agreed the corporal. 'I think his would get anyone's foot tapping.'

'Can you play any other instrument, or just the cornet?' asked Marjorie, keen to get back into the conversation.

'No, madam; just the cornet,' replied the corporal.

'But I thought everyone in a military band had to be able to play at least two instruments, and that the cornet players usually also played the violin,' commented Sir Charles.

'Not in this band, I'm glad to say, sir.'

'Ah well, I must have got that wrong somehow.' The rest of the band were busy packing away their instruments so, not wishing to take up any more of the cornet player's time, he said, 'Well, thanks for putting on a wonderful show and good luck with your tour in Afghanistan.'

They moved away with the rain still beating against St Andrew's stained glass windows. He turned to the two women. 'Doesn't sound too inviting out there. How about another drink before heading homeward?'

'Oh, yes please,' answered Marjorie, enthusiastically, 'but only one, because I have to be at work early tomorrow.'

'Oh, where's that?' asked Lady Harriet, more out of politeness than any real desire for facts.

'I'm a volunteer at the night shelter,' replied Marjorie with some pride as they made their way to the bar area and took a table. 'It's round the clock work, I'm afraid, and we have to put in all sorts of odd hours.'

'Very commendable though,' praised Sir Charles, giving Marjorie a pat on the back before nodding towards the bar. 'What'll it be then? Another gin and tonic?'

*   *   *

Alcohol was certainly creating a feeling of well being in the merry revellers as they rowed their tender back across Malthouse Broad. They'd had a pleasant evening in The Maltsters, managed to knock back several pints of the local brew and were now clunking a slightly meandering course back to their cruiser on the island.

Being on the water in a slightly intoxicated state is not something ever to be recommended, but on this night of driving rain, anything to raise the spirits was perhaps just a little excusable. However, despite two of them having an oar each and the third shouting slightly slurred directions, they were finding it impossible to steer a straight course against the vicious northerly gusts.

Inevitably, that erratic course once again took them back past Tumbledown and with it, thoughts of the Royal Marine and the young woman who was sharing his night at anchor, if not his bed. Perhaps, in their slightly inebriated state, the men didn't intend any eavesdropping but, as they approached the ketch, they leaned on their oars and drifted silently close enough to hear a voice from within. It was the young woman they had seen earlier and her words were clear enough.

'Some things have to be done – don't worry – they'll never find out – I'm so proud of you – I love you and want to marry you.'

With amused expressions the men resisted the temptation to wait for the marine's reply and allowed their boat to be blown clear before again taking up their oars. Well good for them, was their unspoken accolade as they pulled once more against the chop now building in the middle of the broad.

It took some heavy effort and not a few drink induced expletives, but eventually they were back at their boat, climbing wearily aboard and sinking gratefully into their pits. It was now nearly eleven o'clock.

*　　*　　*

Back at St Benet's, it was a heavy thud from for'ard that woke Brenda Morrison.

'Steve, what was that?' she asked, sitting up.

Her husband, still half-asleep, propped himself up on one elbow and listened. Outside, the wind was still howling and the boat shifting and groaning against its lines. He pulled aside the curtain and looked out across the river. It certainly wasn't a night to be out there, with little white horses created by the tops curling off the wavelets. What was reassuring though was that they were still abeam the same area of marsh and it was the river that was moving. 'We're still secure alongside by the look of it,' assured Steve, 'so no need to worry.'

'Well, I definitely heard a thudding noise,' persisted Brenda. 'Do you think it was something falling off the boat?'

'Possibly the mop from off the roof, but it won't have gone in the river.' As if to contradict that statement, there then came from outside the sound of a great splash. 'Ah well, there it goes,' he sighed, 'but nothing I can do about it now.'

'That was no mop. That was something far heavier,' said Brenda anxiously, sitting bolt upright and switching on the light. 'Steve, I think you need to go and check.'

'Oh crikey! Okay, if it'll make you any happier.' Steve climbed wearily out of bed, and made his way to the saloon-cum-wheelhouse where he squinted through the windows. The rain had eased now, but a cold half-moon appeared briefly through the scudding stratus, casting enough light to throw the moorings into ghostly detail. Stark against the background, darker than the darkness, sat the stolid edifice of the ancient gatehouse, all the more eerie in the ethereal moonlight. More importantly, however, he could see that their mooring lines were still attached to the quay, the boat moving to the gusts of wind, but obviously still secure. The rest of the moorings were now devoid of any life. Steve made his way back to the bedroom, checking the time on the saloon clock as he did so. 'Everything looks okay, love, so let's get back to sleep.'

'If you say so,' said Brenda, not totally convinced. 'What time is it now, anyway?'

'Just gone ten thirty-five.'

'Did you see what caused that splash?'

'No, but it's probably nothing to worry about.'

'Well, as long as the boat's all right.'

'It is. The wind's northerly, so it's actually holding us off the quay.'

'I hope this weather clears through like they forecast,' muttered Brenda, turning over. 'I'm looking forward to that walk around the abbey ruins before breakfast.'

'The rain's already lighter,' assured her husband, switching off the light and snuggling down beside her. 'It'll be fine in the morning. Good night, love.'

'Good night, Steve.'

With thoughts of pleasant ramblings to come, they were both soon fast asleep once more.

*   *   *

That clearance, however, was still some hours off when yet more holidaymakers were woken by the sound of a boat's engine. It was midnight at Ranworth Staithe and, as the weather system moved through, the elements were saving their worst until last.

Ranworth moorings look north so the boats moored stern-on to the quay, faced the full force of the gale. With mud anchors holding their bows, they shouldn't have suffered any problems, but the movement and groan of the shifting boats was keeping most crews awake. And then had come the sound of an engine, the throaty growl of a marine diesel, very close to the cruiser on the end of the line, the mother boat of the small lugsail dinghy that had been sailing on the broad the previous evening.

Like Steve at St Benet's, this skipper was loathe to stir from wife and bed on such a filthy night, but there was something urgent in the handfuls of power being used by a boat now very close. It spurred him up on deck, where he found the large ketch he knew to be Tumbledown, bearing down on them. As the motor sailer's bows got nearer, one of her wheelhouse windows slid open and a figure behind shouted across, 'Sorry about this, but we were dragging our anchor in the storm. Can you catch our lines and secure us alongside your boat?'

'I will if I can.'

'Thanks,' shouted the skipper. 'I'll try and get her round first so she's heading into wind.'

The dinghy sailor watched as the larger boat backed away, his eyes particularly on the young woman in weather gear standing in the bows, braving the rain-filled gusts and holding a mooring line, ready to throw it across just as soon as the boat was turned.

But the man at the wheel was having problems of his own, trying to manoeuvre a single screw boat in unpredictable squalls at night with all the windage of a high freeboard and two masts. Added to that, almost maliciously, the storm had chosen this worst of moments to throw its full weight of wind against the turning ketch. Tumbledown was almost round now, just off the moored cruiser, coming about to breast alongside and her skipper giving an extra burst of power to complete the turn. But, even as he did so, a sudden gust caught the boat broadside, paid off the bow and pointed its heavy steel roller straight at the hire cruiser's for'ard windows. There was the roar of the engine going from ahead to astern and cries of, 'Look out!', but all to no avail as, with a shattering of glass and crunch of splintering fibreglass, Tumbledown embedded herself firmly inside the cruiser's saloon.

'Are you all right, love?' shouted the shaken skipper of the hire cruiser, as the young woman on the ketch's foredeck picked herself up.

'Yes, I think so. Can you take this?' she asked, handing across the bow warp she'd been ready to throw.

Tumbledown's skipper also exited the wheelhouse, made his way aft and threw across the stern warp. 'Let's get her secured and then see what we can do.'

In the pouring rain and freezing gusts, the ketch was extricated from the gash and warped alongside the hire cruiser she had so effectively maimed. By this time, stirred by the violent crash, the dinghy sailor's wife was also emerging.

'Are we all right?'

'Yep, but the boat isn't,' explained her husband.

'I'm really so sorry for this,' shouted Tumbledown's skipper, leaning over the guardrail of his boat, 'but that last gust caught the bow and swung me in. There was nothing I could do. Obviously I'll pay for the damage.'

'Can't be helped,' said the other skipper, magnanimously, 'and it's not my boat, anyway. It's the boatyard you'll have to settle with, but I'll need your name?'

'Not now,' complained the wife, shivering in the well of the boat. 'Let's get out of this rain, back to bed and do all that in the morning.'

It seemed the best immediate plan for all of them and, while the storm continued to blow itself out, all retreated back to their beds to catch whatever sleep they could salvage from this very eventful night.

*   *   *

Coming through that night somewhat less scathed were the Morrisons on their cruiser. True to forecast, by early next morning the weather system had passed through, producing a dawn as clear and fresh as the night had been filthy. Streams of sunlight pouring between the cabin curtains had prompted the couple to rise early and set off on their promised pre-breakfast ramble around St Benet's. Stepping ashore though, Steve's first concern was to check the boat for damage. Still in both their minds was the heavy thump heard that night. Now, in daylight, the cause of it soon became apparent.

'The mudweight's gone!'

Sure enough, up there on the bows, the base for the anchor lay empty.

'Well, it certainly couldn't have blown off,' insisted Brenda frowning, hands on hips.

Her husband agreed. 'No, look, it's been pinched, because someone's taken the trouble to uncleat it.'

Brenda shook her head in disbelief. 'But who on earth would want to steal a heavy thing like that in the middle of nowhere and on such a terrible night?'

'It could've been that strange bloke we saw wandering around on the bank.'

'But why and how? It's much too heavy to carry far and anyway, I thought you assumed he'd gone before we went to sleep.'

'Well, it definitely wasn't taken by the skipper of the sailing cruiser, because he'd motored off well before we heard the noise from the foredeck and, in any case, I can't imagine a priest knicking anything.'

But Brenda wasn't listening. Instead she was looking at a bundle on the bank at the end of the moorings. 'Steve, what's that?' she asked pointing.

'I'm not sure, but we'll soon find out.' A brisk walk along the bank soon had them at the scene. 'Just a bundle of old clothes,' declared Steve, gently kicking it with his foot.

'It's an old raincoat and a hat,' said Brenda, taking a closer look. 'Hang on, Steve, I'm sure they're the ones worn by that strange chap pacing up and down last night.'

'But why would he take them off when it was still raining and leave them here by the river?'

At the mention of the river they were both struck by the same morbid foreboding, and tentatively scanned the water near the bank. It was with some relief that they couldn't see any sign of a body, but Steve did notice the last few feet of a rope, floating there on the surface. Clearly it was leading from somewhere at the bottom of the river.

'That must be our anchor rope.'

It certainly looked like it and both of them had the ominous feeling that it wasn't only their mudweight down there on the end of it.

*   *   *

'Jack, it's Bailey.'

The ringing of his bedside phone had brought the ranger out of his sleep with just the slightest hangover from too much wine the night before. Now the cause of that excess was on the other end of the phone at... Jack checked his alarm clock. 'But, it's only six-thirty, Bailey.' He wiped the sleep from his eyes as he felt Audrey stirring beside him. 'What's so important for you to ring at such an unearthly hour?'

'Problems, Jack. A drowning. Suicide by the looks of it, at St Benet's Abbey. We need the moorings there closed for at least the morning. Can you come straight over?'

'Oh, Lord.' Jack checked the clock again. 'Give me twenty minutes, Bailey, and I'll be right with you.'

He swung out of bed and pulled on some clothes.

*   *   *

Chapter Fourteen

'A couple called Morrison, on that hire-boat over there, called us early this morning,' explained DI Bailey as he led Jack onto the St Benet's moorings, indicating as he did so, the solitary cruiser moored close to the gatehouse end.

'Did they see or hear anything?'

'Yep, a strange man wandering about during the latter part of the evening, looking somewhat distraught. Later on they heard a thump, which we now know was their mudweight being removed. In the morning they found out why. It had obviously been our suicide victim using it to weigh himself down in the river.' At the other end of the moorings, two uniformed constables stood beside a white coveralled figure. The latter had just dropped a plastic sheet over the still form lying on the grassy bank. Bailey nodded towards the Broads Beat launch and Fire Service dive boat that lay just off the moorings. 'The divers have finished now, but we're obviously keeping this stretch of river closed until we've removed the body.'

'And one of our launches will be along shortly to help,' added Jack. 'The last thing we want is for our holidaymakers witnessing this sort of thing.'

They were at the scene now with the figure in white coveralls, a grey-haired man with clean features but permanent frown, peeling off a pair of surgical gloves. Bailey approached him. 'Finished your preliminary then doc?'

The pathologist nodded. 'Yes, but with nothing special to report at this stage. All indications so far point to death by drowning.'

'Any idea of time?'

The brow furrowed deeper. 'Always difficult with drowning cases, but he hasn't been in the water long. I'd say sometime between ten and midnight last night.'

'Any signs of violence?'

'None, apart from some abrasion on the ankle where he'd tied that.' The pathologist nodded to one side where a heavy mudweight and its rope lay on the grass verge. 'Get him back to my lab as soon as you can and I'll tell you more then.'

'We will. Thanks, doc. I'll pop along to the mortuary later and see what else you've found.'

The pathologist left, leaving Jack to take in the whole tragic scene. He looked down to the covered lifeless form at their feet. 'Any ID yet?'

'I think so. There's an old mini in the carpark which my DC is checking with registrations, but matey left a note as well.' He nodded towards a sodden coat and hat lying to one side. 'They got soaked by last night's rain, but fortunately he'd put a few last words in one of the raincoat pockets which has stayed dry.'

'And this is where they were found?' asked Jack.

'That's right. The couple from the cruiser saw him wearing them earlier and then noticed them on the bank here when they took their early morning walk.'

'And there's a name on the note?'

'Yes, but before I tell you, I want to see if you can do an identification.'

'You think I might be able to?'

'Possibly. Take a look.'

Bailey pulled back the sheet and Jack found himself staring down at the plain features of a man whose thinning hair lay plastered over small pig-like eyes. 'Yes, I know him,' said the ranger. 'That's Bruce Odell, the bookseller from Cambridge.'

*   *   *

'He was the fellow student who had a bit of a thing for Samantha Waites all those years ago, wasn't he?' asked Bailey.

'That's right, and I have to say, not a man I particularly warmed to when I had that brief interview with him in his shop.'

'Well, he certainly won't warm anyone now,' replied Bailey with a wry smile, as he let the plastic sheet drop back. He turned towards the young female Detective Constable who had just walked back from the car park. 'Any luck with registrations?'

'Yes, sir. They confirm the mini belonged to a Doctor Bruce Odell with a registered address of Boffin Books, Cambridge.'

'Could I see the note he left?' asked Jack.

'Sure.' Bailey nodded to the DC who produced a clear plastic wallet containing a sheet of paper and an envelope, which she handed across.

Jack glanced at the plain envelope and then at the note itself with its few lines:

I can't go on. I'll go on

Bruce Odell PhD

'Hmm, no address on the envelope, but written on Boffin Books' headed notepaper which pins it nicely down to Odell. Rather strange words though.'

'Probably written in haste.'

'No doubt, but what do you think they mean?'

Bailey shrugged. 'Pretty much what they say. Obviously he was a man who'd reached the end of his tether and decided to end it all.'

'Suicide?'

'Of course.'

'Well he seemed determined to make a good job of it,' accepted Jack, glancing down at the heavy mudweight and its rope. 'Presumably, he'd tied that to his ankle?'

'Yep. The rope's the floating kind and the loose end had stayed on the surface. It was that and the pile of clothes that aroused the Morrison's suspicions.'

'And you say they actually saw Odell before he topped himself?'

Bailey nodded again. 'Apparently, earlier in the evening, when he met and boarded a yacht called Foxglove.'

Jack's eyebrows rose sharply. 'Gordon and Rose's boat?'

'That's right,' affirmed Bailey, 'except it wasn't them on the boat, but a priest who sounded Italian.'

'Monsignor Lorenzo Coletti?'

'Had to be. You told me yourself that he was taking the boat to Ranworth alone, so presumably he stopped here with another agenda on the return.'

'And you think he might be involved in Odell's death?'

'Only in as much as it seems he was the last man to talk to him. But he wasn't here at the time of death, because the Morrisons saw him motoring off in Foxglove at nine pm and then saw Odell pacing the riverbank for some time afterwards. But we know Odell topped himself around ten-thirty because that's when the Morrisons heard a loud clunk from their foredeck, followed shortly after by the sound of a large splash.'

'Their mudweight being taken and Odell deep-sixing himself with it.'

'Exactly.'

'All sound's pretty neat, I grant you,' agreed Jack, 'but what's your take on the whole business?'

'Obviously it's all connected to the Samantha Waites business. My guess is that all those years ago, Odell here had an obsessive desire for Samantha and tracked her down to the boat she was staying on in Horning. We know she wasn't interested in him and probably told him to get lost. In a fit of jealous rage, and reckoning if he couldn't have her, no one else would either, he murdered the poor girl and dumped her body in the river. He must have thought he'd got away with it too, until you came along and he saw the game might finally be up.' Bailey shrugged. 'A tragic tale but it does clear up an old mystery.'

'Or creates a new one.'

'Why do you say that, Jack? Doesn't my scenario make perfect sense?'

'Yes, in many ways, but not all. For instance, why did he come all this way to end his life and in the way he did? Why not where he lived in Cambridge and in the comfort of his own home?'

'Perhaps he just wanted to die as close as possible to where Samantha did, and in almost the same manner, as some sort of act of repentance.'

'Okay, but why take the trouble to meet a priest first?'

'For the same reason. Probably to make a confession or receive absolution from his sins before the end.'

'He didn't strike me as a particularly emotional or religious person,' pointed out Jack as they made their way back along the moorings.

'People often turn to religion when the chips are down,' said Bailey, 'but we'll know more when I've talked to the priest myself.'

'You won't learn much if he took Odell's confession,' warned Jack. 'Remember, they're bound by oath to remain silent.'

'Well, we know Coletti was the de Courcey daughter's godfather, so perhaps family friendship might overcome divine confidences.'

'Let's hope so. I'll be interested to hear the result,' said Jack, as they came level with the Morrison's hire cruiser. He glanced towards the couple sitting in their saloon with a uniformed female constable and cradling mugs of hot drink. 'Can't have been a nice experience for them.'

'No, but they're a sensible pair. They'll get over it.'

'I'm sure.' Jack looked back to where the body still lay, guarded by the two constables. 'You know, Bailey, I'm surprised they heard the sound of the splash above last night's wind and rain. After all, their boat's a good fifty metres from where it all happened.'

'I know, but they were already awake and alert from the thud on deck as he took the mudweight.'

In the car park, the coroner's black van had already arrived and two mortuary technicians approached Bailey for instructions. When he'd directed them to the scene, he turned back to Jack. 'Let's hope I get something out of the priest Coletti. As he's staying with the de Courceys, I'll have a chat with them at the same time. We'll talk to the daughter and her vet boyfriend later, but how about you seeing the marine general, Kingsbourne. You say he's staying on the river, so it won't seem that out of place for you to have a few words and just confirm his movements at the relevant times.'

'No problem.' Jack looked over Bailey's shoulder to where a Broads Authority launch was just approaching the mooring. 'If your police boat can hold the fort for a bit longer, I'll slip along to Ranworth in ours and see if he's still there.'

'Sounds good.' Bailey ran a weary hand through his hair. 'Lots to do, Jack, so let's make contact later today and compare notes.' He sighed resignedly. 'Why does something tell me this case isn't going to be just a straight forward suicide?'

'Copper's intuition.' Jack smiled. 'I feel it too.'

*   *   *

146

General Kingsbourne was already about his own business, still at Ranworth, and on board the damaged hire cruiser offering more humble apologies.

'I really am so dreadfully sorry. Have you been in touch with the yard yet?'

The hire skipper, who had identified himself as Malcolm Reynolds, nodded. 'Yes, and they've told me to bring the boat straight back. Apparently, this early in the season, they have plenty of spare cruisers and said they'll upgrade us to a bigger one at no extra cost.'

'Ah, that's good.' Kingsbourne indicated the large towel covering the gaping hole left by the night's collision. 'You told them, of course, that I'll pay for the damage?'

'Yep, and they asked me to get all your details.'

'Of course.' Kingsbourne fished in a pocket of his oilskin, produced a card and handed it across. 'Sorry it's a bit soggy, but that's me and I've written the name and number of my insurance company on the back.'

'Thanks.' Reynolds read the card aloud. 'Major General Gregory Kingsbourne RM. RM?'

'Royal Marines, though I wasn't much credit to the corps in last night's fiasco,' he admitted with a sigh. 'Thirty-odd years around boats of all sizes and this is my first accident.'

'Couldn't be helped,' said Mrs Reynolds as she handed the marine a mug of coffee. 'Would the – err – young lady like a drink?'

'Thank you for asking, but she's no longer on board. After the collision, her father came to pick her up.'

'Best thing too.' Mrs Reynolds smiled sympathetically. 'She must have been soaked through, poor lass, out there in that storm trying to handle the ropes.'

Kingsbourne took a welcome swig of coffee and grinned. 'I know, but Rose is a great girl and she's been around boats all her life and in all weathers.'

'Does she sail with you often then?' enquired Mrs Reynolds.

'No, we've never actually sailed together and Rose only came yesterday to sort out her own boat for a friend. Her partner Gordon's a vet and as he was off on a farm visit and the weather was so lousy, she decided to stay on board for the night.'

'Well, she seems a competent girl, whatever,' said Reynolds. 'Just lucky she was still here to help when things got tricky.' He glanced out of the for'ard windows. 'Hello, you seem to have another visitor.'

Sure enough, a ranger's launch was gliding up to Tumbledown and Kingsbourne recognised Jack Fellows about to make fast alongside.

*   *   *

'Seems like you didn't exactly cover yourself with glory last night, Greg,' chided Jack with a smile. En route to Ranworth, word had already come in from head office about the collision the previous night and the need for statements to be taken. If anything, it provided a good excuse for Jack to check out the general's movements, an aim now being pursued in Tumbledown's saloon, where he had just taken down his account of the incident.

'You could say that.' Kingsbourne placed two mugs of coffee on the table between them and sat down opposite. 'I'm pretty mortified about the whole business.'

'Well, it was a filthy night and at least Tumbledown seems to have come through it pretty unscathed.'

'Yes, she's a tough little ship,' said Kingsbourne, giving the hull a thump. 'It was the other boat that took all the damage, I'm afraid.'

'Don't worry, the boatyard will have her fixed in time for the busy season, and the yard hands will be glad of a bit of overtime at an insurance company's expense.' Jack's eyes met Kingsbourne's over the rim of his mug. 'Lucky you had Rose on board to help as deckhand.'

'Yes, indeed.' Kingsbourne repeated the explanation he'd given to Mrs Reynolds, adding only, 'Rose just loves being on the water, Jack, and she was keen to experience a night on the ketch.' He gave a sharp grimace. 'That is until I nearly wrecked her.'

'Well, if Gordon was happy, who are we to judge. By the way, did you hear what happened at St Benet's last night?'

'No.'

Jack explained, noticing no particular reaction from the general. 'Did you know this Odell character, Greg?'

'No, never heard of him before. Should I have?'

'Not necessarily, but I understand Lorenzo Coletti spent some time here on Tumbledown with you yesterday.'

'Yes, that's right. Arrived here in Foxglove. Lost the halyard up the mast when he was putting in a reef, which is why Rose had to come over.'

'Quite an eventful night for our good Monsignor, as it turns out,' continued Jack, 'because after sailing from here he stopped to meet Odell at St Benet's. In the time you spent together here, did he mention what he had planned?'

'Not to me, he didn't.' Kingsbourne took a swig of his coffee. 'Lorenzo's a nice chap, but I have to admit we didn't have a lot in common. Most of our conversation was about boats.'

'Right.' Jack stood up and rinsed his mug in the galley sink. 'Thanks for the coffee and sorry I can't linger, but that was a bit of a knock you had last night, so I need to go and get a statement from the couple on the other boat.

'Of course.' Kingsbourne saw him to the rail. 'Sorry to have made more work for you, Jack, but I don't do these things often.'

As Jack crossed to the other boat, he couldn't help wondering just what General Kingsbourne was referring to.

*   *   *

'So, Bailey, what did Monsignor Coletti have to say for himself?'

In the saloon bar of The Rising Sun, Jack sat back and relaxed for the first time that day. A brief telephone conversation in the afternoon had arranged this meeting but, with both he and Bailey busy, the discussion had been limited to deciding a time and place. Now, back in this popular riverside watering hole on the edge of Coltishall village, with soft drinks and packets of crisps before them, it was time to exchange findings. Unfortunately, Bailey's were exactly what Jack had predicted.

'Very little other than to remind me that confessionals were strictly confidential.'

'But did he say how and why Odell contacted him in the first place?'

'No, pretty close-lipped about the whole business, but gave me to understand he knew about Odell through the de Courcey family and didn't seem particularly surprised that he'd topped himself after their secret meeting.'

'Hmm, I think our mysterious priest might stand a little more looking into,' mused Jack. 'Did he happen to drop any clues as to what he was doing in Cambridge in the first place?'

'Afraid not. I did try, but got nowhere. The man seemed very distracted, so I didn't push it.' Bailey tore open his packet of crisps and sighed. 'It's just one more aspect of this whole business that I need explained.'

'Yeah, well I've been giving it some thought myself, based on our dinner chat last night,' revealed Jack, 'and I've got a bit of a theory which I'd like you to check out.' He gave Bailey his reasoning.

'Right.' Bailey wrote a well known name in his notebook. 'I'll get someone on to it but, if you're right, it'll put a whole different complexion on what happened last night.'

'Well, we'll see,' said Jack between sips of orange juice, 'but, for the moment, Lorenzo Coletti admits they met at St Benet's for what we assume was a confessional.'

'He didn't say as much, but I got that impression. However, a confession of what, he wouldn't say.'

'No, but we can guess, and surmise that was why Lorenzo was so keen to set off single-handed yesterday afternoon. In my mind, his proposed reason for visiting General Kingsbourne on his ketch was just to cover a meeting that had been arranged sometime beforehand.' Jack leaned closer across the table. 'How about the others? What were they doing last night?'

'Apparently, the de Courceys were in Norwich.'

'At a band concert,' added Jack, 'which we already knew about from Rose.'

'I didn't see the vet, McQuaid,' continued Bailey, 'but according to the de Courceys, he was off on a late evening visit to see a horse on a farm south of Norwich.'

'Yes, I already knew that too. I saw Kingsbourne this morning and Rose spent the night on his boat.'

Bailey's eyes widened slightly. 'Did she now? I thought she and the vet were a real luvvy pair. So what was that all about?'

'Hopefully, not what you think. According to the general, she only stayed because of the weather.'

'Yeah, I can believe that,' scoffed Bailey with undisguised cynicism, 'but, whatever, for someone in his position, it was a pretty stupid thing to do if he didn't want eyebrows raised.'

'Perhaps eyebrow-raising was what it was all about,' suggested Jack.

'You mean, the deliberate drawing of attention for later use as an alibi? Do you think he might need one, then Jack?'

'I don't know, but there's something about all this that doesn't ring true. How about the de Courceys? Anyone to vouch that they actually were at that concert in Norwich last night?'

'Yep. According to Lady de Courcey, there was a rather pushy woman sitting next to them who got chatting and then insisted the three of them went and talked to members of the band afterwards. Sir Charles did have a quick exchange with one of the cornet players who can also probably vouch for them.'

'Possibly, but my experience is that women usually recall conversations better. Did you get the lady's name?'

'Yes, although address-wise, Lady Harriet could only remember her place of work.'

'Would you mind if I had a word with her?'

'Not at all if you think it will do any good. Strictly on the QT though.'

'Of course.'

'How about Kingsbourne and Rose? Anyone to vouch for their being on the boat?'

'The cruiser they smashed into, certainly remembered,' said Jack with a smile, before relating the full story of Tumbledown's midnight encounter at Ranworth Staithe.

'That's an hour and a half after Odell's death though Jack. They could have been involved and still back at their boat in time for all that.'

'Yep, I know,' agreed Jack, 'but I also met a party of chaps on the staithe getting fresh groceries from the store. Seeing my uniform, they asked if it was true about the death at St Benet's. In the ensuing chat, the midnight collision came up and they told me how they'd rowed past Tumbledown just as Foxglove was preparing to sail. They had a chat with Kingsbourne and remembered him saying he might have to shift moorings if the wind got any stronger. One of the party was an ex-soldier himself and remembered the whole conversation.'

'Anything significant?'

'Just something a little odd, that's all.'

'In what way?'

'Oh, nothing important. Just something that didn't quite add up. And then later, when they were rowing back past Kingsbourne's boat, they actually heard Rose talking about her love for him, how they wouldn't be found out and how she wanted to marry him.'

'Not quite the platonic encounter between those two then, that General Kingsbourne led you to believe.'

'So it would seem, but still hard to accept, knowing both Kingsbourne and Rose as I thought I did. You say you didn't get to talk to young McQuaid at Broad View?'

'No, but the de Courceys did remember where he went to see that horse, so I'll check with the farm.' Bailey took a lingering sip of his drink and sighed. 'You know, Jack, what worries me is that all these alibis are just too cast iron to be true.'

'I know what you mean, but hopefully by this time tomorrow we'll know just how solid they really are, so let's get together then and compare notes.' The two men finished their drinks and walked together out into the car park. 'I need to go home and do some serious thinking,' said Jack as he climbed into his car and lowered the window.

Bailey bent down beside him. 'About what?'

'The something from the past that I know has a direct bearing on all this.'

'Still not recalled it then?'

Jack shook his head. 'Unfortunately not. You know how it is? The more you try and remember something, the more illusive it is.'

'Well keep trying, Jack, and it'll come when you least expect it.'

'I hope so.' Jack started the engine. 'In the meantime, though, I'd put money on my theory about Coletti being correct.'

'We'll see tomorrow if you're right,' said Bailey.

We will indeed thought Jack as he drove away and headed homeward. This was one time in his life though when he wished with all his heart he was wrong.

*   *   *

'You know, Jack, I can't help feeling that if you'd just thrown the scanky handbag straight in the bin, that poor Odell man might still be alive.'

'A lot of hanged criminals would still be alive if it wasn't for detection, Aud, but that's not the point. The fact is that the truth always wins out eventually and we only help speed the process slightly.' Jack was stretched out in his favourite fireside chair now, enjoying the last hours of the day with his wife and with something a great deal stronger than orange juice easing his flow of thought. 'And I wouldn't be too quick to feel sorry for Odell either,' he added, emphasising the point with his glass. 'That man was a little creep if ever I saw one and he became very twitchy when I mentioned Samantha's name. I think the chances are that he was responsible for her death.'

'But, you don't *know* that, Jack,' replied Audrey.

'No, but I bet Lorenzo Coletti does.'

'The priest from Rome? You surely can't be thinking ill of a man of the cloth?' Audrey's devout defences were clearly up. 'It sounds to me as if he was the only one trying to help Odell by at least easing his soul.'

'If he was, he didn't make a very good job of it,' pointed out the more pragmatic Jack. He gave a frustrated grunt. 'The sanctity of confession has probably avoided more prosecutions than I've had hot dinners. Add to that a very close-knit family and we'll be lucky to get one word out of any of them.'

Audrey gave a sniff. 'Well, your esteemed marine general doesn't sound a pillar of virtue either. Having an affair with young Rose, for goodness' sake. No wonder he was so keen to spend some time here in Norfolk.'

'We don't know that, Aud, and if it's a fact, then I'm losing my touch when it comes to judging people. I'd have put Kingsbourne down as a pretty decent type and Rose as the loving partner of Gordon McQuaid.'

'People are never quite what we think, are they, Jack? Perhaps even Bruce Odell wasn't basically bad, but just someone who developed an obsession for a girl he couldn't have.'

'But he must have felt some guilt or else he wouldn't have drowned himself.'

'I know, poor man,' sighed Audrey, 'but I wish he hadn't chosen such a religious site as St Benet's for his dreadful last act. Goodness knows what the black friars would have thought.'

'Who?'

'The black friars, Jack. You know, the Benedictine monks who used to run the abbey back in the Middle Ages. Jack, are you still listening?'

But Jack was miles away, rejoicing in the sudden revelation Audrey's words had triggered. 'That's it, Aud. You've got it.' He was both smiling and clenching his fist in triumph.

'Got what, Jack?'

'The thing I've been trying to remember for days now and, quite possibly, the solution to who murdered Samantha Waites.' He gave the chair arm a thump of satisfaction. 'Yes, that must be it.' He got up and headed for the study. 'I need to call Bailey right now.'

And then he was gone leaving a rather bemused looking wife trying to work out exactly what it was she'd actually said.

*   *   *

Chapter Fifteen

'Well, your hunch about Monsignor Coletti has been proved right, Jack.' It was the following morning and, from behind his desk in North Walsham CID headquarters, DI Bailey handed Jack a printed email. 'Cambridge CID just got back to me. The poor chap's got an inoperable brain tumour. He came to Addenbrooks hoping they could operate, but tests showed things had gone too far. They reckon he could go at any time.'

'I'm so sorry to hear that,' sympathised Jack, 'but at least we now know what the poor chap was doing in Cambridge.'

'Yes, one mystery cleared up,' said Bailey, 'but it brings us no closer to finding out what part he may have played in Odell's demise.'

'No, but I have a theory now about what lay behind everything that happened back then when Samantha Waites disappeared.' Jack leaned forward. 'You remember me saying there was some past event I couldn't recall, but which I felt held the key to the whole business. Well, last night, my dear wife said something that finally got my recall functioning again and brought it all back.'

'I knew there had to be a good reason for you requesting a crack of dawn meeting.' Bailey's smile veiled only slightly the weariness in his voice. 'Okay, let's have it.'

Jack relayed a sequence of events that were now as clearly imprinted in his mind as the day they'd happened. It was a long story, interrupted only occasionally when Bailey wanted clarification on some aspect. Finally the young detective sat back and gave a low whistle. 'Crikey, Jack, that's quite a tale. A bit before my time, but you're telling me these are absolute facts?'

'The truth and nothing but the truth. You can read the reports for yourself.'

'But you weren't personally involved?'

'No, none of us at Scotland Yard were, for the reasons I've already explained.'

'But you think it was connected to Samantha Waites' death?'

'Absolutely. It all fits, and the reason you were told to drop the investigation from the start.'

'Phew!' Bailey ran a distracted hand through his hair. 'You getting onto the case in the first place caused enough agro. If I now pursue Odell's death from *this* angle I'll have the Chief Constable on the phone telling me to wind my neck in faster than you can say "forget your pension".'

'Not if you put the thing straight onto the back burner as a clear case of suicide and...' Jack glanced around and lowered his voice, '... you let me do all the investigating.'

'I can't do that,' protested Bailey. 'I've let you get too involved as it is. The Chief would have my guts for garters if he found I was running some sort of enquiry under the table. No, Jack, if what you say is correct, we're both getting way out of our depth here.'

'Which makes it all the more important that we fight fire with fire,' insisted Jack. 'Do you still believe in justice, Bailey?'

'Of course I do.'

'Well then, let me at least ensure it's done in this case, if only for the sake of Samantha Waites. Just give me what you have already and then I'll keep you right out of it.'

Bailey blinked twice and said, 'Okay, Jack, but I don't want to be kept in the dark completely. Let me know what you find out and, once you've reached some firm conclusions, I'll decide what action to take. But, this conversation never took place, right?'

'Right.' Jack shook the DI's hand. 'Now, tell me what's come to light so far. Any post-mortem results yet?'

Bailey pushed an open file across the desk. 'Cause of death was definitely drowning at around ten-thirty, but did you know he was diabetic?'

'Yes, he mentioned it when I first met him in Cambridge. Has his doctor there confirmed it?'

'Yep, and the pathologist also found traces of insulin in his body.'

'Which figures,' said Jack, 'but were they the correct dose for someone self injecting?'

'Hard to say. Apparently that's almost impossible to determine post-mortem.'

'But the pathologist was quite sure that the cause of Odell's death was drowning?'

'Yes, no doubt about that.'

'Strange though.'

'In what way?'

'That someone planning to end it all should choose such a cold and miserable way to go when all he had to do was slip quietly into oblivion by giving himself an overdose of a prescribed drug he already had access to.'

Bailey shrugged. 'Perhaps it was a spur of the moment decision made after baring his soul to Coletti. The autopsy also found a fair amount of brandy in his stomach, presumably imbibed on the yacht, so that dose of Dutch courage might just have been enough to help him end it all there and then.'

'So, the good Monsignor was dishing out a generous quantity of alcohol as well as absolution on his boat.'

'He probably needed a stiff drink himself,' replied Bailey, 'living as he was with the thought of his own imminent mortality.'

'Which could have been a motive in itself for righting a few wrongs before his time was up.' Jack nodded to the other file on the DI's desk. 'How about young McQuaid's alibi, the one about visiting a farm to tend a sick horse?'

'Grange Farm, actually, just to the south of Norwich. I sent my DC there to check the story and it's correct. Apparently the daughter, one...' Bailey glanced at the file, '... Carol Knights, is in charge of the place while her parents are abroad on holiday. Her horse was lame and McQuaid had looked at it earlier in the day. Seems he prescribed some sort of food additive, but found he'd left it at his surgery, so volunteered to drop it off later that night and check the horse again while he was there. Although Miss Knights was at some Young Farmers' meeting, we know that McQuaid did indeed make that visit as, at ten twenty-two, he sent her a text to confirm he'd been and that the horse was okay.'

'Did the DC check the text?'

'Yes, and it definitely came from McQuaid's mobile and was sent from the vicinity of Grange Farm like he said.'

'You gave a very precise time for that visit, Bailey. How come?'

'Because, as well as the exact time of the text, we have a positive sighting to that effect.' Bailey swung his laptop around for Jack to see. 'Luckily, the Knights have a full surveillance system installed at the farm. The DC brought the DVD back with her which shows this.' The screen brought up slightly grainy shots of a battered Land Rover with *VetCare* on the side, driving through Grange Farm's gates and up the farm road to the house and yard. Then it showed the Land Rover stopping at the stable block and a figure in cap and wax jacket getting out and entering the stable itself. And then finally, after a package of something had been placed by the stable door, shots of the vet sitting in the vehicle keying something on his mobile before driving off once more, back down the farm road and out of the gate. Screen information showed the date and time throughout. Bailey clicked it off. 'I think you'll agree it settles that one.'

'Seems that way,' agreed Jack. 'How about the musician in Norwich who de Courcey claims he was chatting to?'

'Yes, I rang his unit and asked if they could make enquiries as to which cornet player it was. A Corporal Jeffries called me back within the hour but, as the regiment's off to Afghanistan in a week, he hasn't time to come in. However, he did confirm that he spoke to what sounded like de Courcey, at the end of the concert.'

'Okay, how about the lady who sat next to them. Any interview there yet?'

'No.'

'Right, give me her work address and I'll go and have a chat.'

'I can't believe I'm doing this,' sighed Bailey as he scribbled the address of the night-shelter and handed it across. 'There, just make sure you don't let on where you got it.'

'I won't.' Jack stuck the address in his notebook and got up. ' I'll call you later and let you know how I got on.'

'I'll call you,' corrected Bailey, ' and best I do it out of the office.'

'Okay.'

Even as his office door closed the DI's phone rang.

*   *   *

Jack was back on his afternoon river patrol the next day when Bailey's promised call came through. 'Hi, Jack, is it a convenient time to talk?'

He eased his launch around another bend in the Fleet Dyke. 'Sure, I'm just heading down to South Walsham to check something out.'

'Really, what?'

'Oh, just something prompted by another look I've just had at St Benet's moorings, something that didn't quite click.'

'Okay, Jack, I know better than to press you. How about your other enquiries?'

'Very interesting. I went to the night shelter this morning and had a talk with Marjorie Reynolds.'

'The lady who chatted to the de Courceys at the band concert. What's she like?'

'Bit of a busy body, but obviously smitten with Sir Charles and, therefore, having complete recall of all he said that night.'

'Which can't have been that interesting.'

'On the contrary,' said Jack, straightening the launch down the last reach to the broad, 'it was very interesting indeed.'

'Really? So, any leads?'

'Just some theories to be going on with.' Jack was abeam the small marina now with Gordon and Rose's yacht, Foxglove, lying on her moorings, a silent witness to just what had transpired aboard her that stormy night. Or, perhaps, not so silent, thought Jack as he slowed down and took a closer look at the old boat, noticing as he did so, something very interesting indeed. 'Hmm, are you still there, Bailey?'

'Yes.'

'Look, I need a big favour.'

'We're in short supply of those right now, Jack. What is it you need?'

'Another underwater search at St Benet's moorings.'

'What! You're joking! We've used the brigade diving team twice already in the last week and now you want a third! I can see me going down as the idiot who blew the complete police budget on diving.'

'Not if it gets the results I think it will. Tell the powers that be that you're looking for Odell's wallet or something.'

'Whereas, what we're really looking for is…?'

Jack explained, adding, 'I wouldn't ask if I wasn't sure, Bailey.'

There was an audible sigh at the other end of the phone. 'All right, Jack, I'll see what I can do.'

'Thanks. If Lorenzo Coletti won't tell us what happened on Foxglove that night, this might be the only way we'll find out.'

'I doubt if Monsignor Coletti will ever tell anyone anything again,' responded Bailey in a sombre voice.

'Why? What do you mean?'

'I mean that I had a call from Sir Charles de Courcey immediately after you left yesterday. They couldn't wake Lorenzo that morning and realised he'd gone into a coma. He's in hospital now, but isn't expected to pull through.'

*　　*　　*

'Oh, poor Lorenzo,' sympathised Audrey on Jack's arrival home from work. 'A brain tumour. How awful.' She shook her head sadly before taking her husband's hand. 'We were all wondering what he was doing here, so how on earth did *you* work it out, Jack?'

'Just simple deduction really,' explained her husband as they walked together into the conservatory and sat down. 'First there was his preoccupation with something, his tired appearance and the fact that, as you pointed out, he'd travelled all the way from Rome by train.'

'But none of those factors were that extraordinary, Jack.'

'No, not singly, but taken together they became quite significant, especially when I discovered he suffered from headaches. That raised in my mind, the possibility of ill-health. All other enquiries as to why he'd travelled to Cambridge had proved negative, so I asked myself if it might be for medical treatment.'

'For which Cambridge is famous,' agreed Audrey, 'what with Papworth and Addenbrook's.'

'Yes, leading hospitals in their fields, but the question was, which one? Papworth is of course renowned for heart surgery, whereas Addenbrook's specialises in brain conditions. I guessed it had to be the latter, because he'd travelled all the way across Europe by train.'

'What had that got to do with it? You suggested yourself that the man probably didn't like flying.'

'Yes, but unlikely when we know he worked for years as a missionary overseas which must have entailed a fair bit of flying. No, there was another very good reason why Lorenzo now couldn't fly and that was because even the slight decompression of air travel can cause undue suffering to anyone enduring a brain tumour. Our poor Lorenzo had to travel by train because flying could have caused him excruciating pain.'

'The poor man,' sighed Audrey. 'And didn't anyone know about this at the time?'

'He told the de Courceys when he arrived, but they'd been respecting his wish for confidentiality. The hope had been that Addenbrooks could remove the tumour, but tests proved that nothing could be done, hence Lorenzo's return sooner than expected.'

'The only positive thing about this is that, even assuming Odell didn't take his own life, it at least eliminates Lorenzo as a suspect.'

'I'm not so sure.'

'Jack! He's a man of the cloth and desperately ill. You surely don't think he would have committed murder.'

'In normal circumstances, no, but his judgement may have been impaired because of the tumour. If Odell, in his confessional, really did admit to Lorenzo that he'd murdered Sam all those years ago, then perhaps the priest, knowing he'd probably be dead before anything could be proven anyway, decided it was time for a bit of divine retribution.'

'But, Lorenzo can't have done it, because we know that he'd sailed off back to South Walsham a good hour and a half before Odell died.'

'According to witnesses, yes, but what did those witnesses really see and hear?'

'Foxglove leave the mooring with a priest at the helm at nine o'clock,' recollected Audrey. 'He even called them a greeting in Italian.'

'Hmm,' mused Jack, 'I wonder. Have you started the meal for tonight yet, Aud?'

'Not yet, why?'

'Well, don't bother, because I'm taking you out for one.'

Audrey frowned. 'I'm not accustomed to spontaneous treats, Jack Fellows, and this doesn't seem the most appropriate of nights for celebration, so what are you up to?'

'Oh, just some things to check, but it's also a way of saying "thanks" for giving me that great lead last night.' Jack glanced at his watch. 'There's just some more stuff I need to look up on the internet and then we'll go. Six-thirty be okay for you?'

'Fine, I'll have a shower and change. Anywhere special you've got in mind?'

'Oh, just a little Italian restaurant I saw in Norwich,' explained Jack as he stood up and departed for the study. 'It'll help get us in the mood for that holiday you're planning.'

*   *   *

Next morning's temperatures were mild, with rays of sunlight just breaking through the overcast. To Jack, patrolling by Thurne Mouth, they heralded the prospect of a beautiful day ahead.

Since leaving base, he'd been shadowed by a pair of Hunter's yachts running elegantly before the fresh easterly breeze, the chuckle of their bow-waves seemingly mirrored by the smiles of their contented crews. Now on the Bure, they waved goodbyes, continuing down towards Acle while Jack turned upriver, at the same time scrolling through the contacts on his phone and ringing the selected number.

'DI Bailey.'

'Jack here. Bailey, I think it's time we had a chat with all involved. Any chance of you calling a meeting with the de Courcey clan?'

'You sound like you have a case, Jack.'

'Yes, I think I do.'

'Right. Well, I'll simply tell Sir Charles that we'd like to update the family regarding the Odell investigation. Otherwise they'll be on to the Chief Constable before I've put the phone down. I don't like lying, Jack, so I'm not even going to ask what exactly it is that you've got up your sleeve.'

'The truth, I hope. If you let me know the time and place, I'll call General Kingsbourne and have him there as well. We'll know if I'm right when we get them all together and run my theory up the flagpole.'

'Well, I just hope it doesn't shred in the ensuing storm,' warned Bailey with grim humour. 'Of course, this gathering won't include one of the main players in the drama.'

'Monsignor Coletti you mean. Any news of the poor chap?'

'Yes, and it's the worst. Lorenzo Coletti died peacefully, without ever regaining consciousness, early this morning.'

*   *   *

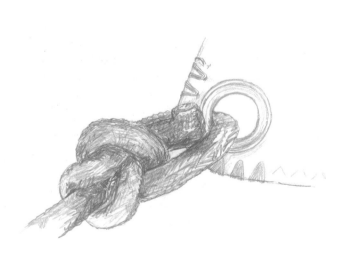

Chapter Sixteen

'I really don't see the need for this meeting.' After pouring himself a stiff brandy and soda, Sir Charles de Courcey waved the glass over the assembled group around him. 'We all really have better things to do.'

Jack and Bailey stood in Broad View's spacious lounge. Seated before them were Lady Harriet, looking strained and drawn and sipping a Martini, daughter Rose and partner Gordon McQuaid on the sofa holding hands, and even General Kingsbourne, his ketch Tumbledown framed in the picture window as it swung at anchor on the broad.

It was two days now since Jack's call to the DI and in that time the diving team had undertaken a more extensive search of the moorings at St Benet's. The results were as Jack had anticipated, but getting the de Courceys to agree to this meeting, had proved somewhat more of a challenge. Only the promise that it would be strictly unofficial and in their home had produced a grudging acceptance. Kingsbourne alone, when Jack had found him alongside Horning Staithe, had seemed more than happy to alter his schedule and sail back to South Walsham.

'I realise this probably isn't convenient at this time,' explained Jack, 'but, nevertheless, we're very grateful that you all came.'

'Not all of us, Fellows,' de Courcey was quick to point out.

'Ah yes, poor Monsignor Coletti. We were genuinely very sorry to hear of his passing and somewhat shocked, seeing as it was only in the closing days of his life that we realised just how ill he was.'

'Yes, such a lovely man,' sighed Lady Harriet, visibly upset. 'Apparently, the brain tumour had been diagnosed a year earlier. The possibility that Addenbrooks might be able to do something for him was his last hope.'

'But, in the end, a forlorn one,' added de Courcey, 'which makes this meeting, only days after his death, all the more inappropriate, Inspector.'

Bailey straightened up. 'We're not insensitive to the situation, Sir Charles, but Bruce Odell is also dead and in strange circumstances, so I want to bring you all up to speed with our enquiries so far.'

'Why?' de Courcey took his brandy to an armchair and sat down. 'How that man died is of no concern to us.'

'But it obviously was to Monsignor Coletti,' said Bailey, 'who was, as far as we know, the last person to speak to him before his death.'

'Suicide, you mean,' corrected de Courcey, downing his brandy in one gulp. 'Look, it's all quite simple isn't it, even for you country coppers? It's blatantly obvious to us all that Odell was responsible for Sam's murder and, up until now, the bastard probably thought he'd got away with it. Then you spooked him with your own enquiries, Fellows, and he knew the game was probably up. Why else would he have decided to top himself now, after living with the guilt for thirty years? How he got to meet Lorenzo, God knows, unless their paths crossed in Cambridge, but the confidentiality of Odell's confession must have weighed very heavily on a dying man's shoulders. I have no doubt at all that the stress of that meeting caused Lorenzo's sudden relapse and ultimate death, so I hold Odell responsible for that too. So, good riddance to him, I say.'

'But, you can't always have disliked Odell,' pointed out Jack, 'because, after Samantha's disappearance, you transferred the money you'd allocated to her research funding to his.'

'How did you know that?' For a second, de Courcey looked stunned, but he soon recovered and explained, 'He caught me at a bad time, Fellows. With Samantha gone and those funds already committed to research, I felt it appropriate that they should at least go to another Darwin student and, even better, to someone she'd known.'

'Even someone who'd subjected her to unwanted amorous attentions?' persisted Jack.

Irritation flashed across de Courcey's face. 'Look here, Fellows, I agreed to this meeting as a form of closure, not to be cross-examined by someone with no authority whatsoever. To put it bluntly, none of this is any of your damn business.'

'On the contrary,' cut in Bailey, 'Jack Fellows is a ranger on these rivers and, as such, what goes on here *is* his business, so just be patient and bear with us, because this is a long story.'

'Which is all very fine and well,' interrupted Gordon McQuaid, 'but I have a practice to run and appointments to keep and, as this Odell bloke meant absolutely nothing to me…' He rose to leave, '… perhaps I can be excused from the rest of this rather boring discussion.'

But Bailey blocked his path. 'Mr McQuaid, this "boring "discussion" will shortly very much concern you personally, so I suggest you sit down again and hear what's to be said.'

'I think we all need to say nothing and listen,' declared Kingsbourne, speaking for the first time at this gathering. There was natural authority in his tone, enough to further stay McQuaid's retreat and, with a pleading look from Rose and a squeeze of her hand, he resumed his seat beside her.

'Thank you,' continued Bailey, with only a touch of sarcasm. 'Right, now let me give you more details regarding the suicide.'

'Which are?' butted in de Courcey, still not prepared to take a voiceless role.

'Which are,' repeated Bailey, ignoring the interruption, 'that it was not a suicide at all.'

'Not a suicide.' de Courccy glanced down at his empty glass. 'You mean it was an accident? Or a heart attack, or something?'

'No, Sir Charles, it was murder.'

'Murder!' Jack saw Rose squeeze McQuaid's hand ever tighter, but it was Lady Harriet who spoke up first. 'I suppose this means that you must suspect dear Lorenzo. Easy, I suppose, to blame a man no longer with us, but there were witnesses who swore that he had sailed off in Foxglove a good hour and a half before Odell's death?'

'Very interesting that you know the timings, Lady Harriet,' observed Bailey, 'because I'm not aware those facts have ever been made public.'

McQuaid quickly jumped to her aid. 'No, but we know that Foxglove was already back on her mooring by nine forty-five because I went and checked her on my way to Grange Farm.'

'Ah yes, the farm visit,' noted Bailey. 'I think we're going to have something to say about that later.'

'Which sounds as though *I'm* now the one in the frame,' growled McQuaid, not failing to notice the cynicism in the DI's tone. 'Don't you believe what I've told you?'

'Actually, I don't believe any of you,' replied Bailey, leaning back against a bookcase, 'but we're all getting way ahead of ourselves without pinning down the basics of the thing, which was Samantha Waites' disappearance over a quarter of a century ago. But why and how did she disappear?'

'We know the *why*, Detective Inspector,' grumbled de Courcey, standing up to pour himself yet another brandy, 'Bruce Odell had formed an obsessive fixation for her which ended in jealous murder. It was a crime of passion. Can't you see that?'

'No, I can't,' replied Bailey, 'because that's not what happened, and you know it.'

'Do I? So, if Odell didn't kill her, who did?'

'For the answer to that, we need to go way back to when you and Samantha first met,' explained Bailey, gently, 'but I'm not the one who's been instrumental in uncovering the truth. That credit goes to Jack Fellows here, so I'm going to ask him to spell it all out.'

General Kingsbourne went to the small bar and poured himself a double whiskey. 'Do you really have the authority to do that, Jack?'

'Not officially,' admitted Jack, 'but I must remind you all that this is an unofficial meeting, so I've as much right to speak here as any of you.' He glanced at Rose. 'I'm not sure if you know the full story, but during the Falklands War of '82, your father and Samantha Waites were engaged in espionage work in Peru for British Intelligence.'

'We told both Rose and Gordon some of the story a few days ago,' interrupted de Courcey.

'Good, but perhaps you didn't explain how the object of that covert work was to stop the sale of Exocet missiles to Argentina through Peru. The general here…' Jack nodded towards Kingsbourne, '… was a young officer at the time, out there on the Falklands and only too aware of how the use of those missiles by the junta could swing the tide of the battle in Argentina's favour. They'd already cost us HMS Sheffield and Atlantic Conveyer and damaged Glamorgan and it was only a matter of time before they got one of our carriers.'

'Which presumably meant the Argentineans were keen to buy more of the missiles,' reasoned McQuaid, now more than interested in the proceedings.

'Desperate would be more the word,' agreed Jack. 'So desperate that they were prepared to pay $4million for each Exocet they could get their hands on. But the problem was that Britain had engineered a complete freeze of all Argentina's overseas assets, plus an effective arms embargo which meant they had to find a way of getting hold of them through the back door. Consequently, it was the world of finance into which control of the situation had fallen and that was where Sir Charles' expertise lay, and in Peru, the very country where we suspected the deal was being done.'

'Intriguing stuff, I grant you,' responded de Courcey, 'but what has any of this got to do with a girl's disappearance in Norfolk?'

'A good question,' replied Jack, 'and one which I'd been struggling with myself until the other night, when my wife Audrey, mentioned the Black Friars, the Benedictine monks who used to inhabit St Benet's Abbey.'

'Benedictines. Black Friars.' de Courcey's bewilderment was laced with contempt. 'What earthly relevance could they have to this whole business?'

'Nothing directly, but the name triggered my recall and I finally remembered that at seven-thirty on the morning of the eighteenth of June, 1982, a man's body was found hanging from scaffolding under London's *Blackfriars* Bridge.'

'A man? What man?' asked McQuaid.

'A man called Roberto Calvi, Managing Director of a large Italian bank called Banco Ambrosiano. It had once been a very religious-orientated organisation, known as "The Priests' Bank", and requiring Catholic baptismal certificates of anyone holding an account with them. But under Roberto Calvi's directorship, they underwent a startling and sinister change that turned them into a very special international institution. Now, Banco Ambrosiano was engaging in just about every crooked financial deal that came its way, including illegal share dealing, laundering money for the mob and undertaking the most illicit of foreign currency transactions.'

'Such as handling the payment for Exocet missiles for Argentina,' volunteered de Courcey with unexpected frankness.

'Exactly. In 1980, the bank had opened a South American subsiduary, Banco Ambrosiano de America del Sud, in Buenos Aires and later, the Banco Ambrosiano Andino in Lima, Peru. It was the latter bank that was handling a guarantee of $200 million for the missiles.'

'But how was this Calvi chap allowed to get away with such dealings?' asked McQuaid. 'Surely the Italian authorities would have been down on him like a ton of bricks.'

'Not in the atmosphere of corruption that existed in Italy at that time,' explained Jack. 'You see, Calvi was also paymaster to P2, a shady pseudo-Masonic lodge that counted amongst its members some of the leading figures in Italian politics, industry, media, military and the intelligence services. P2 was sometimes referred to in Italy as a "state-within-a-state". But, by 1981, the authorities were on to Calvi. He was arrested, tried and given a four year suspended sentence plus a hefty fine for illegal currency exports. Amazingly, he still kept his position in the bank, but time was running out for Banco Ambrosiano as well. In 1982, they went bust with debts of around a billion dollars and Calvi himself went on the run. Three weeks later he was found hanging, his pockets filled with heavy bricks and some fifteen thousand dollars in cash of various currencies.'

'So, banking scandals aren't a purely modern day phenomena,' commented McQuaid.

Jack smiled. 'They certainly aren't, but what made the collapse of Banco Ambrosiano all the more scandalous was the organisation holding the majority of their shares and to which most of that missing money had been milked.'

It was Rose who asked the question. 'And that was...?'

Jack smiled. 'Your father, more than anyone, knows the answer to that one, Rose. It was the Holy See in Vatican City.'

*   *   *

'The Vatican!' Rose blinked twice and turned to her father. 'That surely can't be right, can it Dad?'

'I'm afraid it is,' replied a sad faced de Courcey, 'but I have to point out that the Vatican eventually conceded their involvement and, in 1984, paid Ambrosiano creditors $224million in compensation.' He shook his head and turned back to Jack. 'Calvi was a bad lot, but only the tip of the iceberg when it came to the corruption running through the system.'

Jack nodded. 'Very convenient then that his secrets went with him under Blackfriars Bridge.'

'Another man whose conscience got the better of him,' observed McQuaid.

'Yes, if he really had committed suicide.'

'Was there any doubt?'

'Not if you believed the ruling of the first inquest, but Calvi's own family were convinced he'd been murdered. They knew him to be afraid of heights, so why, they argued, should a man who suffered vertigo go climbing up scaffolding when his hotel room in Chelsea was found to be full of prescribed barbiturates which would have given him a much easier end if he'd so decided?'

'I know you were a Scotland Yard detective, Jack,' interjected Kingsbourne, 'so presumably you were on this case.'

'No, I wasn't, actually,' replied Jack. 'In fact, no Scotland Yard officers were involved at all.'

'Really. How come?'

'Because Blackfriars Bridge marked the Thames boundary of jurisdiction between the Metropolitan Police and the City of London Police and it was the latter who conducted the investigation.'

'Was that significant?'

'Possibly, because the head of the City Police reported daily direct to Margaret Thatcher, whereas the Commissioner of the Metropolitan Police made his to the relatively less senior Home Secretary. You can infer from that what you like,' commented Jack, 'but there was plenty of other material for those suspecting conspiracy in high places. For instance, I mentioned the Italian secret society, P2, but they also liked to refer to themselves as the Frati Neri, "The Black Friars", which was ironic, considering Calvi's place of death.'

'But didn't this Calvi man's family challenge what they considered a wrong verdict?' questioned Rose.

'They did indeed and, in July '83, managed to force a second inquest, but that jury couldn't decide and merely changed things only slightly to an open verdict. Still convinced it was murder, the Calvis then hired a private investigating team which obtained an independent forensic report. That established that at the time of Calvi's death, the water level of the Thames would have been washing around his legs, but there was no physical evidence of that. Nor was there any sign on his clothes of the rust and paint that must have come off the scaffolding when he was climbing up, or any forensic evidence that he'd even touched the bricks in his pockets. "God's Banker" as the old rogue was known, had clearly been murdered and the City of London Police then reopened the case as such.'

'So, who did it?' asked McQuaid.

'They never found out and probably never will. Five men eventually went on trial in Italy, but were aqutitted. Everything pointed to it being the work of the mob, which wanted revenge at losing so much of their cash in the collapse of Banco Ambrosiano, but a more likely motive was simply to keep Calvi quiet. He knew too much about the workings of P2, the Mafia, the Vatican involvement and even deeper conspiracies beyond, and had to be silenced once and for all.' Jack turned back to de Courcey. 'And now to answer your original question of what relevance any of this had to Sam's disappearance. It's relevant because, I believe, in your covert investigations in Peru, you and Samantha uncovered the true source of the money that would have been used to purchase those Exocets.'

'We've already established that it would have come through Banco Ambrosiano,' confirmed de Courcey.

'*Through* them, but where *from*?'

'You tell us, Jack,' said Rose.

'I think,' said Jack, 'that your father and Samantha found beyond doubt that the $200 million guarantee was to have come from the Vatican.'

*   *   *

'Surely that can't be true,' challenged Rose. 'It's one thing to accuse the Vatican of dubious financial transactions, but to say they were also getting involved in arms deals is surely going a conspiracy too far.'

'Not really, though I can imagine, for someone like you brought up in the Catholic faith, it must be pretty hard to stomach,' acknowledged Jack. 'But the Instituto per le Opere di Religione, the Vatican bank, had fingers in all sorts of dubious pies, including arms companies. At the time the Falklands War started, Argentina was drilling for oil just off their mainland. That operation was being financed by the Vatican, but had to stop for the duration of the conflict. So, it was very much in the Holy See's financial interests to get the war over with as quickly as possible and preferably with a win for Argentina. And then, thanks to Samantha and your father here, the money trail for the Exocets was traced and Aerospatiale had to pull out of that deal. The Vatican must have been far from happy.'

'But killing? They wouldn't go that far, surely?'

'I think they would,' declared Jack. 'Remember, just four years before Calvi's murder, we'd had the most dubious death of all in the Vatican itself. Pope John Paul I, newly appointed to the papal throne, had avowed to rid the Holy See of all its financial corruption but, in so doing, signed his own death warrant. Just thirty-three days after his election he was found dead in bed from causes never established because no post-mortem was ever conducted. It's a sad fact that when billions are at stake, the highest and the lowliest with dangerous knowledge, have to be taken out. Just hours before Calvi's death, his own secretary, Graziella Corrocher, threw herself from her fourth floor office in the bank's Milan headquarters. Once again, it was written off as suicide, but it wouldn't take much imagination to suss the real cause.' Jack nodded towards Sir Charles. 'No, you and Samantha, harbouring knowledge that could be devastating to a fifth of the world's population, now realised the perilous position you found yourselves in. Doubtless, British Intelligence were keeping you informed of any likely threat and, in the summer of 1984, your worst fears were realised when they warned you both that dark forces were closing in. Am I correct?'

de Courcey wavered and it was his wife who spoke next. 'Charles, there comes a time when it's useless to resist. I think that's now come and you need to be totally honest with Jack here.'

'All right. Yes, you're correct, Fellows. The intelligence services did indeed warn me that they'd got word we were targets for silencing. With my title and high profile, they'd kept a pretty good watch on me since the Falklands, but had relied on Sam's relatively sheltered life within the confines of Darwin College, to be a safeguard in itself. That, however, was proved wrong and so I took it upon myself to get her somewhere I was sure the forces of evil would never find her.'

'The Norfolk Broads, where the possible appearance of a capybara on the southern rivers had provided the perfect cover,' filled in Jack.

'It seemed the best idea at the time. The Broads are a pretty remote area, and on a boat she'd be constantly on the move. We thought those assassins, whoever they were, would never catch up with her there.'

'But they did, at Horning Staithe,' said Jack, sadly. 'How do you think they found her?'

'It had to be Odell. To complete the cover, Sam had gone through the motions of taking leave from college for field research, so she had to keep in touch with her faculty, and inadvertently let drop to Odell some clue as to her movements. Intelligence told me later that the hit squad had tracked her down to Darwin. I'm sure Odell, still with an axe to grind, was only too glad to spill the beans. By this time, Sam, already pretty twitched at the thought of being on a hit list, had returned to the northern rivers and contacted both myself and Kingsbourne. So, we arranged to meet at Horning, only to find her and the boat gone. As you know, we finally found Cantuta down river, but no Sam.'

'A desperate situation, I grant you,' conceded Jack, 'but what I can't understand is how you were prepared to leave it at that with no attempt to even search for a body.'

'That was a decision by the security services,' explained Kingsbourne. 'They were concerned that any further investigation would expose the intelligence gathering in Peru and, as the government at that time was keen to rebuild South American relationships...'

'... they asked you just to forget a girl who'd died because she once served her country.' Jack gave a snort of disgust. 'Hardly an honourable course of action was it?'

'We had no option, Jack,' conceded Kingsbourne, though with little conviction.

'But the fact is,' continued Jack, 'that you all laid the blame at Bruce Odell's door, which means you all had a motive for murdering him.'

'A nice theory, Fellows,' scorned de Courcey, 'but, as you well know, we were all otherwise engaged at the time, so there was no way any of us could have done it.'

Jack nodded. 'You're right, but one of you did and, against the odds, I've worked out who.'

*　　*　　*

Chapter Seventeen

'The problem, of course,' began Jack, 'is that you all had such watertight alibis.' He nodded towards McQuaid sitting impassively beside his partner. 'You, Gordon, were at Grange Farm tending a lame horse and, luckily, got captured on CCTV.' He then indicated de Courcey and his wife. 'You, Sir Charles and Lady Harriet, were in Norwich at a military band concert where you got into conversation with at least two people who will swear as to place and time.' Finally, Jack nodded towards Kingsbourne. 'You, Greg, were on your boat where you were seen and chatted to by several other boaters and were accompanied by Rose, who had decided to spend the night on board Tumbledown, rather than suffer a soaking in the storm that was due to pass through.'

de Courcey shook his head. 'Of course, you're forgetting one other person aren't you, Fellows?'

'You mean our dear departed Lorenzo,' replied Jack. 'Certainly, a be-collared priest sailing Foxglove on the eve of the worst weather that week was something that people would remember. Like Malcolm Reynolds, the skipper of the hire cruiser that Tumbledown collided with at midnight, who had earlier seen our good Monsignor sailing on Malthouse Broad and with whom he nearly collided. Reynolds remembered the priest's cheerful call not to worry. Likewise, the Morrisons, the couple at St Benet's who witnessed events there and saw him sail off back to South Walsham an hour and a half before Odell drowned.'

'Exactly.' de Courcey smiled. 'So, that's Lorenzo in the clear, God bless him.'

'If it actually *was* Lorenzo they saw,' said Jack.

The smile dropped. 'Explain.'

'Well, what did all those witnesses see and hear exactly? A man in a dog collar who greeted them with a few friendly words of Italian. Malcolm Reynolds had enjoyed several holidays in Italy and prided himself in being reasonably proficient in the language. So, he remembered the words exactly, "Non preoccuparti fratello". Now, for starters, I knew that Lorenzo spoke quite reasonable English, so I asked myself, why should he call out in Italian?'

'Just the stress of the moment,' answered Kingsbourne. 'I was there and saw the two boats almost collide. Surely it was only natural for the poor chap to break into his native tongue when things looked a bit dodgy?'

'Yes, if he'd used correct Italian, but he hadn't,' explained Jack. 'I took my wife to an Italian restaurant in Norwich the other night and the waiter was kind enough to translate "Non preoccuparti fratello" into English, which was "Don't worry, brother".'

'What's wrong with that?' asked McQuaid. 'It seems a friendly enough greeting from one sailor to another.'

'It would be if used in English,' explained Jack, 'but used in Italian, "fratello" or "brother" equates to our expression of "mate", which might be chummy enough here, but is surely not a greeting to be used by the head of a seminary.' Jack paused before asking, 'Have *you* ever been to Italy, Gordon?'

Rose gave her partner a quick nod and McQuaid shrugged. 'Yes, Rose and me had a holiday together in Naples a year ago.'

'And therefore decided that the few Italian phrases you picked up then would come in handy posing as Lorenzo.'

The vet's laugh sounded slightly forced. 'Now you really are going too far, Jack. You saw for yourself on that CCTV footage that I was miles away at Grange Farm at the time.'

'Ah yes, let's watch them again together, shall we,' suggested Jack with a thumbs-up to Bailey, who took a DVD from his pocket and slipped it into the player for the large screen TV. 'Here we have your Land Rover arriving at the farm gates,' he narrated as the grainy images came on the screen. 'And there's the vehicle continuing up the drive.' Jack paused the image. 'As you can see, Grange Farm's drive is wide, so what can anyone tell me that's odd about the way Gordon is driving up it?' There was silence before Jack spoke up again. 'Okay, I'll tell *you*. He's driving up the right-hand side.'

All present could see the truth of Jack's observation, but it was de Courcey who broke the silence. 'Meaning?'

'Meaning that VetCare's Land Rover was actually being driven by someone who'd managed to cope well enough on the main roads with other traffic as a guide, but who, without white lines, had instinctively gone to the side he was most used to. And that man was, of course...' He glanced around at the impassive faces watching the screen, 'Monsignor Lorenzo Coletti.'

Again, McQuaid shook his head. 'But if you continue, you'll also see shots of me actually arriving at the stable block and getting out.'

'These ones, you mean,' said Jack, again pressing PLAY and fast-forwarding to the relevant scene, 'where we can certainly see images of someone in a cap and wax jacket like yours. But, like so many security cameras, this one doesn't show the face clearly and so we only have the clothes to go by. Again, an easily contrived deception.' A nod from Jack, and the DVD was stopped again at an image of the figure in the car holding a mobile phone. 'And then we have the texts. One from Lorenzo at Ranworth to Rose and the one Carol Knights received from Gordon telling her that the horse was okay.'

'Exactly,' interjected McQuaid. 'The police checked those messages and they were sent from the correct phones and from the correct places.'

'Of course they were, but not from the people we were led to believe.' Jack clicked off the DVD. 'It was the easiest of things for both Lorenzo and you, Gordon, to swap phones and send those texts.'

'You're forgetting one thing though,' protested McQuaid, 'and that's the language factor. If Lorenzo had sent that one to Carol, it would have been bound to include at least one error of English. As it was, it was in the usual texting abbreviations that any English sender would use.'

'Whereas, Lorenzo's to Rose that was in slightly iffy English,' said Jack. 'But what if you each keyed in the message on your phones before exchanging them? Then, at the appropriate time, all you each had to do was press SEND, and two very personal and feasible messages were received for later evidence.'

'And, on this very dubious premise, are you saying it was me helming Foxglove at Ranworth and even later at St Benet's?' asked McQuaid.

'Yes, that's exactly what I'm saying,' confirmed Jack. 'My theory is that you knew Carol Knights was going to be away from Grange Farm that night and deliberately forgot the bute you'd prescribed for her horse, thereby providing the perfect excuse for you, or someone, to be revisiting at the vital hour. But the figure getting clocked on CCTV had to be Monsignor Coletti, because I thought it strange from the start that you and Rose would allow a man who hadn't handled a boat in a while and was unused to the Broads, to go sailing off in your much-loved Foxglove. Boats invariably occupy a very special place in their owners' hearts.' Jack managed just the wisp of a smile. 'Sometimes even more than partners.'

'I take it that was directed against me,' reacted Rose, sitting up. 'Okay, I admit I spent the night on Tumbledown with Greg, but that was for reasons of pure convenience.'

'Or, possibly, to look after the boat when he'd gone off to St Benet's in Foxglove with Gordon.'

'Ah, so I'm in the picture now as well am I?' challenged Kingsbourne, stirring himself. 'The trouble with that theory, Jack, is that I was seen on Tumbledown *after* Foxglove departed.'

'Not exactly, General. I spoke to those men who'd encountered you while they were rowing ashore to the pub. Even if it was you they had that conversation with on Tumbledown, there was still time for you to slip aboard Foxglove between then and when they saw her sailing out of the broad with a priest at the helm. What I'm saying is that you, or someone, was hiding down below at that time and stayed on board until Foxglove moored at St Benet's.'

'What do you mean, me "or someone"?'

'I mean, I don't think it was you, either on Tumbledown or hiding below in Foxglove.'

'Of course it was me on Tumbledown,' protested Kingsbourne. 'You said yourself those men saw and talked with me.'

Jack gave a little laugh. 'I'm sorry if this whole discussion seems to be revolving around costume-changes, but that's what happened once again. Those men described a tall figure in white roll-neck, but there was something which told me that it couldn't have been you they were talking to.'

'Really. And what was that?'

'It was after you'd explained you were in the marines and one of the men told you in return that he'd been a "pongo" himself,' explained Jack. 'He told me he'd been surprised that you seemed unfamiliar with that expression, one that all navy men use for army soldiers. Now, it's inconceivable that you, as a long-serving marine, had never heard of it yourself. No, Greg, it wasn't you talking to those men and it wasn't you who later, at midnight in the storm, collided with the hire-cruiser at Ranworth Staithe. I've seen you handle a boat and know how expert you are at it. You would never have allowed Tumbledown to get into a situation like that.'

'So...' Kingsbourne glanced out of the picture window towards his beloved ketch at anchor on the broad, '... if it wasn't me on board her, who was it?'

Jack nodded towards the other tall figure in the room. 'It was you, Sir Charles.'

'Me?' de Courcey closed his eyes. 'This tale is getting more fanciful by the minute. You know for a fact that Harriet and I were at a band concert in Norwich when Odell died.'

'I agree Lady Harriet was there,' acknowledged Jack, 'but it wasn't you with her, it was General Kingsbourne here.'

'Greg? Are you mad?'

'Not at all, and I'd advise you, if you ever intend such a deception again, not to use a military man at an army band concert.'

'What do you mean?'

'I mean,' continued Jack, 'that the lady who thought she was sitting next to Sir Charles and Lady de Courcey, remembered the conversations of that night quite well. In particular, she recalled the one with the young musician at the end when Sir Charles assumed he also played the violin and seemed surprised that he didn't play any other instrument.'

'Music interests me,' responded de Courcey, 'so what's wrong with that?'

'Nothing, except it gave away that it was Greg and not you attending that concert,' explained Jack. 'You see, it's only in *Royal Marine* Bands that musicians are proficient in more than one instrument and where standard practice is that the cornet players usually double as violinists. As a famous British actor once said, "Not many people know that", and in this case, probably only a Royal Marine.'

'Even assuming all these ridiculous allegations are correct,' hedged de Courcey with a slightly forced smile, 'please tell me why on earth we would we go to such absurd trouble?'

'To cover for each other while a murder was taking place,' said Jack, moving more into the circle of family. 'The murder by you, Sir Charles, of Bruce Odell.'

*   *   *

Jack glanced towards the small lounge bar. He could have done with a stiff drink himself by this time, but instead he pressed on.

'Let me paint my scenario of what I think happened that night. I'm assuming you somehow had a family conference and all decided Odell had to be disposed of. Just why, we'll come to later. But die, he must, and so a meeting was decided for him to meet Foxglove at St Benet's, a nice isolated spot for a bit of dark-deeding and fittingly close also to the site of Samantha's own murder. You're all a pretty bright lot and felt quite confident in committing the perfect crime. Essential to this was that you all had good alibis and witnesses to prove them. In my opinion, you went a bit overboard on that and seemed to go out of your way to draw attention to yourselves, which is always a giveaway.'

Jack glanced around the room, but no one spoke up in contradiction, and so he pressed on. 'So, Gordon and Lorenzo swapped identities at Broad View, as did Sir Charles and General Kingsbourne, probably in The Malsters when Lady Harriet brought Rose out to Ranworth. With the pub full that night, it must have been easy for you both to do a quick change in the gents' toilet. Afterwards, Greg would have gone with Lady Harriet to the band concert while it was Sir Charles, now attired in white polo neck and oilskin, running his daughter out to Tumbledown. While Rose was then going through the act of sorting out Foxglove's halyard, those men rowing to the pub came close and you had a chat with them to establish the alibi. And then it was off to St Benet's, with Gordon helming and Sir Charles stowed below.'

'If there's *any* truth in this fantastic tale,' spoke up McQuaid, 'why would I go too? If Sir Charles really intended to murder Odell, why didn't he just take the boat, leaving me on Tumbledown with Rose?'

'Because you had a very special part to play at St Benet's, Gordon,' explained Jack, his expression hardening. 'After Odell boarded Foxglove on some pretext and been encouraged to take a good shot of brandy, the next thing was to sedate him. It isn't only humans who suffer diabetes. Dogs and cats do too and are also prescribed insulin for their condition. So you, Gordon, as a vet, certainly had access to that drug and were well used to injecting unwilling animals. My guess is that while Sir Charles was restraining an already sozzled Odell, you injected him with a dose of insulin way over his prescribed limit.'

'So, it's me you're actually accusing of the murder now?'

Jack shook his head. 'No, only assisting in the act of. To give you or, supposedly Lorenzo, a good alibi, Odell's time of death had to be after you'd been seen to sail off back to South Walsham. No, you only put Odell into a hypoglycemic coma and probably helped haul his unconscious form ashore and out of sight over the bank. There, Foxglove's mudweight was tied to his ankles and an hour and a half later, Sir Charles tipped him into the river.'

'But that couple saw Odell walking on the quay heading after Foxglove had gone,' protested Lady Harriet. 'And they later heard *their* mudweight being taken and, shortly after, a splash as Odell drowned himself with it.'

'Once again, they only *thought* they saw and heard that,' responded Jack. 'As Odell was unconscious, it would have been the easiest thing in the world for your husband to don his old coat and hat. In the rain and darkness, the Morrisons assumed the stooping man they saw pacing the mooring was the same one they'd seen earlier waiting for a boat. After a good interval and when they seemed to have gone to bed, Sir Charles did indeed haul the mudweight off their boat, but that wasn't the one found weighing Odell to the river bottom.' Jack frowned. 'I'd always worried how the Morrisons heard that splash so far away and over the noise of the storm, but the following day, when I passed Foxglove's mooring, I noticed *her* mudweight was also gone. So, yesterday we had divers go down again, and they found the hire cruiser's mudweight close to where it had been moored. It's a reasonable assumption then that Foxglove's had been the one used to weigh down Odell, and dumping the Morrison's had only been to complete that illusion and draw their attention to the time. My theory of the sequence of events, Sir Charles, is that after ensuring you'd been seen pacing up and down the moorings dressed in Odell's coat and hat, you then stripped them off and piled them nearby before rolling his unconscious body into the river. You then noisily hauled the Morrison's mudweight off their deck and slung that in the river also, completing the picture of a man committing suicide alone and an hour and a half after Foxglove had departed. Somehow, you then made your way back to Ranworth where, sometime before dawn, you and General Kingsbourne here swapped back to your true identities and the plan was complete.' Jack paused before going over to the bar and pouring himself a large Scotch. He raised it in toast. 'Here's to the perfect murder that almost was.' He knocked back a good measure of his drink. 'So, how did I do?'

But de Courcey wasn't ready to capitulate just yet. 'You're forgetting the suicide note found in Odell's coat, Fellows. Pretty good proof of his intentions, so how do you explain that?'

'Ah that was one of the easiest bits,' smiled Jack. 'It was quite ingenious, but too brief for what it was intended to portray and lacking even a date. Strange words those – "I can't go on – I'll go on", but admittedly written in Odell's own fair hand. I put them into the search engine of my computer and found they were actually the title of a book by the renowned Irish author, Samuel Becket. Being written on Odell's bookshop notepaper, I assumed they'd probably been penned there also. Lorenzo, we know, was in Cambridge in the week prior to Odell's death, so the odds are he somehow contrived, perhaps using the pretext of searching for that title, to get the bookseller to write and sign that note. On the day in question, he gave it to you to slip into the coat pocket and, heh presto, we have a suicide note.'

'So, now you're saying Lorenzo really was involved in the plan,' said Rose.

'Oh yes, but with very extenuating circumstances. He was a close friend of this family and the poor chap had just been told he'd only a short time to live, and so probably felt he had very little to lose.'

'But he was an ordained priest, Fellows, and fearing for his mortal soul,' argued de Courcey. 'Surely he'd be the last man to get involved in murder when he knew he'd be shortly meeting the greatest judge of all.'

'Not, if what he was doing was in some way also serving the church to which he'd given his life,' replied Jack. 'You've admitted yourself that he was your confessional in Peru, and so probably knew all about the part his beloved Vatican had played in the acquisition of those Exocets. Doubtless his elevation, soon after, from mere missionary worker to rector of a large seminary in Rome, was part of the pay-off the Holy See used to buy his silence. But, being a totally devout man, I'm sure Samantha's death played on his conscience and, in his diseased mind, helping get rid of Odell seemed in some way to have paid the forfeit.'

'Very clever, Fellows,' acknowledged de Courcey with a slow insincere handclap. 'A good tale, if a little far-fetched. If I was left at St Benet's as you claim, how on earth do you think I returned home, because it's an awfully long walk to the other side of the river via either Wroxham or Acle Bridge?'

'Probably by Rose picking you up in Tumbledown's tender and taking you back to Ranworth,' replied Jack. 'My guess is you'd probably been hoping there'd be no boats moored at St Benet's that stormy night and, when you saw there was, you had to do some pretty fast thinking. So, after dispatching Odell into the river with Foxglove's mudweight and then deep-sixing the one belonging to the cruiser, I reckon you simply scuttled over the bank and made your way through the marsh the short distance to the River Ant. There, Rose picked you up and took you back to Tumbledown where, to your doubtless horror, you found the ketch dragging her anchor in the storm. It would have been midnight by that time and the last thing you wanted was Greg's boat to go drifting aground, so you started the engine and motored to the staithe for shelter. You wanted any witnesses to think Rose had been on board all night, so it was okay for her to be seen on the foredeck, but *you* had to stay out of sight in the wheelhouse. But I'm guessing that this was the first time you'd handled any motor sailer, let alone Tumbledown, and you made a complete hash of it.'

'But the skipper, Malcolm Reynolds, was the same dinghy sailor who'd seen me on the broad the evening before,' pointed out Kingsbourne. 'He had no problem recognising me when I went aboard his boat the next morning to apologise.'

'No, because by that time, soon after the collision, Lady Harriet had dropped you back at Ranworth and Rose and Sir Charles had gone home with her, leaving you to dish out the apologies in the morning.' Jack gave Kingsbourne a sympathetic smile. 'Knowing you, it must have been pretty galling having to say "sorry" for something you would have never done yourself, but it did at least strengthen the identification deception.'

'All very intriguing,' declared de Coucey with a forced smile, 'but purely surmise and conjecture on your part. You haven't one iota of solid proof that any of this improbable tale is correct?' He turned to Bailey. 'No, my guess is that if you had, you would have arrested me already and this conversation would have taken place at the police station.'

Bailey could only nod agreement. 'No, much as it pains me to admit, Sir Charles, we have nothing that the DPP would even consider as evidence for a prosecution. I learned long ago in my police service that there's a mountain of difference between suspicion and proof and this is a case in point. I shall, of course, make a personal report to the Chief Constable and no doubt the coroner will give an open verdict on Samantha's recovered remains and one of suicide on Odell and that, sadly, is where things will probably rest.'

'And how about you, Fellows?' asked de Courcey. 'It was, after all, your meddling that started this whole fiasco in the first place. Are you going to accept that all your wild theories are completely without proof and let sleeping dogs lie?'

Jack stood immobile, sipping the remains of his Scotch, but obviously weighing deep personal convictions. Finally, after what seemed an age to those awaiting his decision, he downed his drink, shook his head and spoke. 'All my working life,' he started in a quiet voice, ' has been devoted to pursuing truth and justice. That's what coppering is all about. There was never any excuse accepted for murder in a court of law, and that's how it should always be.' He glanced quickly towards Rose de Courcey. She was biting her lip and tightening her grip of McQuaid's hand. Likewise, Lady Harriet seemed about to crush the glass in her own. Only de Courcey and Kingsbourne stood immobile. 'But you're right, all I have in this case is up here…' he tapped his head, '…and that's probably where it will stay. This whole business only started with me indulging in a bit of fishing and perhaps that's where I ought to apply my future endeavours.' Once again, Jack shook his head. 'No, if any of this ever comes out, it won't be from me.'

'Good. And now I think we could all do with another drink,' suggested de Courcey, playing well the part of a man content that common sense was prevailing.

But it was undisguised relief that seemed to fill Broad View's lounge. As Lady Harriet and Rose exchanged tearful hugs and Kingsbourne and McQuaid, thankful handshakes, Bailey went to take his leave. de Courcey raised his glass to him. 'Goodbye, Inspector. Sorry we couldn't oblige you with a confession and I'm assuming we'll hear no more on this subject.'

'Not until further evidence comes to light, Sir Charles.'

'And that won't happen, I can assure you.' With Bailey gone, de Courcey edged alongside Jack. 'Drink up, Fellows. You can probably guess you're no longer welcome here either.'

'I don't doubt it,' agreed Jack, before himself easing de Courcey to one side and well out of hearing of the others, 'but what you should thank me for, is that I didn't elaborate further on what lay behind Odell's death.'

'I'm not sure what you mean.'

'Yes you do. I *mean*,' continued Jack, 'that there was more than pure revenge motivating this family to plot Odell's perfect murder. Assuming that he was somehow involved in Samantha's death, the question I kept asking myself was, why did you wait over a quarter of a century to exact retribution? The answer was that my investigation had triggered something else.'

de Courcey frowned. 'Oh really. And what was that "something"?'

'Blackmail, Sir Charles. Odell was threatening to spill the beans unless you…'

'… once more handed over a considerable amount of money,' completed de Courcey. 'Yes, you're right, we had a telephone call from him very shortly after your first visit. If it had been a simple cash transaction, we would have probably paid up just for peace of mind. But this time, as we soon found out, he'd made demands from Rose as well.'

'Rose! I wouldn't have thought she was good for much money.'

'She's not, as she told Odell at the time, but he had an alternative scheme.'

'Which was?'

'That she spend the night with him. I told you the man was a sexual predator, and the years hadn't diminished his craving,' said de Courcey before suddenly realising what he was saying and concluding, 'so, thank God the man committed suicide like he did.'

'Indeed,' responded Jack with undisguised cynicism, ' but it takes some pretty damning knowledge on his part to make demands like that, Sir Charles. Okay, there were dark deeds being done back then, but they were linked to national security and the intelligence people would have taken care of anyone seeking to cash in on that. No, there was something even deeper that Bruce Odell knew about, something that could have ruined everything you and your family stood for.'

It was de Courcey's turn to narrow his eyes, but his smile was one of acceptance. 'And I think you've also guessed what that was.'

'Yes, I think I have, Sir Charles but, this time, I'd prefer *you* to tell *me*.'

The financier glanced around to where the rest of his family were chatting happily. He ushered Jack towards his study. 'All right, Fellows. It seems I owe you. Let's go somewhere quiet, and I'll do just that.'

* * *

Epilogue

'Go on, Spike. Fetch!' Audrey watched as the border collie tore off down the riverbank to retrieve the stick thrown by Jack. She turned to her husband. 'It's good to be able to just relax together again.'

'Yes, it certainly is. That case gave me more heartache than most I care to remember.'

She sighed. 'And, in the end, it all came to nothing anyway.'

'No, there won't be any charges brought in the near future, but at least we solved the mystery of the lost handbag.'

'Gosh, that all seems a long time ago now,' said Audrey. It was the day after the final denouement at Broad View and the Fellows were enjoying a quiet stroll as Jack explained all that had transpired. Now, as Spike came trotting proudly back, stick in mouth and tail wagging, Audrey sought to clarify a few points of her own. 'One of the things I don't understand, Jack, is that young vet Gordon McQuaid allowing himself to get involved in such a dark business, or the lovely daughter Rose, for that matter. They both seemed such nice level-headed young people.'

'And so they are, Aud, but they're young and in love and want to get married and there was the snag.'

'You mean Sir Charles and his strict Catholic faith putting up that ridiculous barrier against his only daughter marrying an agnostic. But this is the twenty-first century, Jack, and young people don't worry about that sort of thing anymore.'

'So we're led to believe, but most youngsters, brought up within a faith and keen to please parents they love, will still find it hard to swim against the tide. Rose certainly did. But then came this opportunity to even the odds, a family crisis in which Gordon could finally prove his worth and where his medical knowledge and skills could help rid them once and for all of the Sword of Damocles that was Odell. What better way to win over an opposing parent.'

But Audrey was still unconvinced. 'Millions of young men battle with disapproving prospective fathers-in-law, Jack, but they don't assist in murder for it.'

'They do if it also means getting the one you love out of a fearful predicament.'

'Ah yes, Odell's dreadful demands regarding Rose.' Audrey closed her eyes in disgust. 'Blackmailing for money was unforgivable in itself, but to include *that* demand was beyond the pale.'

'Or the product of a sick mind,' reasoned Jack. 'It explains though why Odell was prepared to meet at such a desolate spot as St Benet's. It was Rose he was expecting to arrive there in Foxglove for a night of ...'

'Don't even say it, Jack,' broke in Audrey, holding up her hand. 'It must have been a shock when, instead, it was her father and partner and the means to his end. Compared to that, I suppose people thinking Rose was indulging in a night of hanky-panky with General Kingsbourne aboard Tumbledown, was relatively harmless. But was she really alone, Jack? That's something else that puzzles me, because didn't you tell me those men, rowing back to their boat, actually overheard her in very intimate conversation with someone?'

'Yes, but not with Kingsbourne or anyone on that boat,' explained Jack. 'Those words about "somethings have to be done" and "no-one will find out" and "I love you and want to marry you" were intimate all right, but ones with her own partner, Gordon. He admitted to me himself that, with the deed complete and his own conscience giving him trouble, he'd rung Rose on her mobile and she was trying to console him.'

'As only a loved one can.' Audrey smiled. 'I know she was involved in the plot as much as anyone, but I still think she's a very decent girl. How can that odious Odell have even thought he could get away with such an immoral suggestion?'

'Because he was convinced he held all the cards, possessing as he did, such dangerous knowledge.'

'You mean Samantha's murder and the cover-up that followed?'

'More than that, Aud. Something that would have turned the de Courcey's idyllic lives upside down for ever.' Jack paused to re-throw Spike's stick before giving his wife a meaning look. 'What I'm going to tell you now is something not even Bailey, knows about.'

'My goodness, this sounds serious stuff, Jack. Presumably it still relates to Samantha's murder?'

'It does indeed, but that's the crux of the whole mystery. You see, Samantha Waites was never murdered.'

'Never murdered! But, Jack, the divers found bones at the scene.'

'I know, but they weren't Samantha's.'

'Whose were they then?'

'Lady Harriet de Courcey's.'

Audrey stroked her forehead in disbelief. 'But she's alive and well and living with her husband.'

'No, Audrey. Samantha Waites is alive and well and living with Sir Charles.' Jack saw the continuing look of utter confusion in his wife's face. 'Let's start from the beginning, when Sir Charles and Samantha had been warned by our security services that assassins from the mob were in this country and out to get them.'

'But, if what you're saying is right,' interrupted Audrey, 'and the mob murdered Calvi in 1982, why did they wait another two years to target Sir Charles and Samantha?'

'It probably stemmed from that second unsatisfactory coroner's verdict, after which the Calvi family launched their own investigation. I think that was when the mob, realising an eventual trial was inevitable, decided to clear up any loose ends that might compromise them in court.'

'Which had to include Sir Charles and Samantha?'

Jack nodded. 'Unfortunately, yes, which was when Sir Charles decided to get Sam away to some remote location. And, what better than on his boat researching some wild story about a monster spotted down on the River Waveney? But Sam, possibly sensing imminent danger, came back to the northern rivers where Sir Charles set off to meet her. In the meantime, Odell, having learned of her location at Horning, tipped off the mob who were sniffing around Darwin, and they closed in.'

'What a hornet's nest,' sighed Audrey. 'So what happened then?'

'Something no one had anticipated, which was that Lady Harriet, presumably already harbouring deep suspicions as to her husband's fidelity, got wind of this Norfolk tryst and headed there herself to put a stop to things once and for all. I gather the real Lady Harriet wasn't a particularly nice person and doubtless wouldn't have spared the young student's feelings, but when she located Cantuta at Horning and went on board for a confrontation, Sam wasn't there. Correctly suspecting she was only briefly ashore, Lady Harriet let herself in with her own key and settled down to await her return.'

'That would certainly have given Samantha a nasty shock.'

'Yes, but in the end it was poor Lady Harriet who had the nastiest shock anyone could imagine. You see, fate dealt her a cruel blow by being in just the wrong place at just the wrong time.'

'You mean the assassins murdered her by mistake, thinking she was Sam?'

'Exactly, an easy mistake when you consider there wasn't that great a difference in the two women's ages. When the mob arrived they were looking for a twenty-something female alone on that boat and in Lady Harriet, they thought they'd got her. Samantha returned to Cantuta to find the most appalling scene imaginable and with little doubt that it was she who'd been the intended target. Luckily, Sir Charles and Kingsbourne were soon there with her and immediately realised the ramifications of what had happened. They straightway enacted a cover-up plan, the first part of which was to get the boat out of Horning and somewhere well away from prying eyes.'

'To that spot where you first found Sam's handbag?'

'The very place. Sir Charles' own secret service experience had obviously given him the ability to think on his feet and, with his wife dead and Sam needing to be protected, the security services were contacted and a long-term plan worked out in which the two women's identities were swapped.'

'In other words, our own government colluded in covering up a murder.'

'That's the harsh way of viewing it,' admitted Jack, 'but, let's face it, Aud, nowadays even murderers are given new identities on their release, so it certainly seemed justifiable at that time to protect a girl who'd done the country invaluable service. The main priority was ensuring that no further attempts were made and to do that they needed to preserve the mob's erroneous impression that they'd eliminated Samantha. Admittedly, it was a plan that gave the loving couple the life they'd dreamed of and with the security of state backing. And so the late Lady Harriet was silently disposed of into the river along with Sam's handbag in case the remains were ever discovered and, to all intents and purposes, Samantha Waites ceased to exist.'

'How cold-blooded.' Audrey gave a shiver. 'But surely they couldn't have hoped to get away with such a deception forever. What about friends and relations?'

'There weren't any relations and all the friends were in London. Broad View was purchased immediately and Sir Charles and the new Lady Harriet, whose appearance wasn't drastically unlike the original, were duly installed to live a happy, but relatively reclusive life. Happy, that was, until Odell happened to spot them in the background of a magazine photo taken at some charity event. He immediately recognised the "Lady Harriet" in the picture as really ex fellow-student Samantha Waites and, being an intelligent but unfunded PhD student himself, wasn't slow to cash in on that knowledge.'

'So, the transfer of research funding, originally allocated to Samantha, to Odell's own highly emotive project was, in reality, his first attempt at blackmail?'

'Yes, and a successful one at that,' confirmed Jack. 'With his newfound happiness in jeopardy, Sir Charles immediately complied. Fast-forward then to the present and yours truly reopening the bag of worms by discovering Samantha's handbag. My going to interview Odell that morning in Cambridge told him that the case was alive once more. And then, when the news broke that actual remains had been discovered, he saw that as a way to rescue his near-insolvent second-hand book business. This time he made a much heftier demand.'

'Which included daughter Rose,' completed Audrey. 'He must have been mad to make such an obscene proposal. Sir Charles would probably have paid up if it wasn't for that.'

'I agree, but you have to look at it through Odell's perspective, Aud. In his warped mind he was levelling the score with Sam who'd rejected him all those years before. So, now he was going to make her pay for it by demanding a night with her daughter instead.'

Audrey closed her eyes in disgust. 'A sick mind, indeed. But how on earth did you even *suspect* such a deception, Jack?'

'A number of reasons, actually, and from quite early on in the proceedings when I first met the-now Lady Harriet out rowing. On reflection, that seemed out of character when Sir Charles gave me the impression that his wife had been an unadventurous lady who'd refused to leave the comfort of her home and join him in Peru. But Jean Hendricks told me that Samantha used to go for early morning boat race training sessions with Greg Kingsbourne. And he himself said they took a sailing holiday together on the Broads when they were students. Now, romance apart, there was a girl with an interest in rowing and boats and it wasn't hard to link both those pursuits to the Lady Harriet we know now.'

'Right. What else?' asked an ever-intrigued Audrey.

'Well, with that suspicion, I cast my mind back to Odell telling me of how he'd seen the de Courceys in that photo at the charity event in aid of endangered species. It prompted the question of why would they be attending such an event? The answer, of course, was that it was a cause dear to Samantha's heart and deepened my belief that it was she and not the real Lady Harriet in that photo. We know now, of course, that it was that revelation that set Odell on the course to blackmail, because why else would Sir Charles, a man supporting animal charities, suddenly change his funding to one involved with animal testing? And then there was Rose herself.'

'Rose?'

'Yes, a veterinary nurse with a love for animals. From whom did she inherit that trait? Again, the answer pointed to Samantha being her mother rather than the woman we thought. And finally, only yesterday, Sir Charles said how Odell had known Sam was in Horning by her inadvertently letting it slip while reporting back to college. How did Sir Charles know that if he hadn't spoken to her after the event?' Jack shrugged. 'All small points but adding up to a big suspicion which eventually became hard fact.'

'But one which must forever remain a secret.' Audrey shook her head sadly. 'Poor Lady Harriet lying all those years at the bottom of the river without even a Christian burial. And no one ever taken to account for her murder.'

'And lack of further evidence means Odell's murder will probably never come to trial either,' admitted Jack. 'In some ways, Aud, I hope it stays that way.'

'That doesn't sound like the Jack Fellows I've always known,' said a shocked Audrey. 'I thought truth and justice came before everything in your book.'

'Not any longer.'

'My goodness, Jack. Why this change of heart?'

'Well, for a start, I came to like that family and the friends around them. Yes, they conspired to carry out a meticulously-planned premeditated murder, but Odell was certainly no loss to society and who's to say any of us wouldn't have reacted the way they did if our family were threatened.'

'But no person is justified in taking on the mantle of judge and executioner, Jack. You've always told me that yourself.'

'I know, but there's another factor here which I can't quite come to terms with.'

'Which is?'

'That Odell's murder would never have happened if I hadn't become obsessed with solving a mystery. My going to see him triggered the whole tragic sequence that followed. I can understand the de Courcey's feelings towards me. They thought that whole tragedy thirty years ago was literally dead and buried. Instead, I had to go and resurrect it and drive them to commit a desperate and appalling act.'

'And yet, Jack, in the end, I think this last terrible business has actually brought them closer together than they've ever been. Certainly Gordon, risking all he did, showed the de Courceys that family loyalty far surmounts religious bigotry and I'm sure he and Rose will soon be tying the knot and Broad View will be echoing to the sound of little feet.' Audrey sighed. 'You know, it's General Kingbourne I really feel sorry for. He's been left with no-one and it can't have been easy for him, all those years, knowing the girl he once loved was with someone else.'

'I think he dealt with it by devoting himself to his career in the marines,' answered Jack. 'But, chatting to him, I got the impression that that career might well be coming to an end anyway. He made no secret of his distaste for a proposed life behind a desk at the MOD, and realises how much he's enjoyed these last few weeks on board Tumbledown. I suspect his only duty in Whitehall will be to write out his resignation and then happily sail off into the sunset.'

'And so, in the end, Jack, everyone will have discovered their best course in life.'

'I'm not sure if I have, Aud. Perhaps it really is time for me to give up this sleuthing and devote myself to fishing.'

'Oh no, not fishing, for goodness' sake!' protested Audrey. 'It was that that got you into this whole mess in the first place.'

'Yeah, I guess you're right, love,' admitted Jack, allowing himself a smile at the irony of it all. 'It certainly seems a long time ago now since

I brought home that stinking handbag and we went on the trail of the Waveney River Monster.'

'Ah yes, the river monster. I always thought that was a pretty far-fetched tale anyway,' scorned Audrey. 'When they were looking for an excuse to get Samantha away on a boat in Norfolk, they could have come up with something more feasible than that.'

'I know, but it served its purpose at the time,' reflected Jack, turning for home and looking about him. 'Where's Spike?'

'Over there, barking at the ducks,' said Audrey, pointing a hundred yards beyond, to where the collie was yelping over the riverbank.

'Spike, don't you dare go in. Leave them alone and come here,' yelled his master.

Spike, being a naturally obedient dog, paused in his barking, his only form of defence as he stared into the eyes of a strange brown-haired creature gazing back at him from the water below. Those eyes were set above wide flared nostrils and the sheer size of this living thing was causing Spike's own hackles to rise in instinctive fear. Then came a whistle from his master and Spike was snapped out of his fixation, gave a final defiant yelp and ran with all his might back along the riverbank.

Yards away, the strange creature also turned, dipped once more beneath the river's calm surface, and swam away into continued obscurity.

THE END

186

Other books
in the
Jack Fellows
series of murder-mysteries

WaterProof
ISBN 978 0 903094 23

is the first in the Jack Fellows series of Murder Mysteries set on the Norfolk Broads.

Patrolling the Norfolk Broads as a Navigation Ranger is, to ex-Scotland Yard detective Jack Fellows, the perfect job.

That's until the cold hand of violent death touches even this idyllic corner of East Anglia. Murder on the Broads is rarer than a bittern, but the police soon have their man. Or have they? Jack is sure they've got it wrong and sets out to prove it. Amongst the tranquillity of this unique setting he discovers a simmering cauldron of bitterness and deceit with suspects aplenty.

Relationships, livelihoods and reputations are in jeopardy, but whose will be sacrificed as he pursues the truth.

The WaterProof can be obtained from your local bookseller, price £5.95, or direct from the author via his website:

www.chriscrowther.co.uk

or by sending a cheque for £5.95 + £1.50 p&p to:

Chris Crowther
PO Box 1239
Norwich
NR12 8XF

Still Waters
ISBN 978 0 903094 24 5

is the second in the Jack Fellows series of Murder Mysteries set on the Norfolk Broads.

Backpacker Sally Becket has inherited a boatyard she didn't know existed from a grandfather she never knew she had. But these are the least of the mysteries confronting her when she comes to live in a small Broadland village. Who really was "Captain Charles", and was his drowning an accident, suicide... or murder?

Even Ranger Jack Fellows' deductive skills are stretched to their limits as he seeks to separate myth from reality in this tale of family secrets and love beyond the grave.

Still Waters can be obtained from your local bookseller, price £6.95, or direct from the author via his website:

www.chriscrowther.co.uk

or by sending a cheque for £6.95 + £1.50 p&p to:

Chris Crowther
PO Box 1239
Norwich
NR12 8XF

The Water Frolic
ISBN 978 0 903094 26 9

is the third in the Jack Fellows series of Murder Mysteries set on the Norfolk Broads.

A month's secondment to the southern rivers finds Ranger Jack caught up in local discords of bigotry and suspicion. A joint endeavour might just bring harmony between two very different communities but, as plans go ahead, old grievances surface as surely as a sinister secret from the broad itself. Tensions run high, but no one can predict just how tragically events will ultimately turn.

The Water Frolic can be obtained from your local bookseller, price £6.95, or direct from the author via his website:

www.chriscrowther.co.uk

or by sending a cheque for £6.95 + £1.50 p&p to:

Chris Crowther
PO Box 1239
Norwich
NR12 8XF

Water Under The Bridge
ISBN 978 0 903094 27 6

is the fourth in the Jack Fellows series of Murder Mysteries set on the Norfolk Broads.

Navigation Ranger Jack Fellows finds himself involved in the most baffling case of his career, and this time it's much closer to home with his youngest daughter, Amy, at the centre of the investigation. But how do you solve a crime, so strange in its circumstances, that it had to be impossible in the first place?

Water Under The Bridge can be obtained from your local bookseller, price £6.95, or direct from the author via his website:

<u>www.chriscrowther.co.uk</u>

or by sending a cheque for £6.95 + £1.50 p&p to:

Chris Crowther
PO Box 1239
Norwich
NR12 8XF